W9-AGB-185

THE RENEGADES

This Large Print Book carries the
Seal of Approval of N.A.V.H.

THE RENEGADES

GREG HUNT

THORNDIKE PRESS
A part of Gale, a Cengage Company

Farmington Hills, Mich • San Francisco • New York • Waterville, Maine
Meriden, Conn • Mason, Ohio • Chicago

Copyright © 1988 by Greg Hunt.
Thorndike Press, a part of Gale, a Cengage Company.

ALL RIGHTS RESERVED
This is a work of fiction. Any resemblance to actual people, places or events is purely coincidental.
Thorndike Press® Large Print Western.
The text of this Large Print edition is unabridged.
Other aspects of the book may vary from the original edition.
Set in 16 pt. Plantin.

LIBRARY OF CONGRESS CIP DATA ON FILE.
CATALOGUING IN PUBLICATION FOR THIS BOOK
IS AVAILABLE FROM THE LIBRARY OF CONGRESS

ISBN-13: 978-1-4328-6333-3 (hardcover alk. paper)

Published in 2019 by arrangement with Cherry Weiner Literary Agency

Printed in Mexico
1 2 3 4 5 6 7 23 22 21 20 19

In memory of Frank Elliot —
A fine friend and fallen comrade.

I guess there was quite a bit
of outlaw in all of us back then,
wasn't there, brother . . .

PART ONE

PART ONE

CHAPTER ONE

February, 1866

Light flurries of snow were beginning to gust through the air as William Bird hurried down the street toward the Clay County Savings Bank. He was late for work again and he knew there would be hell to pay if he reached the bank after Mr. Morrison, the owner, arrived. Few people were on the streets of Liberty, Missouri on this cold Tuesday morning, and those who were out hurried on their way with heads ducked and collars raised against the brisk wind blowing in from the northwest.

It would be a slow day at the bank, William thought and smiled. That would give him plenty of time to relive in his mind the delightful events of the previous evening.

He had been seeing Wanda Bowers for nearly three months now, but last night was the first time he had actually been alone with her for any appreciable length of time and he was amazed at how easy it had been to cause all his long-cherished fantasies about her come to fruition. He had been planning his strategy — the boysenberry brandy, the lavish compliments, and the vague mentions of a long happy life together — almost since the start of their affair but it had taken this long for the right moment to arrive. Then last night when he went to see her, he learned that her mother was away visiting relatives, and her little brother was spending the night with a friend. The brandy had hit her pretty quickly, and his smooth words had done the rest. . . .

Absorbed in his reverie, his head down against the blowing snow, William almost knocked down Mrs. Stevenson, the apothecary's wife, before he noticed her. He stepped aside and touched the brim of his hat in apology, then proceeded on his way after she had passed.

Of course, he had no intentions of marrying the girl. Her father, before his death, had been a mere day laborer at the lumber yard, and her mother was a maid in the home of Colin Burke, one of the more prosperous businessmen here in Liberty. Her background was entirely unsuitable for the wife of a successful banker, which William Bird planned to be someday, and even now, after only one true liaison with her, he could tell that he would eventually grow tired of her. But still it would be an enjoyable dalliance for a while, and certainly it would do Wanda no harm to be known for a time as the girlfriend of such a respectable and enterprising young fellow. It very well might open the door to better things for her, William thought magnanimously.

He paused at the entrance to the bank and looked inside. His father, Greenup Bird, was already there as usual, seated at his desk behind the low rail which separated the front portion of the bank from the rear area where the employees did their work. Fortunately, however, there was no sign that Mr. Morrison had arrived yet. He was safe again.

"Good morning, Father," William said as he entered the bank and headed to the tiny storage room in back to deposit his coat and hat. "It looks like we're in for a real storm before the day is out."

Greenup Bird simply glanced up over the rim of his thick glasses and cast his son a quick look filled with reproach, a look which William chose to ignore.

"I would have been in sooner," William explained, "but as I was dressing I realized I didn't have a fresh shirt and I had to wait while Mother ironed one for me."

His father simply grunted, not even bothering to acknowledge William's lame excuse. He would remain disgruntled for a while longer, William knew, at least until Mr. Morrison arrived and Greenup Bird fell into his customary role of clerical subservience.

A year ago, when William first began working at the Clay County Savings Bank, he vowed to himself that he would never end up like his father, imprisoned behind the same desk, working for the same unappreciative employer, for most of his adult life. Now that the war was over, there were too many other opportunities to take advantage of, and he had promised himself that he would only work here long enough to learn the ways of banking and finance before moving on to greener pastures.

But for now he must play the game, he reminded himself, as he sat down at the desk beside his father's and surveyed the day's work before him.

The fire in the wood stove near the front of the bank had nearly melted the frost inside the front windows by the time Mr. Morrison arrived. Both the Birds, father and son, greeted their employer courteously, and received the customary nods and mumbled replies in return. Without removing his overcoat, the bank owner marched to his large desk in back and picked up the previous day's accounts, which Greenup Bird had placed there for his inspection. When he was finished examining them, he turned to the elder clerk and said, "I'll be out of the office today, Greenup. I have to ride out to Cal Chase's and discuss some business with him. You'll be in charge while I'm gone."

"The storm looks like it's settling in," Bird replied. "I don't envy you the ride out there."

"Business is business, Greenup," Morrison replied. "Cal Chase is considering borrowing six thousand dollars to purchase some new land, and I'm not about to let a little snow stand in the way of a deal like that."

"No sir, of course not," Greenup agreed.

All the time that Morrison was in the building, William remained bent over the accounts in front of him, but as soon as the owner left he rose and made himself a cup of tea. Then, when he returned to his desk, he leaned far back in his chair, rested his feet on the corner of his desk, and sipped the steaming brew.

"The old man stands to make a handy profit off this Chase deal," William mused. "After the papers are signed, it might be a good time to ask him for a raise in pay."

"You might give some consideration to earning what you get now before asking for any more," his father replied.

"You act like it's your money, Father!" William complained. "How long have you worked here now? Nineteen or twenty years? And where has it gotten you? You're still in the same job, sitting behind the same desk that you had when you started. And during that same time, Old Man Morrison has gotten rich off your hard work."

"Someday you're going to slip and call him that when he's here, and then you'll be in big trouble," the elder Bird cautioned his son. "If there is one thing Mr. Morrison expects from his subordinates, it's respect. That and complete honesty are requirements for a good bank employee."

"Yes, I can see where all your respect and honesty have gotten you, Father," William said condescendingly. "I can count on the fingers of one hand the number of raises he's given you over the years, and all the while he's continued to get richer and richer through your hard work. Well it's not going to happen to me. I'm not going to grow old hunched over a desk totaling up how much money somebody else has made. I want my share, too."

14

Tiring at last of his son's tirade, Greenup Bird glanced up from his work, removed his wire-rimmed spectacles and raised his hand to rub the marks they had made on the bridge of his nose.

"It's good to dream big, son," he said, "but there is something to be said for simply earning an honest living, too. I may not have been able to give you all the things that Mr. Morrison has provided for his children, but there has never been a time when you didn't have food to eat, a roof over your head, and decent clothes on your back. I have always provided for you and your mother as best I could."

"Yes, I know that Father, but . . ." William paused, realizing that there was no use in continuing. They'd had this discussion many times before, and he knew that what it always boiled down to was that his father simply didn't think big. Whatever great ambitions he might once have had were long gone, and by now he was resigned to his lot in life. But that didn't mean William had to settle for anything but the best. There was a whole continent outside the doors of this place, a vast nation bursting at the seams with growth and opportunity.

His reflections were interrupted by the opening and closing of the front doors of the bank. The two men who entered were both slightly older than William, perhaps in their early twenties. The shoulders of their blue soldier's overcoats and the broad brims of their dark hats were dusted with powdery snow, and the red glow of their noses and bearded cheeks were evidence of the fact that they had been out in the elements for quite some time. One of the men turned aside to warm his hands at the stove, while the other withdrew a bank note from his pocket and started to the teller's window. William Bird rose from his desk and walked over to the counter.

"Can you change this?" the man asked, surrendering the note.

William accepted it and inspected it briefly. These days there was a lot of strange paper money floating around, and Mr. Morrison had laid down strict guidelines about which kinds his bank would and would not accept.

"Yes, we can take this," William announced, "but we have a five percent discount —" He glanced up, intending to explain to his customer precisely what the note was worth in gold U.S. dollars, but suddenly the words caught in his throat and a shudder of unexpected fear swept over him. The man, who had seemed so normal

16

and friendly only an instant ago, now held a cocked revolver pointed at the center of William's chest!

"If you make any noise, I'll shoot you," the stranger warned him. His voice was low and even, but something about the calmness with which the man spoke erased all doubt in William's mind about his ability to carry out his threat.

"But what . . . who . . . ?" William stammered. He glanced around in desperation, only to realize that the second newcomer, the one near the stove, had also pulled a gun and was now pointing it at his father. Greenup Bird remained seated behind his desk, staring dumbstruck at the weapon which threatened him.

Instinctively William began to back away from the counter, but he was stopped short by the desk a couple of paces behind him. The man in front of him placed one hand on the counter and quickly vaulted over it. All the while the aim of his revolver never strayed, even for an instant. Across the room, the second gunman had prodded William's father to his feet and was herding him toward the back of the room.

"What do you men want here?" Greenup Bird asked at last. "Did you come to kill us?"

"It won't come to that if you do what you're told," the second gunman answered. "All we want is the money."

Until that instant, William had been as confused as his father about the intent of these two men. He had never heard of anybody stealing the money from a bank at gun point. How could they hope to get away with it? It was daylight, and they were in the middle of town. It just wasn't done!

The man nearest to William thrust a cotton flour sack into his hand, then took him by the arm and spun him roughly toward the open door of the bank vault.

"Fill it up!" the thief demanded.

When William hesitated, the man struck him hard in the middle of his back with the butt of his revolver, then shoved him harshly forward. Gasping in pain, William stumbled clumsily into the vault and began scooping the stacks of currency off the shelves and into the sack. Needles of pain shot through his back, and his mind seemed numbed by what was happening to him. He had lived through the entire war without ever having to go into the Army, and without ever facing even a moment's danger, but now it suddenly occurred to him that either of these men could, and very possibly might, take his life. Terror stirred a rebellion in his bowels which he was only able to control with great effort.

While William was busy with the money, the second robber, who remained outside the vault, was busy collecting the contents of the tin cash box under the counter. William's father stood slightly to the side, watching in horror as the bank's assets disappeared into the cloth sack.

It took only a moment to gather up all the money. Then the man outside began prodding Greenup Bird toward the door of the vault. Greenup hesitated, trying to reason with the thief.

"Are you young men so sure you want to go through with this?" he said. "You're going to be in a lot of trouble when you're caught. The sheriff of this county —"

"Get in the vault!" the thief demanded. "Get in there or I'll shoot you down and throw you in!"

"All right. All right, I'm going," Greenup said hurriedly and scrambled into the vault.

The thieves forced their victims to move to the rear of the small vault, then they swung the door closed, plunging father and son into complete darkness. They simply stood there awhile longer, still too stunned by the suddenness of the whole incident to know what to do or say.

Then slowly William reached out a hand until he touched the lapel of his father's coat. He needed the contact to reassure him that they were still all right.

"It wasn't our fault, Father," William said, his voice strained and laced with hysteria. "They had guns and there was nothing we could do. Nobody can say it was our fault. We won't lose our jobs, will we, Father?"

"It'll be alright, son," Greenup Bird assured William. "We couldn't have stopped them, and I'm sure Mr. Morrison will agree that our safety is much more important than whatever cash those men took. He'll understand." But even as he spoke the words, Greenup found himself wondering how much truth they actually contained.

The street outside the bank was vacant as the two robbers emerged and started toward their nearby horses, each carrying a cloth sack heavy with loot. Both had thrust their weapons into the pockets of their overcoats so they would not attract attention to themselves, but they were still ready to draw and shoot in an instant.

"Did you see how much *money* we got, Frank?" one of them said quietly to the other. "I never had any idea a little bank like this kept so much cash in it. And it was so easy. There was nothing to it!"

"We made a good haul, brother," the second man agreed with satisfaction as he stuck his foot in the stirrup and swung astride his mount. Both quickly tied their sacks to their saddles, then swung their horses around toward the south edge of town. Meanwhile, throughout the town, over half a dozen other men were casually mounting up. The thieves had not come alone, and now that the job was done, their companions were preparing to leave town with them.

The two robbers had ridden only a few dozen feet down the street when one of them noticed a pair of men stopped beneath the awning of a store nearby. Both were gazing toward the street, talking quietly to one another.

"Those two are staring at us," one of the men told the other anxiously. "I think they might suspect something!"

Even as he spoke, one of the bystanders reached down and thrust a hand inside the heavy winter coat he wore. Before he had a chance to withdraw whatever it was he had been reaching for, the two gunmen opened up with their own revolvers, firing a hurried fusillade in his direction. The man collapsed forward immediately, struck by one of the shots, but his companion was somehow able to leap aside and dodge into the doorway of a nearby hardware store.

As if the first few shots had been a signal, suddenly all the men in the band began to fire wildly into the air, shouting at the top of their lungs as they goaded their horses at full speed toward the road leading south out of town.

A few townspeople risked hurried glances out the windows of their businesses and homes as the mounted band thundered out of sight, but many others remained hidden until the danger had passed, remembering well the destructive powers of men such as these during the recent War Between the States.

CHAPTER TWO

Captain Jack Marshall had one of those lined, wizened faces that by itself told the story of a lifetime spent in adventurous pursuits. He wore no beard, but his thick moustache drooped down on both sides of his mouth almost to his chin, and his hair was streaked with gray. He had a friendly, fatherly sort of face, one that inspired trust and confidence.

Mollie Hartman could only hope that the man was as trustworthy as he appeared because, despite the fact that she had only known him a few short days, she had just turned over a small fortune in gold coins to his keeping.

"All right, there's the full amount that we agreed on," Molly concluded. "Four thousand dollars in gold. And in return, I am to receive one-quarter of the profits from your party's prospecting expedition to Montana Territory. All the papers are signed, so I guess that concludes our agreement." She reached out to bind the pact with a handshake, and though Marshall was slightly surprised by the gesture, he accepted her hand in his and gave it a firm pump.

"Today's a day you'll remember for the rest of your life, Miss Hartman," Marshall told her with a confident smile.

"With pleasure, I hope," Mollie replied. "It wasn't easy coming up with that much gold on such short notice, but either you are the most convincing con man in the West, or you really do have a way to make a fortune for both of us."

"Oh the gold's there, a'right, ma'am," Marshall said. "The whole story is true, just the way I told it to you. I came acrost the spot in the winter of 'sixty-four, lost as a goose, half-starved, and damn near froze to death. Those nuggets I showed you was some of the ones I picked out of the gravel in that creek bed before a storm forced me to push on down to Moose Hennessey's cabin."

"And you will remember to make inquiries about my brother in every place you visit?" Mollie reminded him. "His name is Tyson Hartman, and we last heard from him in 'fifty-nine when he sent a letter from Fort Bridger."

"Yes ma'am, I'll ask around every chance I get, but it's like I told you before. You shouldn't get your hopes all built up, 'specially if it's been that long. It's a hard land out there, and there's more ways than you could ever count for a man to die. Seven years is a long time to stay alive in the Rockies."

"Well, you are living proof that some do survive, aren't you Captain Marshall? And anything at all that you happen to find out about him will be more than we know now."

"Yes ma'am," Marshall agreed.

After the frontiersman was gone, Mollie put the papers they had signed in the small safe in her office, then closed and locked the heavy metal door. This was, without a doubt, one of the biggest financial gambles she had ever taken, but now that it was done she felt no regrets about her decision. Crook or not, Marshall obviously knew the ways of the frontier well, and the other members of the eight-man group he had put together to develop his discovery all impressed Mollie as being competent, hardworking men. There was always the chance that she would never hear from Marshall or any of the others again, but if she did, the possibilities were good that the news would be about all the money they were making in the Montana gold fields.

A light knock sounded on the door to her office, then the door swung open and her bookkeeper, Winfred Marks stepped into the room. Marks was an odd-looking character with an elongated neck and thick wire-rimmed glasses that made his eyes appear to bulge out of their sockets, but despite his curious appearance, he had proved to be a loyal, competent employee. He kept track of Mollie's finances as meticulously as if they were his own, and in the eighteen months he had worked for her she had never found the slightest reason to doubt his honesty.

"There's a man waiting outside the stage door, Mollie," Marks announced. "He says he's an old friend of yours and has asked to see you."

"Did he give his name, Winfred?" Mollie asked

"He said his name is Younger. Coleman Younger."

"Cole . . . ?" She spoke the name so quietly that Marks only saw her lips move. The announcement came as such a surprise to Mollie that for a moment she simply left her assistant standing there, waiting in confusion for some sort of instruction about what to do with the visitor.

"I can tell Hank to make him leave,"

Marks suggested tentatively.

"No, no! I want to see him!" Mollie protested urgently. "It just surprised me to find out he was here. Bring him in right away!"

After Marks left, Mollie fluttered around like a nervous schoolgirl, taking a quick swipe at her hair with a comb, straightening the wrinkles out of her skirts, and wishing briefly that she had taken the time to apply a bit of rouge before she left home that morning.

But all those petty concerns were forgotten the instant Cole Younger appeared in the office doorway. Without thinking, she bounded across the room and threw her arms around him, kissing his cheek warmly as tears of joy welled in her eyes.

"If I'd known a reception like this was waiting for me," Cole announced, a broad grin on his face, "I would have come to see you a long time ago."

"It's just so wonderful to see you, Cole," Mollie said. "I've missed you so much. It seems like you've been away forever!"

"It *has* been two years," Cole said. "And I have to admit there have been a few times in there that I'd have given my right arm to lay eyes on you again, Mollie." Taking her gently by the arms, he moved her away from

27

him a bit so he could get a better look at her. He was glad to see that she still wore her blond hair long, letting it outline her beautiful face and sweep down across her shoulders. The dress she wore was simple yet attractive, with just enough lace around the neckline and sleeves to add a charming elegant touch. Her figure seemed slightly fuller than it had before, but at thirty-two she still had the slender waist and graceful curves of a woman years younger.

"I swear, Mollie," Cole exclaimed after his unabashed examination of her, "you're made out of the stuff a man dreams about on cold winter nights!"

"You old smooth talker!" Mollie exclaimed. "How long have you been back from California?"

"Nearly a month," he admitted.

"And you're just now coming to see me?"

"Well, I've spent most of my time at home with Mama," Cole told her, "and the rest traveling around visiting family and friends. And to tell you the truth, Mollie," he added more soberly, "I wasn't all that sure you would want me to come here . . . not after the way things were the last time we saw each other."

Mollie nodded her head in understanding, remembering how strained and upsetting their last encounter had been for both of them. It had taken place at her brother's farm in Clay County back when the war was still going on. Cole had been preparing to leave for Texas with the band of Confederate irregulars he rode with, but before he went Mollie had felt it her obligation to reveal to him the love affair she was involved in with a Union officer.

They had had a bitter, painful argument, and when Cole had mounted his horse and ridden furiously away, Mollie had not been certain that they would ever see each other again. But that had happened during the worst of times when both their lives had been completely caught up in the turmoil of the war. Now the war was over, and Mollie was delighted to realize that time and the ending of the conflict had washed away all the hard feelings which had once stood so firmly between them.

"I heard what happened to your man right after I got back, Mollie," Cole revealed. "To be honest, I can't say I was sorry that he was killed because he was a Yankee officer, but I am sorry that you lost somebody that you cared so much about."

"It was awful, Cole," Mollie admitted. "When I first heard that Kurt was dead, I thought for a while that I would surely go crazy from the pain of losing him. But you know what's so strange about it now? When I think back about those times, it's like it was all unreal, or that it happened to somebody else. I was living in a dream world back then . . . but. . . ." She paused and shook her head, as if to clear the shadows of the past from it, then said, "But there's no need to go into all of that right now. Let's talk about the present. How long do you plan to stay in Kansas City?"

"I don't have any definite plans," Cole told her. "Since the war's been over I've had a little trouble figuring out what I should be doing with myself, so for now I'm just drifting around and doing pretty much whatever pleases me."

"Where are you staying?"

"I don't have a place yet. I came straight here as soon as I hit town."

"Well, I'm glad you haven't taken a room yet, because I want you to stay with me," Mollie announced. "I guess you've heard that I have a house now."

"Yeah, your brother told me that the rich old lady you used to live with died and left you everything she had. As a matter of fact, he told me that you're doing pretty well for yourself all around."

"It seems like I am," Mollie told him,

"although it surprises me as much as it does anybody else. The whole thing started about nine months ago when the man that owned this theater, Brian Kerr, decided to sell out and head to California. He'd fallen in love with a little trollop named Kate Bonnette, and when she left him and headed west, suddenly nothing would do for Brian but to run after her and try to get her back. So he made me a deal on the theater that I just couldn't turn down, and almost overnight I quit being an actress and started being a businesswoman.

"Then three months after that, poor old Ginnie passed away. I had no idea before she died that I was even in her will, let alone that she planned to leave me everything she had. But suddenly I was the owner of a big house on Quality Hill, and I had thousands of dollars in the bank that I didn't know what to do with. So I started investing a little here and there, making a sort of game out of trying to figure out how Kansas City would grow, and most of my guesses have turned out all right. So far, at least, I've been right more times than I've been wrong."

Talking about her good fortune seemed to embarrass Mollie however, and so she soon turned the conversation in another direction. Brushing her fingers against the fine material of Cole's suit coat, she remarked, "From the looks of things, I guess I'm not the only one who's doing all right. Back when I knew you before, it took a wedding or a funeral to get you this dressed up."

"Well I took to gambling out in California when I saw that it would probably be a better way to earn a living than prospecting or working in somebody else's mine," Cole explained, "and it seems like there's a certain way a man's supposed to look if he's going to make a go of it in that line of work. Then even after I gave that up and decided to come on home, the habit of dressing like this just stuck."

They talked for a while longer before Mollie called Winfred Marks in and announced that she was leaving for the day. Cole had a buggy waiting outside with his gear in back, so they headed straight to Mollie's house to get him settled in.

The house which Mollie had inherited from her close friend and former landlady, Genevieve de Mauduis, was located in one of the older and more exclusive residential areas of Kansas City called Quality Hill. The white two-story Victorian mansion sported a spacious yard and elaborate latticework trim on the outside, and a dozen spacious, high-ceilinged rooms inside. Living alone, with only a housekeeper and handyman to help out, it was far more house than Mollie needed but she loved the place far too much to ever consider selling it and moving someplace else.

There was a moment of awkwardness as they entered the house and started up the front stairway toward the second floor. Not until that moment did it occur to Mollie that every other time Cole had been here, he had stayed in her room and slept with her. Before the war, and even for a time after it started, she and Cole Younger had been lovers. Neither of them could have begun to count the times that they had found pleasure and refuge in one another's arms, but despite that fact, their involvement always had been different from a true love affair. In the beginning, it had sprung more from the depth of their friendship and the longings of their bodies than from the romantic feelings that were supposed to bind a man and woman together forever. Over the years, Mollie had seldom entertained the notion that she and Cole might someday be man and wife, and she could never recall Cole giving any indication that that possibility existed.

Everything had changed between them

when Kurt Rakestraw, the Union officer, had entered Mollie's life. With him she had found romantic love in its purest and most desperate form, the kind of love that Mollie somehow knew she and Cole Younger would never share. And now, though Kurt was dead and Cole was here, more handsome and appealing than ever, Mollie knew that the two of them could not go back to the way things had once been.

Cole seemed to know it too, for when they reached the second floor hallway he told her, "If one of these rooms happens to have a bed that's firmer than the rest, that's the one I'd like to use. Over the past few years I've gotten so used to sleeping on a blanket on the bare ground that somehow a soft mattress just seems to swallow me up and smother me during the night."

"If that's the case, I think you'd like the bed in here," Mollie said, leading him to the second room on the right and opening the door. "Ginnie had boards put under the mattress, and she used to come in here to sleep when her back started bothering her."

Cole set his luggage on the floor, tested the mattress with one hand, and pronounced it acceptable. Then, turning back to his hostess, he said, "I appreciate your hospitality, and I promise I won't wear out my welcome here. I don't know for sure how long I'll stay in the city, but I know it won't be long. These days it seems like no matter where I light, after a little while I start getting restless and ready to be on the move again. I guess it has something to do with the war and with California. Since 'sixty-one, there've been damned few places I've stayed at long enough to call home."

"The longer you stay the better, as far as I'm concerned," Mollie assured him. "It will be a nice change to hear somebody besides myself bumping around this big empty place in the mornings, and having you so close will give us plenty of time to catch up on all that's happened over the last two years."

"That sounds good to me," Cole said, "and we might as well start this evening. I want to take you out to the best restaurant in town to celebrate our reunion."

They made a handsome couple, Mollie in her white satin gown and Cole in his broadcloth suit. For this special occasion Mollie selected the restaurant in the Benton Hotel, which was famous throughout the area for its French chef and its remarkable wine selection. The Benton was one of the newest hotels in Kansas City, and the lavishness of its furnishings was reflective of the growing affluence of many of the city's residents since the war ended. After over a decade of almost constant strife and bloodshed, it seemed to many that, at last, Missouri was finally coming into its own.

The tip which Cole gave the maître d' assured them a private booth in the rear of the restaurant, and once they were seated, the wine steward appeared almost immediately to give them his recommendations. Cole ordered a bottle of champagne, then selected a second bottle of wine to drink with dinner.

"I'm very impressed, Cole," Mollie teased her companion lightly. "The roughneck Cole Younger that I knew a few years ago would not have even wanted to come into a place like this, let alone known how to order the best bottle of wine in the house."

"I guess I picked up a thing or two out west in places like San Francisco," Cole explained. "The city's still young, just like Kansas City, but where there's as much gold as there is in California, somebody's bound to come up with expensive things for people to spend that gold on."

"Well you haven't said much about it yet," Mollie noted, "but you must have done all right for yourself out there."

"There were good times and bad," he said.

"When I was on a roll and I had the money for French wine, that's all I drank, and when I didn't, mescal or rotgut whiskey got the job done just as well."

"What made you quit Quantrill's Raiders and go west before the war was over, Cole?" Mollie asked at last. "I know you were very upset with me when you left here and rode with them to Texas, but surely that wasn't it. Even my nephews John and Daniel who were there with you said they never knew exactly why you did it. They told me that one day you just said you were leaving, and then you got on your horse and rode away."

"No, it really didn't have anything to do with you," Cole assured her. "It's just that things were crazy for us in Texas. That was the third year of the war, and by then a lot of the men were so wild that even Quantrill couldn't do anything with them. Finally he lost control completely, and then the group started breaking up. Some went off to join the regulars, and most of the others fell in line behind either George Todd or Bill Anderson.

"I could tell by then that the war was lost, but what bothered me even more was that all the fighting we had done here — supposedly in the name of our own people, the people of Missouri — hadn't helped any-

37

body a damned bit. After a while, it actually looked to me like we were doing them more harm than good by keeping the Federals constantly stirred up like a nest of hornets."

He sipped his champagne, and his eyes took on a faraway look as he recalled those tragic and tumultuous times.

"I promise you, Mollie, that it was one of the hardest things I ever did," he said, "just riding away and leaving John and Daniel and a lot of others that I had fought with for three long years. But I guess I was starting to get scared . . . not of being killed or wounded, but scared that if I kept on the way I was going, pretty soon I'd turn into a mindless killer, just like Bill Anderson and Arch Clement and some of the others already had. It was becoming so goddamned easy to kill a man . . . so easy. . . ."

A moment of stillness fell over them as the waiter appeared at their table. Bringing themselves back to the present momentarily, they ordered their meal and waited for the waiter to leave.

"Well I'm glad you left if that's what might have happened to you," Mollie said. She reached across the table to take his hand in hers as she added, "And I'm glad you're here now, too. You know, Cole, you're the best friend I've ever had in my life, and probably the best one I ever will have."

"We've lived a lot of history, haven't we, Mollie?" Cole said.

"Yes, and I hope we have a lot more left to live," she replied. "That terrible ordeal is finally over, and maybe things will get better from now on. Now that the killing has stopped, maybe everybody can just settle down and live their lives in peace."

"Maybe . . ." Cole said without conviction.

After another momentary pause, Mollie decided the time was right to move on to more pleasant topics. "You told me you've been to see my brother and his family recently," she said. "How are they? Is there any news?"

"Jason and Arethia are doing well. Your brother and Ben are working the farm alone this year, and John and Daniel are making a crop on your father's land. They're all fine, just like you'd expect. The one that surprised me the most, I guess, was your niece Cassie. The last time I remember seeing her, she was just a little pigtailed girl with jam on her face and one shoe untied. But now, my God! She's seventeen years old, but she looks twenty and thinks she's twenty-five. After I was there a couple of days I kept noticing her looking at me and smiling all the time. Finally it hit me that she was trying to *flirt* with me. Can you believe it? With me!"

"It's in the blood of the Hartman women," Mollie said and laughed. "We like to keep our skills honed, which means that we have to practice as often as we can with any man that's available. And I'm sure you appear to be quite a dashing figure to her. I know you do to me."

Cole smiled at her, and for an instant she glimpsed that old light shining in his eyes. Mollie knew that at that moment they were both recalling the times they'd been lovers. . . . It made her feel old suddenly to realize how long ago all that had been, and how much had happened since to change things between them. But she let the mood rule her for only an instant before remembering the pleasure she felt at being reunited with Cole once again.

"I think I'd like a little more champagne before our food arrives, Cole," Mollie said, sliding her glass across the table toward him. "It's been a long time since I let my hair down and just got giddy and silly, but perhaps tonight's the night for it. At least I know if I do get drunk, I'm with someone I can trust."

"The last time I heard words like those,"

Cole told her, a teasing smile on his lips, "they were spoken by a pretty young senorita in Monterrey . . . and she found out later that evening how trustworthy I really was."

"Then I guess I'll just have to take my chances," Mollie laughed, pushing her glass a little closer to her friend. "Pour the wine, Cole."

CHAPTER THREE

Ridge Parkman stood in the doorway of the farmhouse, a cup of coffee in one hand and a cigar in the other, gazing out over the broad, lush field of corn across the road. It was good land, rich and productive, and the sights and smells of the farm stirred memories of the years he had spent growing up in a place like this. Now, after more than a decade away from such a tranquil setting, he found those memories had a nostalgic quality. He had difficulty reminding himself of the backbreaking, dawn-to-dusk work that it took to make a farm as profitable as this one appeared to be.

Behind him, two rooms away in the kitchen, his mother was clattering around putting away the last of the pots and pans she had used to cook their lunch. It had been a simple enough meal of homegrown meat and vegetables, but because it had been prepared by his mother's hands, and

42

because it had been so long since he had settled down at his mother's table, the food had seemed particularly delicious.

Unexpected circumstances had brought him here, and Ridge had not even been able to give his mother any warning that he was coming home. Several days before, his superior in the United States Marshal's Office in Denver had asked for a volunteer to escort a prisoner back east to Kansas City for trial, and Ridge had accepted the assignment because it would bring him so close to his mother and the rest of his family. Before leaving Denver, he had requested a month's leave so that he would have some time for a proper visit with his family.

Sarah Parkman now lived on a farm which had been started by her brother, William Hartman, in the early 1850s. William had been not only a knowledgeable farmer, but also a shrewd businessman, and with the help of the stable of slaves he owned he had turned the place into a thriving enterprise before his death at the hands of a band of Kansas abolitionists in 1858. A year later Sarah had traveled west to Missouri from Virginia along with her father, her brother Jason and his family. Jason, his wife Arethia, and their children still lived on the farm they'd established nearby, and Sarah and

43

her father Will had set up housekeeping here on William's place.

Will Hartman, the patriarch of the clan, had been killed during the war, but even after his death, Sarah had somehow managed to make a go of the place by herself, sometimes using hired hands when they were available, but more often hitching up a team and working the fields herself. Things were better now, though, Ridge thought. After the war ended her nephews John and Daniel, both sons of Jason, had moved in here with her and were working the lands on shares. The fields of ripening corn and wheat which now surrounded the simple farmhouse were their doing, and Sarah had happily reported to her son during lunch that once the crops were in and the spring loans were repaid, there would still be a decent profit to be split three ways by her and her nephews.

This place had never been home to Ridge Parkman, though. He had left Virginia the year before his mother moved west, and within a short time had signed on as a U.S. Marshal in Washington D.C. His various assignments during the war had taken him farther and farther west, and by the time Lee surrendered at Appomattox, he was spending most of his time deep in the Rocky mountains tracking down some of the many outlaws and undesirables who plagued the mining districts there.

Ridge Parkman had visited this place only twice since his mother moved here, but they had kept in contact by mail, and during the worst days after Will Hartman's death he had regularly sent home a portion of his meager monthly wages to help her get by.

Although she was only forty-six, the hard country life had aged Sarah Parkman surprisingly since the last time her son had seen her. Her dark hair was starting to take on a steely gray cast, and the lines around her eyes and mouth had begun to deepen. Inside, however, she was still the same woman — quiet, reserved, deeply loyal to her family and her religious faith, resigned and uncomplaining about the life she led and the fate which was hers.

In recent years, Ridge had begun to view his mother as a vaguely tragic figure. Widowed a few months before her son's birth, she had never been able to forget her husband or give herself to any other man. From family stories, Ridge gathered that once during her girlhood Sarah Parkman had been a gay, spirited young woman, but the tragic death of her husband Randolph when she was only fifteen years old had somehow drained all the liveliness and gaiety out of her forever. To Ridge's knowledge, she had never allowed another man to court her since that day in 1835 when a horse thief's bullet had ended the life of dashing young Randolph Parkman.

Ridge heard his mother walking quietly toward him across the living room, and he turned to smile at her. She smiled back readily, her eyes aglow with the pleasure of his unexpected presence. Together they went out onto the front porch and took a seat on the swing which hung by chains from a beam overhead.

"Now that I'm here," Ridge admitted, "I feel guilty about not coming to see you sooner. Two or three times over the past couple of years I've planned trips back, but something always seemed to come up, some matter that the captain thought was important enough to cancel my leave and keep me in Colorado."

"Don't feel bad about things like that, son," Sarah told him. "Your life and your work are there now, and I understand. I'm proud of you for becoming the man that you have, and I'd never fault you for not being able to make the long trip back to Missouri as often as you'd like." She paused a moment, then added, "But I must confess, do worry about the danger you must be in sometimes. We all thanked the Lord when the war ended and John and Daniel were both able to return safely to us, but I can't forget that for you the danger is still as great as it ever was."

"It's not always a bed of roses," Ridge agreed, "but I have become a very cautious fellow, and without sounding boastful, I also have to admit that I'm pretty darned good at my job. Somebody's got to do what I do if this land's ever going be safe for decent, hardworking folks to live in."

"I suppose so, son," Sarah said. "I suppose you're right."

They were quiet for a moment, swaying slowly to and fro on the swing. Then Ridge asked, "So you say John and Daniel plan to be back this afternoon? I'm anxious to see them and to thank them for the good job they've been doing around here."

"Well they said when they left yesterday morning that they should be home this afternoon," Sarah told him. "They just rode over to Stockdale to look at some horses, and it's only a forty-mile round trip."

"They were off fighting somewhere the last time I was home, and so I haven't seen either of them for more than six years. I bet both of them have changed so much that I wouldn't even recognize them anymore."

"They have changed, Ridge," Sarah agreed. "Of course, they're both grown men now. Daniel is twenty-one and John is twenty-three. But riding with Quantrill's Raiders for three years put more age on them than the simple passage of time ever could. Long after they came home, I didn't think either of them would be able to settle down to this kind of life anymore. But they've worked hard at it, and so far they've done all right."

"They sure have," Ridge said, surveying the nearby fields once again. "I remember the last time I was here, most of this land was fallow. Between the Jayhawkers and the bushwhackers, you didn't have any stock left but a few scrawny chickens, and the only crop that was growing was a few dozen acres of corn and vegetables that you had planted and tended by yourself."

"That's true, but still and all, I was far better off than hundreds of other people who lived in these parts. At least I was still alive, and I had a roof over my head and food to eat. Back in the summer of 'sixty-four when things got really bad, sometimes I would try to feed ten and twelve folks a day who passed by here near to starvation and with no place to go. A lot of them were

48

women and children with no men left to take care of them and not a cent in their pockets to get them to anyplace safe. I remember times when I would just cook up big pans of cornbread for everybody because that was all that was left here to eat, but even then I still knew I was lucky to be lying down each night in my own bed in my own home."

"You're a good woman, Sarah Parkman," Ridge told his mother. "To give up so much to people you didn't even know."

"I couldn't have done anything else, son," Sarah replied quietly. "I couldn't have turned them away, not as long as there was a single mouthful of anything left here to feed them with. If you could have only looked into their eyes and seen the fear and desperation there. . . . But times are much better now," she added brightly. "They say that a lot of people who were driven from their homes in Jackson County by the Jayhawkers and the Union soldiers are starting to come back, and the market prices for everything are starting to go up. We're finally beginning to do well again."

"All I can say is that you deserve it," Ridge told his mother. "After all you've been through, you deserve every bit of good fortune that comes your way." He stubbed out the butt of his cigar on the heel of his boot and tossed it into the yard, then drained the last of the coffee from his cup and rose to his feet.

"I'm going up to the barn to take a look at that stone bruise on General Grant's hoof," he announced. "It didn't seem to be bothering him on the ride up from Kansas City, but I want to keep an eye on it for a while longer anyway."

"That's sure a fine name for a Virginia boy to give his horse." Sarah complained lightly as he started away. "It's a wonder my mules, Stonewall and Memphis, can stand to stay in the same barn with a creature named that."

"Well I haven't heard any ruckus from that direction since I stabled General Grant a couple of hours ago," Ridge said, chuckling, "so I guess they worked it out amongst themselves."

The sun was nearly down and Ridge was walking the fence row along one side of a field of corn, thinking of times long ago. All of his childhood years had been spent living in his grandfather's home, where Sarah had returned to stay immediately after the death of her husband. They had farmed there too, of course, and from the age of six, Ridge

50

had been accustomed to putting in long hours in the fields with his grandfather all during the summer months. Things had been different back in Virginia, though, because the land they worked had been nearly farmed out, and it had been a constant battle each year to persuade the stony hillsides to yield even a meager crop. Back then, he thought, many a Virginia farmer would have sold his soul to produce a stand of corn like the one he was now walking by.

Despite the struggles, Ridge still remembered his childhood fondly. His grandfather had been a stern but caring man, deeply devoted to his family, and his grandmother, until her death in 1851, had been one of the most good and loving people Ridge had ever known. He had been only slightly younger than his Uncle Tyson and his Aunt Mollie, and the three of them had grown up more as brothers and sister than as nephew, aunt and uncle. He learned from his mother that Tyson had gone west to the frontier even before Ridge had headed in that direction, but their paths had never crossed during the years Ridge had spent in Colorado. And as far as Mollie was concerned . . . well, Ridge planned to have a good long visit with her in Kansas City before he headed out on his way back to Denver.

He stopped beside one of the stalks of corn, which rose a couple of feet higher than his head, and grasped one of the two fat ears which the stalk had borne. Beneath the husk he could feel the kernels of corn, thick and mature. He pulled the ear free, stripped back the husk and took a bite, savoring the sweet flavor in his mouth like a long-forgotten treat.

It was funny, he thought, standing there with the ear still in his hand, that such a simple act as this could invoke such a vivid recollection. He could practically see his grandfather in his faded old bib overalls, standing at the edge of a corn field, tasting the fruits of his summer's labor to gauge whether harvest time had arrived. And Ridge remembered himself at that time, a shirtless, unshod, towheaded boy of eleven or twelve standing nearby with an ear in his hands as well, solemnly imitating the old man.

"Mister, I'd like for you to hold your hands out away from your body and turn around real slow so I can get a look at who you are," a stern male voice announced from somewhere behind Ridge.

A momentary flash of panic shot through Ridge as he realized that his gunbelt still lay on the table beside his mother's sofa and that he was out here completely unarmed and unprepared for trouble. But close on the heels of that instinctive reaction came the realization of who the man who had just spoken must be. A grin was already starting to spread across his face by the time he completed his turn.

Each of the two men who faced him held a cocked revolver in his hand. Beneath their full beards, Ridge managed to recognize the still boyish visages of his cousins John and Daniel.

"We don't want any trouble and we have no plans to harm you," the taller of the two said calmly. That, Ridge decided, was John. "We just want to know who you are and what you're doing wandering around out here in our field."

"I guess you haven't been by the house yet," Ridge said with a grin.

"Why?" the second man asked with a sudden edge of tension in his voice. "What's happened at the house?"

"Nothing in particular, I suppose. But I'd guess that my mother is cooking our supper by now, and if the three of us stand around out here jawing for much longer, it's sure to be cold by the time we get there."

"Ridge Parkman?" John exclaimed in disbelief. "Cousin Ridge?"

53

"None other," Ridge replied. "Now if the two of you will holster that iron and let me put my hands down, I'd say it's about time we got on to some handshaking!"

Recovering from the unexpectedness of the encounter, both John and Daniel quickly put their weapons away and stepped forward to greet their cousin with handshakes and hearty backslaps.

"I'm real sorry about the guns and all, Ridge," John explained, "but old habits die slow, I guess. We spotted you out here as we were riding down the road, and it seemed like you might be trying to slip around the edge of the field toward the house."

"All our enemies didn't go away just because the war ended," Daniel added. "There's still a lot of hard feelings in this part of the country because of what was going on two and three years ago, and there's still some fellows around with a mind to settle a few old scores."

"It never hurts for a man to be cautious," Ridge told them. "And judging from how easy it was for you two to get the drop on me, I'd say I wasn't cautious enough."

The three of them turned and started toward the house, stopping briefly along the way to get the horses which John and Daniel had left out of sight on the far side of the field. Near the house, Daniel turned aside to lead the two mounts to the barn while Ridge and John went on inside.

In the kitchen Sarah was just setting the table for supper, as Ridge had predicted. Daniel came in a few minutes later, and while her son and nephews were washing up, she began to bring large bowls of food to the table.

"So how did the horse buying go?" Ridge asked. "I saw that you didn't bring any back with you except the two you were riding."

"We bought six head," John explained, "and the man is going to deliver them later. Daniel and I are thinking about getting into a little breeding. There's good money in it, and the time's finally come when the Army doesn't sweep through the countryside every few weeks buying every saddle horse they can find from the civilians for twenty dollars a head."

"Back when we were fighting the Federals, we came to appreciate the value of good horseflesh," Daniel commented casually. It was the first mention anyone had made about how the Hartman brothers had spent their time during the recent war, and it caused a sudden, uneasy silence to fall over the table. They were all uncomfortably aware of the fact that Ridge and his cousins had been on opposite sides of the conflict, although Ridge's involvement in Colorado had been less direct than that of John and Daniel in Missouri.

Finally Ridge swallowed a mouthful of fried chicken and said, "You're right about that, Daniel. I've learned that having a good animal under you can sometimes give you that little bit of edge when it counts the most. I gave four hundred dollars for that horse I ride now, but he's paid for himself many times over since I bought him."

"I saw him when I was up in the barn," Daniel replied. "He's a fine animal, just the kind John and I are looking for."

"Well you can forget that," Ridge told him, grinning broadly. "They haven't minted enough money yet to buy him from me."

After a few more minutes of conversation, John and Daniel began telling their aunt the bits of local news they had picked up during their trip. They told her of a new Methodist church which was being built in Richmond, and related the sordid details of how the wife of a store owner in Liberty had run off with a traveling farm implements salesman, only to be abandoned by him in Springfield to make her way back home in disgrace.

"Speaking of Liberty," Sarah said, "have they had any more word about who might have taken all that money from the bank there back in February?" There was an odd note of concern in her voice that made Ridge pause and look up at her.

"There's a lot of names being tossed around," John said, "most of them former Quantrill men, of course. But nobody really knows anything for sure. The truth is, even the two clerks in the bank couldn't agree on the descriptions of the two men who actually went inside. And as far as the others who waited outside, well, they say it was snowing that day, and hardly anybody was out on the street."

"I heard about that robbery all the way out in Denver," Ridge commented. "And after I read the story in the paper, I thought it was a funny thing that nobody had ever thought of robbing a bank before. How much was it that they took?"

"We heard it was about sixty thousand dollars," Daniel answered. "But I'd be willing to bet it wasn't that much. There's a lot of reasons why a bank owner might lie about a thing like that."

"I suppose so," Ridge said. "But no matter how much it was, it's going to cause some real problems from now on. After those fellows showed how easy it was to rob a bank, I guess we'll be seeing it happen all over the country now."

"Maybe," John commented. Then he added more bitterly, "And maybe some of these big dog bankers need to have their pockets emptied once in a while. A lot of them have gotten rich by taking everything away from ordinary people who got behind on their notes when times were hard. I've got no sympathy with the bankers, none at all."

"Well, I can't argue with you about that," Ridge said, "because I know what the bankers sometimes do to folks. But as far as these fellows who robbed the bank in Liberty are concerned, I have my doubts about whether they thought they were making some sort of point on behalf of the ordinary people. I expect they just did it so they could have the money, plain and simple."

"Maybe, Ridge," John replied. "Maybe so."

After they finished eating they remained in the kitchen awhile. Daniel helped his aunt clear the table, then dried and put away the dishes while she washed. Ridge and John sat at the table smoking and drinking coffee.

"In one of her letters, mother told me that you and Daniel had some problems getting parole after the war was over," Ridge commented to his cousin. "How did that all turn out?"

"Nothing was ever settled about it," John replied in disgust. "The Federals made allowances for Confederate regulars to take an oath and get a parole so they could go home, but Quantrill's men never got that opportunity. They said we were outlaws instead of soldiers, and that if we wanted to turn ourselves in we would have to face trial for the things we did. But nobody's ever tried to enforce that. Most of the bushwhackers Dan and I knew finally did the same thing we did. After a couple of months of hiding and waiting to see what would happen, we just got on our horses and went home. And so far it's been all right. We settled in here with Aunt Sarah, and nobody's tried to bother us, but technically we're still fighting."

"There's still plenty of hatred and distrust just under the surface around here," Daniel added from over by the cupboard. "The people are still pretty much divided in their thinking according to the way they felt back during the war. We have our friends scattered all over who think that Quantrill's

Raiders were the only reason that this whole part of the state wasn't completely destroyed by the Federals and the Jayhawkers. And then there are those who believe that we're the lowest dogs that God ever accidentally made. You can bet that any time a hen house gets raided or a folding knife gets swiped from a hardware store, there's going to be somebody who will stand up and swear that a former bushwhacker must have done it."

"At this point, I wouldn't try to fault you for doing what you believed you had to do," Ridge told his cousins. "But surely all the bushwhackers didn't take to peacetime life as quickly as you two did. There must have been some bad apples as well."

"Sure, there were plenty of them," Daniel said. "Especially toward the end when things got so wild and dangerous that no completely sane man would have stuck it out. We had our share of madmen just like any outfit. Maybe more."

"Well what happened to them?"

"Most are dead, I guess, which is probably just as well for some. I can't imagine men like Bloody Bill Anderson or George Todd ever going back to walking behind a plow or stocking shelves in a dry goods store. But the point we're trying to make is, that the war created a lot of deadly, desperate men all over the nation, and not just here in Missouri among Quantrill's bunch. And yet all those other men were given the chance to go home and turn their lives around and live in peace . . . but not us. Every day we still live with the threat of being arrested and hauled into court for the things we did as soldiers."

"Why do you think we were so careful with you out there in the field before we found out who you were, Ridge?" John asked quietly. "We've been home for a year now, but we still never know what day a posse might show up and try to take us in."

Having lived with danger so much of the time during the last few years, Ridge could easily understand the strain that his cousins were under. And yet he also knew that during the war, the bushwhackers had not considered it their obligation to live by the same rules that other soldiers lived by. They gave no quarter to their opponents, and seldom if ever did they let enemy prisoners, even helpless unarmed ones, remain alive. The targets they chose were as often civilian as military, and some of their acts ranked near the top of the list of ruthless atrocities committed during the war. Listening to his cousins' arguments, it was easy to understand the sense of injustice they felt, and yet he still was not convinced that all the irregulars who rode with men such as William Quantrill deserved the same sort of postwar leniency and forgiveness as did the line troops in the regular Confederate forces.

But he still had enough sense not to press the issue. It was his first day home, and he was much more concerned with visiting with his mother and becoming reacquainted with his family than he was with starting an argument which could only raise an ugly barrier between himself and his cousins.

After the dishes were cleaned and put away, Daniel announced that he was going to ride over to his parents' home, which was about two miles away, and tell them of Ridge's arrival.

"Tell them I'll be over to see them tomorrow," Ridge said. "I have a whole month before I have to report back for duty, and I plan to spend every day of it with my family."

"I'll tell them," Daniel said, "but if I was you, I wouldn't count on getting much sleep tonight, Ridge. When I get back, I can almost guarantee you that at least my father and my brother Ben will be with me."

"Well if they decide to come," Ridge said, "we'll get Mother to put on another pot of coffee and we'll make a night of it. We've all got a lot of catching up to do."

CHAPTER FOUR

A long line of people waited to congratulate the cast of the play. Mercedes Lovejoy had been the shining star of the event, and now, even after the final curtain, she was still performing with the same casual mix of innocence and seductiveness that she had used earlier in the evening to captivate her audience, or at least the male portions of it.

Mollie Hartman stood to one side of the backstage area which had been cleared for the opening night party. She watched her cast receive the shallow praise of their admirers with fixed smiles and stock expressions of gratitude. She preferred to remain in the background herself, to attend to the myriad details of orchestrating the event, to keep the champagne flowing and the serving table well-stocked with catered delicacies.

Mollie actually hated these affairs, although she was the inspiration behind them

and they had proved to be consistently successful publicity ploys to boost attendance
at the theater. Gaining an invitation to one
of them had become quite a coup among
Kansas City's burgeoning class of social elit-
ists, and heavy attendance by members of
the city's press corps usually guaranteed
good reviews in the local papers.

The thing she disliked most about these
gatherings, Mollie decided, aside from the
expense, was the airs that so many of her
guests adopted. Formal evening attire had
long ago become the standard, and the
majority of the attendees spent the entire
evening gliding and mincing around the
backstage area like peacocks on parade.
Most of the people there represented first-
generation wealth, and they usually ended
up appearing merely as sad parodies of the
sophisticates they believed they had become.

Mollie watched as a man named Simon
Gill, a short, heavyset fellow in his early for-
ties, leaned forward to whisper something
in Mercedes Lovejoy's ear. Mercedes
feigned shock at his remark and lightly
slapped his cheek in mock reproof, but all
the while the smile never left her pretty
powdered features as he passed on down
the line letting another man step forward to
take her hand and speak his piece.

Mercedes had been a real find for Mollie, coming along when Mollie had been in need of a dazzling leading lady. After buying the theater and leaving the stage herself, Mollie had gone through a succession of mediocre actresses, trying to find just one who had the charm and acting ability to keep the customers coming back time after time as she herself had done. And then one day Mercedes simply walked in off the street and asked for a job.

She had been traveling through town with a medicine show, playing the part of Delilah in a play about Samson's downfall, but a fight with the owner of the show had left her adrift and penniless hundreds of miles from her Louisiana home. Strictly on the basis of the girl's looks, Mollie had hired her on the spot and given her a part in a play.

A curious relationship soon developed between the two women. They cared very little for one another on a personal level, as is often the case with beautiful women, but each saw something in the other which she believed she could use to her own advantage.

Mercedes Lovejoy quickly realized that her looks and talent far outstripped those of the other actresses currently available to

Mollie, and she used that knowledge to seize the leading role in the next play Mollie produced. Of course her salary demands were commensurate with her rapid rise to stardom.

Mollie's own time on stage gave her the ability to recognize what Mercedes could become with the proper training and guidance and how much money the young actress would bring into the theater. The first thing she did was hire a dressmaker to create a completely new onstage wardrobe for her young find. The clothes which she helped design herself were neither flashy nor overtly sensual, but in various subtle ways all of Mercedes' new outfits served to emphasize her slender, twenty-four-year-old figure.

Next Mollie undertook the task of teaching Mercedes to act for the particular productions she appeared in. No great Shakespearean qualities were required here. In the simplest of terms, she needed to speak loudly and clearly without appearing to shout, to exaggerate the inflections in her voice and the expressions on her face so that each member of the audience in every part of the theater, would understand clearly what emotion was being portrayed.

But beyond these elementary techniques

and changes, Mollie knew that she could take little credit for the local sensation that Mercedes Lovejoy had become. Because of her flirtatious manner, admirers flocked around the young woman, offering her everything from lavish overnight dalliances to lengthy trips abroad in exchange for her attentions. Rumors circulated about her constantly, but none had the power to lessen the overwhelming popularity that she had experienced during her first year as a full-fledged star.

Mollie knew, of course, that eventually she would lose Mercedes. Someday some man would come along with enough looks, charm and wealth to purchase her affections, or she might decide that even grander opportunities awaited her in some other city like New York, San Francisco or even London. But for now all was well, and each of the women was satisfied with the advantages which the present situation afforded her.

Off to one side of the backstage area, Mollie saw a waiter duck behind a curtain long enough to drain three glasses of the champagne he was serving, and she hurried over to inform him that the price for his little indulgence would be deducted from his wages. By the time she returned to her station at one end of the buffet table, she saw that the reception line was dwindling and that the members of the cast were beginning to circulate among the guests. Each had stern orders to take it easy with champagne and to stay sober, but Mollie knew there were a couple among them who would still bear watching.

Mollie spotted a tall man heading in her general direction but paid him little attention until he came right up to her and said, "I noticed that you don't have a glass of champagne, ma'am. Would you allow me the privilege of bringing you one?" His manner of speaking was cultured and smooth, rich with Southern charm and chivalry.

Mollie's first impulse to refuse, but then she decided that perhaps the party was going well enough for her to relax a little.

"Yes, I would like some. Thank you," she told him. As he turned away to find a waiter, she found herself watching him cross the room. He was a tall, not overly husky fellow with wavy black hair, charming brown eyes and darkly handsome features. He was dressed in formal garb similar to that of her other guests, but on him the striped pants, black coat, white shirt and bow tie looked somehow more natural and appropriate than it did on most of the other men.

"Permit me to introduce myself to you,"

the stranger said as he returned with a glass of champagne for Mollie. "My name is Bedford Lee."

"It's a pleasure to meet you, Mr. Lee," Mollie replied, accepting the glass with one hand and surrendering the other to him. "I'm Mollie Hartman."

"Yes, I know," Lee said with a smile. "I wouldn't be a very good guest if I didn't know who my hostess was, would I?"

"I don't recall ever hearing your name before, Mr. Lee," Mollie admitted. "Are you new in town?"

"Yes I am. I found myself passing through Kansas City a few days ago, and I discovered that I liked the place and the people here so much that I decided to stay for a while. That's one advantage of being in the business I'm in. You can practice your trade just about anywhere."

"And what trade might that be?" she asked.

"Well, you might say I'm involved in financial matters." Lee grinned. "I help people transfer their funds . . . usually from their pockets to mine. I'm a professional gambler."

"I see," Mollie said. She had suspected him to be something of the sort, but hearing him so casually confirm it still put her on her guard. Men like this one usually brought trouble with them in some shape or form.

"I suppose you're wondering what I'm doing at your party," Lee continued. "The fact is, Miss Hartman, I am here uninvited. During tonight's performance I heard the couple next to me talking about the affair that was to be held afterward, and I just decided to see if I could slip in. As I told you, I'm new in Kansas City, and this seemed like a good opportunity to meet some of the more interesting and cultured people here."

"And some of the more wealthy as well?" Mollie asked lightly.

"Well, I'm never opposed to such a thing," Lee confessed openly. "High-stakes games with men who have plenty of cash to spend on their vices is one of my specialties, but I assure you that that was not my main motive. It's like I said before. I hardly know anybody in this city, and I am a man who enjoys good friends and satisfying companionship."

"The truth is, Mr. Lee," Mollie told him, lowering her voice so her comment would not be accidentally overheard, "that many of the people here probably do have more money than they know how to handle intel-

71

ligently, and if you can manage to get your hands on some of it by any legal means, then more power to you. All I ask is that you wait until you're away from here to do whatever it is you do to lure them into your clutches. I hold these parties to build good will among my patrons, and it simply wouldn't do for them to think I had anything to do with setting them up as prey for a card sharp."

"You make me sound like quite a predator," Lee noted, tempering the remark with a smile to show that he was not offended. "But I can assure you that I am not. There are times in a game when everything I do is wrong and I find myself losing money hand over fist just like everybody else. The only difference between me and most of the people I gamble with is that I don't lose as often as I win."

Lee noticed that Mollie's glass was empty and was about to get her more champagne when Mercedes Lovejoy appeared suddenly at his elbow. Her appearance seemed to surprise Lee, but Mollie was not surprised at all. Since Lee was one of the most attractive men in the room, and apparently unattached as well, Mollie had known it would only be a matter of time before the young actress would be compelled to come over and make a stab at adding him to her stable of worshippers.

"Mr. Bedford Lee," Mollie said, "may I present Miss Mercedes Lovejoy, the star of tonight's performance of *Unkind Destiny.*"

Taking Mercedes' hand in his, Lee said, "I'm glad I have the opportunity to meet you so I can tell you how wonderful you were in tonight's performance. I'm sure this is something you hear often, but there were a couple of times tonight when I wanted to just come up on stage and put a bullet between Bart Teasdale's eyes because of how badly he was treating you."

Mercedes laughed. "Less than a month ago a slightly intoxicated gentleman tried to do just that. Fortunately the members of the orchestra stopped him before he could get on stage, but it disturbed Tommy Smith, who plays Bart, so much that he could hardly finish the play."

"Mr. Lee is new in town and has come here tonight seeking satisfying companionship," Mollie explained to Mercedes. She was surprised by the sharply sarcastic tone of her own words, but the two people with her scarcely seemed to notice the brittle comment. Mercedes was bringing the full force of her charms to bear on this handsome stranger, and as each moment passed,

73

Lee seemed to become more and more fascinated by the beautiful, young actress.

"He strikes me as a gentleman who would seldom have trouble finding that," Mercedes said, smiling intimately.

"But the key word here is 'satisfying', Miss Lovejoy," Lee said, never taking his eyes from hers. "And you might be surprised how difficult that is to come by sometimes. Especially for a traveling man like me."

Mollie decided that she couldn't stand any more of this. "If you will excuse me, Mr. Lee," she announced crisply, "I must go and make sure the needs of my other guests are being met as well as yours seem to be." She turned abruptly and started away, imagining that her absence would not even be noticed by the pair she left behind. She was soon absorbed into the general throng of guests, and for the next few minutes she made it a point to keep her eyes and her attention distracted from the area where she had left Mercedes Lovejoy and Bedford Lee together.

The party continued for about another hour. Eventually Mercedes began to circulate again, but now it was with Lee at her side. She introduced him to a number of prominent local residents and newspaper people, but she seemed to make every effort to steer him away from the other young women who played lesser parts in the play. Her intentions toward Lee were obvious, as they usually were when Mercedes Lovejoy selected a man that she considered worthy of her attentions.

When the guests began to leave at last, Mollie busied herself with the details of seeing them off. At one point she saw Mercedes and Bedford emerging from the young actress's dressing room. Mercedes had her wrap on and was clinging tightly to his left arm, laughing gaily at some remark he had just made. Together they disappeared behind some scenery, heading toward the small, private entrance at the back of the theater.

Mollie tried to convince herself that it was for Mercedes' sake that she hated to see the two of them going off like that. Despite his charm and good manners, no one knew anything at all about this tall, handsome stranger. By his own admission he was a member of a profession which bred rogues and rowdies, and despite Merdeces' considerable talents at bending men to her will, Mollie doubted that her young employee could be any match for a man of this sort. God only knew what kinds of trouble Lee might convince Mercedes to get into if he chose to do so.

But it was none of her business, Mollie resolved. She had never interfered in Mercedes Lovejoy's personal affairs before, and she was not about to start tonight.

After the last guest was gone, Mollie paid off the servers and sent them home. Then she gave instructions to two stagehands who remained to turn out the last of the lamps before leaving. Both had already consented to come in the first thing in the morning and finish cleaning up the backstage area and putting everything away. Fifteen minutes later Mollie watched the last employee go home.

The exhaustion of the long day finally began to catch up with Mollie as she started toward her office. The theater was completely dark now except for the bubble of light radiating from the small candle lantern which she carried. The place seemed oddly still after the hubbub and confusion of the party, but Mollie enjoyed the quiet and she relished the thought that within another half-hour, she would be home in bed with this business of opening night behind her for at least another few weeks, the time it would take for *Unkind Destiny* to run its course and for another play to begin.

In her office she made sure the door to

her heavy iron safe was closed and locked. Then she retrieved her cape and started to leave. As she was locking the office door, she detected a faint noise somewhere behind her in the shadowy expanse of the backstage area. It sounded, she thought, like the scrape of a shoe on the bare wooden floor.

For a moment she remained still, trying to calm the sudden rush of tension which swept over her. A place as filled with equipment and scenery as this theater would almost constantly be making faint sounds in the middle of the night, she told herself. Stacks of backdrops would shift slightly in their piles, curtains would rustle, and lamps would moan and pop as their metal parts cooled and contracted. Even the building itself would be responsible for a variety of noises. Floorboards could creak and the very walls would send out slight audible sounds as they settled. Everything was fine, she told herself. But an instant later she knew that was far from the truth.

The man didn't bother to hide as she started across the backstage area toward the door. The moment she saw him, she realized that she had not locked the side door after the last stagehand left. She had only planned to be in the place another minute, and it had seemed unnecessary.

It took Mollie a moment to recognize the intruder because he now wore a heavy jacket, and a dark cap was pulled down over his brow. But then she realized that it was the waiter whose wages she had cut because he had drunk some of the champagne. At the moment she couldn't even recall his name. All she could remember about him was that he was an acquaintance of a stage-hand named Tom Porter and that she had hired him for the night on Porter's recommendation.

"You'll have to leave now," Mollie told him as firmly as her jangled nerves would allow. "I'm locking up and going home."

'I'll be leavin' by and by," the man said, "but first we've got ourselves a bit of unfinished business to take care of." The leer on the man's face looked extremely menacing in the dancing candlelight, and he seemed to weave slightly back and forth as he spoke. He had seemed a little tipsy earlier in the evening when Mollie had paid him off, and she remembered thinking then that the three glasses of champagne she had seen him drink were probably not the only ones he had put away while he was working at the party.

"If you're referring to the dollar I held back from your wages," Mollie said, "re-

78

member that I warned you when I hired you that I didn't allow my serving people to drink on the job. You're lucky I didn't fire you on the spot and send you away with nothing." Even as she spoke, her hand was easing down toward a hidden pocket in the lining of her cape where she carried a small, two-shot derringer.

"So ol' Fred Small ain't good enough to take a nip of your high-toned champagne with you and your high-toned friends," the man accused. "Is that it, lady? Is that what you think?" As he took a menacing step toward her, Mollie's hand fumbled anxiously with the button of the pocket which held the gun.

"It's not a matter of anyone being better than anyone else," Mollie said, stalling, hoping she could get the gun out before he reached her. "The simple fact is that I hired you to do a job, and you broke our agreement."

"To hell with your agreement!" Small snarled, advancing toward her more decisively now. Mollie started to back hurriedly away, but she tripped on a coil of rope on the floor and tumbled over backward just at the second that her fingers closed around the derringer. The candle lantern went flying out of her hand, extinguishing as it hit the floor, and in the same instant the derringer went off. A searing pain raced across her rib cage and she screamed at the top of her lungs.

In another moment Fred Small was on top of her. He tried at first to tear at her clothes, but soon his hands were too busy protecting his face and eyes from her clawing fingers to attempt to undress her. Mollie tried once to bring her knee up between his legs, but the weight of his body held her too firmly pinned to the floor for her to strike any effective blow.

"You're not going to rape me, you piece of worthless trash!" Mollie vowed, trying to lock her teeth into his ear even as she screamed the words. "You might be able to kill me, but that's the only way you'll get what you want."

"Shut up," Small grumbled, backhanding her across the face with casual callousness.

The blow stunned Mollie, but it hardly lessened the ferocity of her resistance. At one point she bucked and heaved so violently she almost dislodged him from on top of her, but he squirmed immediately back on her. Then he struck her again, so hard this time that she wondered for an instant if she would be able to cling to consciousness. All the strength suddenly drained from her body, and Small was able to corral both of her wrists in one viselike grip, which left the other hand free to do as he chose.

Deep within her mind came the realization that she was being overcome by the terror and pain of the attack. She struggled to hold on to consciousness, to continue fighting back, but another force, one which was beyond her control, seemed to be dragging her deeper and deeper into a hopeless void. It was too late. . . .

During the next minute, Mollie was only barely aware of what was going on. Her arms, released from their confinement, fell limply on her chest. Then the feeling of being weighted down by Small's body disappeared. Finally she heard voices and had to wrestle with the unexpectedly difficult task of understanding their meaning.

"Now just hold on, mister," she heard Small say. "It ain't what you think. I wasn't really going to go through with it. I just wanted to throw a scare into her. She made me real mad awhile ago, and I just wanted to scare her a bit . . . kinda put her in her place, if you know what I mean."

"Move over there! Get way over there. Completely away from her," another voice said.

"Sure, mister, sure. But just you be careful with that thing."

A form stooped beside Mollie, and she cringed as a hand lightly touched her cheek. "It's all right now. Are you badly hurt?"

"I . . . I don't think so," she muttered, realizing her ordeal was over. As her mind and her vision slowly began to clear, she saw she was gazing up at the face of Bedford Lee, the stranger that she had met for the first time that evening at her party. He held a small revolver in his hand, and even as he checked on her he was also keeping an eye on his prisoner several feet away. A lit lamp sat on the floor nearby.

"There's blood on the side of your dress," Lee said. "Did he do that to you as well?"

"My derringer went off," Mollie said. "It hurts, but I don't think it's serious."

"You just stay here and rest for a minute," Lee told her. "I have one small matter to attend to, and then I'll be back to take care of you."

"Please hurry," Mollie replied weakly. "I just want to get out of here. I just want to go home."

"In a minute," Lee promised, rising to his feet and picking up the lamp. As he led Fred Small away at gunpoint, Mollie decided he was probably going to tie him up until the police could be summoned to take him away. The two men moved beyond her vision, but she could still hear the sound of their voices, Lee's quiet and determined, and Small's more high-pitched and desperate. Then a sudden gunshot terminated the conversation.

A moment later Lee was back at her side. He had put the gun away, but the smell of gunsmoke still clung to him.

"What did you do?" Mollie asked in alarm. "That shot . . . my God!"

"I killed the bastard," Bedford Lee announced calmly.

"You mean you just took him over there and shot him?" she asked, hardly able to believe her ears.

"I didn't want you to have to see it," Lee said. His voice was so completely devoid of remorse that for an instant Mollie felt a stirring of the same sort of fear she had experienced minutes before when Fred Small had attacked her. But then she considered the man who had died, and what had almost happened to her.

"With him dead, no one but you and I need ever know what he tried to do to you here tonight," Lee explained. His tone was beginning to soften as he knelt by Mollie's side and gently helped her to her feet. "We can simply tell the police that he was a burglar who knocked you around while he was trying to make you open your safe. Then I came in, caught him in the act, and had to kill him. This way, you need not bear the shame of having people know the truth."

Searching her heart, Mollie realized she was almost happy that Fred Small was dead. In fact, if things had not happened as they did, she herself would probably be dead by now. It seemed unlikely that a man like Small would have been willing to leave her alive to identify him later. And if, during the heat of their struggle, she had had it in her power to kill her attacker, she would certainly have done it without hesitation.

But something about the situation still bothered her. Finally it occurred to her to ask, "Why did you come back here tonight, Mr. Lee? I thought you and Mercedes . . . well, that you would be otherwise occupied by now."

"Miss Lovejoy asked me to see her home, which I did," Lee replied.

"And that's all?" Mollie asked. She tried to hide the incredulity in her voice, but realized it was there nonetheless.

"We kissed," Lee added, smiling.

"All right, then, but that doesn't explain how you happened to be here at just the precise moment to save me from that man. Please don't think I'm not grateful to you because I am deeply so, but I'm still curious."

"It's simple enough, Miss Hartman," Lee said. "I wanted to see you again. A little while ago I was outside in my carriage waiting for you to come out so I could offer you a ride home. I heard a shot and I came inside to see what had happened. But we can talk about all that tomorrow, there are other matters to be taken care of tonight. First I must get you to a doctor so he can look at that wound on your side, and then I suppose I'd better visit the authorities and tell them that a thief was killed here tonight. Do you feel well enough to walk to my carriage by yourself, or shall I carry you?"

"No, I can walk," Mollie assured him. "I feel a little weak, but I'll be all right."

The sun was rising by the time Bedford Lee finally delivered Mollie to her house. She dozed off and on during the ride home, but awoke when Bedford stopped the carriage along the curb and stepped out.

"This place is a welcome sight right now," she said as he helped her down. "I'm so tired that I think I could lie down right here on the street and go to sleep if I had to."

"Well in another few minutes you'll have a soft bed instead," Lee told her.

"Bed . . ." Mollie said with a tired smile as they started up the walk toward the front door. "Isn't that a marvelous word?"

Considering the circumstances, everything had gone fairly well after the killing of Fred Small. After leaving the theater, Lee had delivered her to a doctor, and then had gone off to inform the authorities of the shooting. Later the police came to question Mollie at the doctor's house, and she repeated to them the story she and Lee had agreed on. Small had come back to rob Mollie, and had battered her around because she refused to open her safe for him. Then, just in the nick of time, Lee had burst in. The thief had attacked him, and Lee was forced to shoot in self-defence. The policeman who questioned Mollie did not seem to doubt a single detail of the tale she told, and he left her with the promise that the dead man's body would be removed from the theater by morning.

The wound on Mollie's side proved to be a minor gash about three inches long, more painful than serious. The doctor who took care of it for her promised that if she would clean it twice a day and keep it covered until it began to heal, she should have few problems with it. It still hurt even now with a healthy dose of laudanum in her system, but the bone-deep tiredness which she felt occupied her mind more than the burning ache in her side.

When they reached the front door, Lee took the key from her and opened it for her. Before going in, Mollie turned to him and gave him a light kiss on the cheek. "So much has happened during the last few hours that I haven't taken the time yet to thank you properly," she said. "But I am deeply grateful, Mr. Lee. Thank you very much for everything."

"I'm just glad I was there when you needed me," he replied.

"Well, if there's anything you ever need in return and it's in my power to give it, consider it done," she vowed.

"As a matter of fact, there is one thing," Lee said and smiled. "I told you earlier that I came back tonight because I wanted to see you again, but this wasn't exactly what I had in mind. Perhaps in a few days when you're feeling better. . . ."

"You killed a man for me tonight," Mollie told him. "How could I say no to you now? I'll be pleased to see you again any time you like." Then she paused for a moment, thinking of something else, and asked, "But what about Mercedes?"

"I'm thirty-eight years old, Miss Hartman," Lee explained, "and she's what . . . twenty-two or twenty-three?"

"Twenty-four," Mollie told him.

"At her age, she's not ready for a man like me," he continued, "and I'm certainly not the kind of man to be led around like a favorite toy for a short time until someone else comes along to light up her eyes. It didn't take me long to take Miss Lovejoy's measure, or to decide that she's not for me."

"Well I'm not at all sure that I'm ready for a man like you either, Mr. Lee," Mollie admitted softly. "But we can give it a try."

"Yes, let's try it out," Lee agreed. "If there's one thing I've learned in my years as a gambler, it is that there are no sure bets . . . at the poker table or away from it. You pay your money and you take your chances. But I like you and I've got a feeling, a hunch, about us."

"You pay your money and you take your chances," Mollie repeated as she kissed him again and turned to go in. "Yes, I guess that's pretty much the way things go."

CHAPTER FIVE

Jason Hartman sat in his father's old rocker on the front porch of his house. The pipe he held in the corner of his mouth emitted a faint trail of aromatic smoke, and once in awhile he pursed his lips and drew some smoke through the stem, puffing just enough to keep a small glow alive in the bowl.

Somewhere out in the yard a mockingbird was reciting its repertoire of imitations. Through the trees to the west the last reddish glow of dusk was fading from the sky, and a faint breeze was starting to blow up from the south, tempering the uncomfortable June heat and bringing with it the promise of a welcome shower sometime during the night.

Jason heard the screen door squeak open and turned to see his youngest son, Benjamin, coming outside. After settling on the porch swing a few feet from his father, Benjamin took some tobacco and paper out of his shirt pocket and began to make a cigarette. Like most other boys, he had been smoking off and on for years, but only recently, just since his nineteenth birthday, had he found the gumption to do it openly in front of his mother and father. They both disapproved, of course, but never said anything. Young or not, Benjamin was pulling a man's share of the load around the farm, and Jason felt that he deserved to enjoy a man's pleasures and vices as well.

"I think Sal will probably drop her calf within the next couple of days," Benjamin commented as he lit a match and brought the flame to his cigarette. "I saw her in the pasture on my way in from the fields and she's showing all the signs."

"I wouldn't mind getting her up in the barnyard before she does, Ben," Jason said. "She had both of her other calves just fine, but it wouldn't hurt to have her close by in case she needs help this time."

"I'll take care of it in the morning when I feed the stock," Benjamin promised.

Jason heard his daughter Cassie's voice rise in sudden, brief defiance from somewhere back in the house. "But it's the style now, Mama!" the girl announced insistently. "I saw one just like it in a magazine Aunt

90

Mollie brought with her the last time she visited!"

"Maybe back East," Arethia answered in a firm yet calm tone of voice. "But thank heavens young women haven't started dressing like that here yet. Either you cut that neckline at least two inches higher or you won't be going to the dance and you won't be wearing that dress anywhere outside your own bedroom."

"But Mama . . . !"

"No 'buts,' Cassie, and that's final. I'm not going to change my mind about this."

Frowning, Jason tapped his pipe on the arm of his chair to dislodge the loose ashes and final few shreds of tobacco, then stuck it in the pocket of his shirt. Scenes like this one between Cassie and her mother were becoming uncomfortably common, and he was getting damned tired of his daughter's continual defiance.

More than once in recent weeks Cassie had caused his temper to flare, but each time he had wanted to whip some discipline into the girl, Arethia had talked him out of it. And in his calmer moments, Jason agreed that whipping wasn't the answer, not for a headstrong eighteen-year-old like Cassie.

But still it was frustrating for both of them to see her so eager to prove her womanhood and to establish her independence. At her age, Cassie could not fully realize the possible consequences of her rebelliousness, nor would she heed any of the warnings that her parents gave her.

It was the age-old story, Jason knew. Every generation was fated to make its own mistakes and to gain what wisdom it could from its own experience.

"How's the leg tonight, Daddy?" Benjamin asked, drawing his father's thoughts away from Cassie.

"Better," Jason said. "If I have a good night, I think I might be able to put in at least part of a day in the fields tomorrow."

"Well just don't try to do too much too soon," Benjamin counseled. "It would be better to stay off of it for another day or two than to hurt it again before it's completely straightened out."

"I know, son, but I just feel bad about leaving all the work to you during one of the busiest parts of the year."

Jason's left leg had been causing him serious problems ever since a Union canister round nearly took his life during the Battle of Wilson's Creek. From time to time since then, various mishaps around the farm, and occasionally even sudden changes in the weather, inflamed the old wound, bringing on spells of nauseating, disabling pain. This time the trouble had started when he'd wrenched his leg climbing down off the back of a wagon. For the past week he had been forced to sit impatiently around the house while the leg slowly healed.

If any good at all had come from his enforced idleness, it was a renewed appreciation of his youngest son. From dawn to dark each day, Ben worked the fields, tended the stock, and took care of the myriad other tasks which always need doing around a place like this, but never did a complaint or a hint of dissatisfaction come out of his mouth. Of his three sons, Jason thought, Ben was the most like he himself had once been, a born farmer, dedicated to the land, and seemingly content to spend the rest of his days tilling the soil and harvesting the fruits of his labor.

It was just that sort of peaceful existence that Jason had envisioned for himself and his family when they had moved west from Virginia more than a decade before. He had dreamed of lush crops growing on cheap, abundant land, of an escape from the crushing poverty they had known back east, and of raising all of his children to be hardworking, honest, God-fearing and moral.

Life along the frontier in Missouri had

not exactly unfolded according to Jason Hartman's dreams, however. Looking back now on the ten or so years just past, he could not recall a single one of them which had not involved some sort of tragic loss or terrifying danger. First there had been over five years of incessant border warfare with the Kansas abolitionists, and close on the heels of that had come the war, which had devastated the western half of Missouri more thoroughly than anyone could have ever thought possible.

Peace had come at last, as it inevitably must after even the most bitter strife, but it had hardly left the Hartman family unscathed or unchanged. The years of fighting had claimed the lives of his father, two brothers, and his eldest daughter. The close friends and neighbors who had also perished were too painfully numerous to count. Even those who had somehow survived the chaos now bore scars, both physical and spiritual, which they would carry with them for the rest of their lives.

But if there was one thing that a man of the soil always believed in, it was that each season, good or bad, would inevitably arrive in its own due time. Spring followed winter, rejuvenation and growth followed death and decay, hope followed despair. The times were better now. Some had died, and all had changed, but it was the responsibility and the blessing of those who survived to get on with their lives and to make the best of the years ahead.

". . . And then after the crops are laid by," Ben was saying, "I figured I might go to work on clearing that patch of woods north of the creek. I keep hearing more and more people talk about how much money there is to be made on even a small tobacco crop, and it seems to me that might be a good spot to give it at try. . . ." For the past few minutes Jason had been only half-listening to his son's words, his thoughts roving far afield, but now he began to bring his full attention back to the conversation. "We won't be risking much if we start with just ten acres or so of new ground next year," Ben went on, "and then if it seems like a good thing and it makes us any money, we can talk about growing more the year after next."

"It seems like a good plan, son," Jason agreed, "and I've got an idea that we could even talk John and Daniel into coming over to help with the clearing. We could sell the timber on shares so your brothers would make a little money on the deal, and with what we learn from our first tobacco crop, we could probably give them some advice if they decide later to put some in over at Sarah's place."

"I'm sure they'll be glad to help," Benjamin said, "but it'll surprise me if they ever decide to plant even a row of tobacco. Horses seem to be their passion these days, Daddy. I never saw anybody as obsessed with fine horses as those two are."

"Well, it's probably because of the war, son," Jason explained. "Back when they were riding with Quantrill, having just the right horse could easily mean the difference between life and death for a man. I guess that appreciation for good horseflesh just stuck with them."

In a minute the door creaked again, and Arethia came out onto the porch. She had a cup of coffee in her hand, which she gave to her husband before sitting down in a chair beside him. "So what are you two plotting and scheming about out here?" she asked with a tired smile.

"Ben's planning how we can get rich," Jason told her. "He wants to put in a tobacco crop next year."

"Tobacco, huh?" Arethia said, a faint note of disapproval in her voice. She had brought some knitting out with her, and though the light was dim, her fingers flew to work with practiced ease.

"I just want to clear a few acres and try it out, Mama," Benjamin explained. "I don't know if it will make us rich or not, but I do know that a lot of people are making money growing it."

"Well, I guess somebody has to grow the nasty stuff," Arethia replied.

Jason looked at his wife, knowing that something was distracting her thoughts. The argument with Cassie was probably still on her mind, he thought. He reached out and put his hand on her arm in silent consolation, but decided not to bring the subject up until they were alone.

For a while longer Benjamin talked enthusiastically about what he'd heard farmers say about growing tobacco. There was something special about being a man of the earth, Jason thought as he listened to his son's monologue. It was hardly the most exciting profession someone could choose, nor was it the most secure or profitable. But somehow it got a grip on a man and held him, like the soil gripping the roots of a plant, giving it support and nourishment and life itself. And no matter how bad things got, despite the droughts and floods and fires which sometimes destroyed a whole year's labor in a single sweep, there was always next year. There was always the hope of better things to come.

Finally Benjamin rose from his chair, stretched his long, muscular arms and yawned. He was young and strong and healthy as an ox, but twelve straight hours of manual labor still took its toll, even on a man like him.

"I guess it's time for me to hit the hay," he announced. "I know I'm going to hate to hear that old rooster crow in the morning if I don't turn in now."

"Good night, son," Jason said. "If my leg feels better in the morning, I'll go to the fields with you and put in a few hours."

"All right, Daddy. I'll see you at break-fast." Benjamin gave his mother a light peck on the cheek as he passed, then went to his room. In a moment the nighttime silence settled in once again around Jason and his wife, broken only by the sounds of the crickets and the gentle rustle of a breeze through the trees.

For a while Jason sat watching his wife, enjoying the nearness of her and the simple feeling of contentment her presence always gave him. They had married young back in Virginia — both had been only fifteen when they took their wedding vows — and think-ing about the quarter of a century which had passed since that day, Jason could not recall a single moment when he had regretted taking her for his bride. She was a fine woman, loving, courageous and loyal, and he knew that without her, he would never have survived the war or some of the tragedies which had befallen their family.

"I wouldn't worry too much about the girl, Arethia," Jason said at last, knowing his wife's thoughts even though she had yet to speak them. "She reminds me a lot of my sister Mollie at that age, fiery and spirited and eager to plunge head-on into life. But she's got good blood in her, and that makes the difference. No matter what mistakes she makes along the way, I know she'll turn out fine after the wildness runs its course."

"I believe that too," Arethia agreed, "but I also know that some mistakes can't be undone simply by regretting that you made them. Don't forget that I was a young woman like that once myself, and I remember quite clearly the kind of feelings she has now." She paused from her knitting and glanced up, a look of soft disapproval on her face, and then added, "And I remember what young men that age are like, too, what they want and what they'll do if they think they can get away with it. I was just lucky that I made my mistakes with a man who loved me and wanted to marry me, but I'm afraid she might not be so lucky."

Smiling the smile of one whose transgressions are so old that they can now be viewed as amusing, Jason remembered those times as well. Before their marriage there had been occasions when Arethia had been forced to muster all her strength to resist his urgent advances, and a few times during that magic spring, when they were betrothed but not yet wed, her strength had failed.

"You should have seen the changes she wanted to make in that dress pattern," Arethia went on, turning back to her knitting again. "I'm not silly enough to believe that making her dress more modestly will make her act more modestly as well, but I still won't have her leaving this house looking like a strumpet, no matter how she plans to act once she's away from here. Before long she'll want to lace herself up in a corset and paint her face like the women in the city do."

"Well, at her age, I guess she's just naturally going to push the rules as far as we'll let her push them. But there's something else at work here as well," Jason said. "All our children — Cassie included — grew up in extraordinary times. That's bound to have an effect on how they are now."

"Probably you're right," Arethia replied, "but knowing the 'whys' still doesn't make any of this easier. I just wish she was married and settled down. She's old enough for that, but she's always saying that none of these boys around here interest her."

"God only knows the kind of man that eventually will interest her," Jason said, a faint note of dread in his voice. "I still remember the kind of men that Mollie was drawn to when she was that age, and damned few of them were ever the bring-him-home-to-meet-the-family type."

The faint patter of raindrops on the leaves of the trees and the roof of the house heralded the arrival of a shower. For a few minutes Jason and Arethia remained on the porch, listening to the rain and savoring the sweet clean smell it brought. When at last the wind began to pick up, blowing the fat drops up onto the edge of the porch, they rose and went inside. On the way through the house, Jason extinguished the lamp which sat on a table in the living room. Then he slipped his arm around his wife's waist, and they headed toward the bedroom.

The following Sunday, the first since Ridge Parkman had left his mother's farm, John and Daniel came to dinner, bringing Sarah with them. It was a weekly tradition in the family, one which had been going on since the time they all lived in Virginia and Jason and his bride had come each Sunday to eat dinner with his parents.

Arethia fried two chickens for the meal, and Sarah brought over a huge bowl of potato salad, her specialty, on these occasions. The table which Benjamin set up under the trees behind the house was covered with a variety of fresh produce from their garden, and John and Daniel contributed a watermelon, one of the first to ripen this year.

After Jason blessed the table, the various bowls and platters of food began circulating in all directions. While this was happening, the talk turned almost immediately to the recent killing of a man named Thomas Little in Warrensburg. Little, a former bushwhacker and long-time friend of both John and Daniel, had been arrested. There had been several bank robberies throughout Missouri in the last few months, and Little had been accused of participating in the most recent one. Before he could be legitimately tried for the crime, a mob of citizens had forcibly removed him from the jail, and lynched him.

"The word we got was that several prominent people in Lafayette County had signed affidavits saying they saw Tom in Dover on the day of the robbery, so he couldn't have been there when the Richmond bank was robbed," John stated angrily. "But those fools in Johnson County were so anxious to pin the blame on one of Quantrill's men that they took him out and hanged him anyway."

"Well since three men in Richmond were killed during the holdup, including their mayor," Jason pointed out, "I guess tempers were bound to be running pretty high over the whole thing."

"Sure, but it still isn't fair for a man like Tom to be killed for something he didn't do," John said. "I'll bet none of the men who actually did it would have been afraid to face the music if they'd been caught fair and square. But mad or not, what's the use in killing an innocent man?"

"And Tom was a good fellow, too," Daniel added. "You'd search hard to find a straighter shot or a better friend when the chips were down."

"When terrible things like this happen," Arethia told her sons, "it always makes me wonder if the same kind of trouble might eventually come to the two of you. When you finally came out of hiding after the war was over, your father and I hoped that you would be allowed to live in peace, but I guess we were naive to believe that it would be so easy. There were too many years of hatred built up, and too many old scores left unsettled."

"Don't worry about us, Mama," Daniel assured his mother. "We keep to ourselves most of the time, and we've showed everybody in the county that we know how to live law-abiding lives."

"That's right," John agreed. "We've even made a special effort to make friends with Sheriff Watson so if some problem was to come up, he'd be on our side from the start. Shoot, he thinks Dan and I are fine fellows after the deal we made him on that sorrel horse a couple of months ago."

"You know, you boys might be right about some of Quantrill's men being unjustly persecuted lately," Jason said. "But there's one thing that still bothers me about this whole situation. This is the part of the country where Quantrill was strongest during the war, and here is where most of his men came home to after it was over. And now that these bank robberies have started up, they're all happening here, too. It just seems like quite a coincidence, and I could see how a lot of people would find it easy to jump to conclusions."

"Well Daddy, we're not saying it isn't some of the old bunch doing these things," John said. "There were plenty of men with Quantrill who were capable of it, and quite a few who wouldn't feel so bad about it either, because of the way most of us bushwhackers got treated after the fighting stopped. The only thing we're saying is, if they're going to accuse any of Quantrill's men for these robberies, they ought to make damn sure they've got the right men before the lynchings start."

"You almost sound like you think these bank robbers have some sort of right to be doing what they are," Jason said. The odd tone which entered his voice made both of his sons look up at him, and each of them instinctively recognized the need for caution from this point on.

"No, it's not exactly that, Daddy," Daniel replied. "But you know that during the war a lot of rights and wrongs got all muddied up until sometimes it was hard to tell one from the other. A thing might be wrong to do unless you were doing it against an enemy of yours, and then it wasn't wrong anymore. It was right. And sometimes your enemy might be doing a thing that he thought was right and honorable, but because he was doing it to you or yours, you thought it was low-down and absolutely wrong.

"Now the thing about these damn bankers is, a lot of people think they took advantage of too many honest folks during and just after the war, and so they think that maybe some of the money those banks have in them now was just as much as stolen from ordinary people like us in the first place." As Daniel's glance fell on his brother's face for a moment, he saw by the dark look on John's features that he was saying too much.

"No matter what sort of reasoning you might come up with," Jason said, "it's still not right, son. I realize that you and John might even know who's doing the robberies, that they might be old comrades of yours from the war, but don't let that cloud your understanding. These robberies and murders are crimes, and eventually the men responsible for them must stand accountable for their deeds."

"I know, Daddy. I know you're right," Daniel answered, wanting simply for the conversation to end. Both he and his brother agreed that deceiving their family was the most difficult part of the double life they led. Most of the time it was fairly easy to fool their Aunt Sarah, whose simple, loving heart seemed to have no room in it for suspicion. But their father was more astute, and wiser to the ways of violent, warring men. They realized that from time to time he was bound to wonder whether his sons were among the bank robbers whom he so firmly condemned.

But at last the conversation was taken in a different direction by Benjamin, who was eager to discuss his new moneymaking scheme. As soon as he brought up the subject of tobacco, both John and Daniel feigned great interest in what he was saying.

"I've checked it, and that ten acres I want to clear is as rich as any on the place," Ben explained to his brothers enthusiastically. "It won't be a picnic getting it cleared, but the oak, pine and walnut trees we cut should bring a couple of hundred dollars at least, which isn't bad for a month or so of hard work."

"We can help you with that, Ben," John volunteered. "Our crops will be laid by about the same time yours are, and you might even talk Mule Fredrickson into bringing out that small, steam-powered sawmill to cut the trees up into lumber right on the spot. That alone would save days of work hauling the trees off to another sawmill someplace else."

"I told Ben you two would be willing to help," Jason said.

"Of course we are," Daniel agreed. "We're Hartmans, aren't we? We'll always be here if you really need us."

After the meal and the watermelon which followed, the women began clearing the table while the men went to the front porch to smoke and talk. In a little while Jason, his bad leg up on a stubby, three-legged stool, began to doze in his father's rocker, and Benjamin went into the house for a more formal Sunday afternoon nap. Stubbing out their long, slim cigars, John and Daniel wandered out into the yard so their talk would not disturb their father. Their meandering route took them around the fringes of the yard and back toward the footpath which led to the barn.

"Do you remember the night the abolitionists came, Dan?" John asked his younger brother. "The night when old John Brown showed up here and nearly whacked off my head with that damned sabre of his?"

"Sure. It was back in 'fifty-six or 'fifty-seven, wasn't it? How could I ever forget?"

"You know, I still have dreams about that night sometimes," John admitted. "I hear Mama's screams, I feel that terrible old man's hand on the back of my neck like a steel trap, and I always see that look of absolute hate on Daddy's face. And sometimes I think about how different everything might have been if Old Brown had never come. Except for that night, Daddy might never have gotten involved in the fighting, and if he had been left alone to stay neutral like he wanted, you and I might never have been driven away from home during the war. We might never have joined up with Quantrill."

"Maybe," Daniel replied. "But something tells me we would have gone anyway. We were just the right age to do something crazy like that even if nobody made us do it."

"But if we hadn't, we could be just like Ben, settled and content here, happy just to grow crops and tend stock for the rest of our lives. I envy him that."

"He's who he is, and we're who we are," Daniel replied. "I'm glad Ben didn't have to go through the war, and I'm glad he's been able to dig in his heels and live the kind of life that our parents want for all of us. But just remember that there were times when we weren't given a hell of a lot of choice about things. The fact is that we were driven off, and after we joined up with Quantrill it was root hog or die most of the time for the next three years."

"I know, little brother," John said. "I remember. And I also remember that even after the war was ended, they still wouldn't cut any slack for the likes of us. They passed out paroles like circus fliers to the regular line troops in the Confederate Army, but there weren't any to spare for the men who rode with Bill Quantrill, George Todd, and Bloody Bill Anderson. The only thing they had to offer us was a short rope and a long drop."

Their stroll led them to the edge of the fence barnyard, where they stopped to lean their arms on the top rail of a fence. A couple of dozen feet away a newborn calf nuzzled and prodded at its mother's udder, slurping greedily as it sucked the warm nourishment from one teat and then another. The docile old cow volunteered only a casual, unconcerned glance in their direction, while her ravenous offspring ignored their presence entirely.

"You know, Dan," John continued, "I think I might have felt differently about the whole thing if somebody in the government or the Union Army had just said to us, 'That's all right, boys. We all did the best we could, but the war's over and the thing for all of us to do now is figure out a way to make the peace work.' But instead they call us outlaws and blame us for everything from horse stealing to filching pennies out of the Sunday collection plate."

"We might as well be robbing banks," Daniel said, "because even if we aren't, we're going to be blamed for a dozen other things that we didn't do anyway. If a man's going to be an outlaw, at least he ought to have the good sense to make his choice because of something he *did* do rather than something he didn't."

"You're damn right!" John agreed. Then, turning to his brother with a grin on his face, he added, "And besides that, the money's not bad either."

On past the barn, they started down a field road, admiring the neat rows of crops on either side of them as they walked.

With his pocket knife, Daniel shaved a splinter of wood off a dry oak twig he found and began to pick his teeth with it. "I guess I'm riding over to Clark's Crossing tonight," he said, trying to sound as careless about the trip as possible.

"That'll be the third trip you've made over there this month," John said, grinning over at his brother. "Is this thing with Becky Clark getting as serious as all that, little brother?"

"I don't guess there's much risk of it getting all that serious with her," Daniel answered. "It seems like Becky's got her sights set on marrying somebody a whole lot different from me . . . a lawyer, maybe, or somebody like that . . . but she's figured out that it doesn't hurt for her to have her fun with some ordinary fellow until the right man comes along. That arrangement suits me just fine, and believe me, Miss Clark does know how to have her fun."

"Well, you just be careful of her," John warned lightly. "It's those women who say they don't want anything from you that'll walk away with everything you've got and leave you wishing you still had more to give."

CHAPTER SIX

Cassie Hartman rode to the dance in the back of a wagon with her friends Marianna Taylor and Beatrice Winger. Marianna's younger brother Paul drove the wagon, and along the way he stopped off to pick up his pal, Tom Ford. They left early in the afternoon in order to drive the ten miles to the Laclede farm where the dance was being held. Marianna had covered the bed of the wagon with a thick pad of blankets so the long ride was not uncomfortable, and the three girls were having a wonderful time.

Although he was only sixteen, Tom Ford had somehow managed to get his hands on a quart fruitjar of homemade whiskey. He had carefully hidden it beside the road near his house, and they stopped along the way to pick it up as they were leaving. It was clear, biting stuff that slid down the throat like blazing kerosene and hit the stomach like molten lead, but it had the desired

113

impact, even on the girls, who took only a swig or two just to be daring.

The sky was clear, the day was sunny and Cassie Hartman felt wonderful as they rode along through the rural countryside in the noisy, jolting wagon. Getting away from home felt to Cassie like being released from prison for a short time, and she was determined to enjoy the event to its fullest. She and the other girls had already made arrangements to spend the night at the home of a friend near the Laclede farm, which meant that they could stay at the dance much later than if they had to make the long trip back tonight.

To Cassie's thinking, things were getting worse and worse at home. First there had been the incident about the dress she was making for the dance, and only two days later her mother had found the small container of rouge which Cassie had bought during her last trip to see her Aunt Mollie in Kansas City. That had caused yet another major fight with her mother. Then, on the Sunday afternoon following the discovery of the rouge, her father had refused to let her take a buggy ride with Harmon Firston simply because of some idle talk he had heard about Harmon and the underage daughter of a blacksmith over in Gower.

Suddenly the rules she had to live by seemed terribly harsh and unfair. It was as if the whole pattern of her life was being dictated by her parents, and she was rarely allowed to stray in even the smallest way. She was told everything — when to go to sleep, when to wake, when to eat, when to work, when to go, and when to stay.

But this dance was going to be different. There would be no one from her family there to tell her what to do or to report back to her mother and father if she seemed to be having a better time than they thought she should. Her brother Benjamin had decided to attend a stock sale in Independence with John and Daniel instead of going to the dance, so even he would not be around to approve or disapprove of Cassie's pleasure.

At first the small group sang a few songs together to pass the time, but after a while Paul and Tom got tight enough off the whiskey that they lost all interest in singing. Then the three girls turned to talking excitedly among themselves, speculating on who would be at the dance and which young men were the most attractive.

Although she only mentioned him to the others casually in passing, the man Cassie secretly hoped would be there was named

William Bird. The two of them didn't know each other very well, having met only a few times before, but her interest in him had been sparked earlier in the spring when she met and talked with him during a trip to Liberty.

William was different from most of the other young men Cassie knew. For one thing, he wasn't a farmer. He lived in town and worked in a bank, which automatically qualified him as a prize catch. He was reasonably handsome and dressed quite nicely as well, and he had a bold, flirtatious smile which sometimes made even a forward young woman like Cassie feel the urge to turn her eyes away in shyness.

But what had attracted her most to William Bird, Cassie thought, was his grand talk of wealth and adventure in faraway places. During their last meeting, he had explained that he only planned to stay in Liberty long enough to learn about the world of banking and finance. Then, armed with that knowledge, he would seek his fortune elsewhere in some larger and far more interesting place. It all sounded pretty exciting, and Cassie couldn't help but fantasize about being at his side when he left to seek his fortune in some city like New York, Boston or Philadelphia.

The sun was nearly out of sight in the west and the sky had taken on a lovely orange hue by the time they reached the Laclede farm. The Laclede family had been sponsoring these annual gatherings for the young people in the vicinity for over ten years, and though the tradition had been suspended during the worst part of the war, they were back in business now.

Scores of people were already at the party, and more were arriving all the time. Wagons, buggies and saddle horses had been left all over the large open pasture north of the two-storey farmhouse, and to the south between the house and the barn, several long tables were covered with food and beverages. Near the barn on a low platform erected for the occasion, a fiddler, a mandolin player and two guitarists were playing a lively tune. Several couples were already beginning to twirl and stomp around the open area in front of the bandstand.

Cassie and her friends were greeted by a number of female acquaintances as they carried their covered dishes to the tables. For the time being the young men were still remaining somewhat apart, standing in clusters around the fringes of the yard, smoking and talking among themselves as they covertly examined the ranks of available young ladies. From her experiences in years past, Cassie knew they would become more bold in the hours ahead as the whiskey they had smuggled in began to do its work.

Trying to act as inconspicuous as possible, Cassie eyed the scattered groups of men, searching for William Bird, but he didn't seem to be here yet and she began to worry that he might not come at all. In truth, they had made no firm agreement to meet and be together at the dance, but she had mentioned the subject during their last conversation and she had thought at the time that an unspoken understanding had passed between them. Perhaps she was wrong, or even worse, perhaps some other girl had caught his eye during the intervening weeks and all her plans and hopes for the evening would come to nothing.

After depositing their dishes of food, Cassie, Marianna and Beatrice headed for the house to greet their host and hostess, Matt and Carrie Laclede. The Lacledes were a childless couple in their mid-fifties, and legend had it that they had started holding these gatherings simply so they could occasionally enjoy the company of young people. But whatever the Lacledes' motivation, their dances had become one of the major annual events in Clay County, and growing old enough to attend one marked a major milestone in the lives of many of the area's young men and women.

The Lacledes were greeting their guests in the front parlor of their home. The room was packed and Cassie and her friends stayed only long enough to say hello to hosts Matt and Carrie, before going back outside.

"I saw Tine Brookshire over by the bandstand when we first came up," Marianna told her friends, "and he couldn't take his eyes off of me the whole time we were out there. I just hope he doesn't make a nuisance of himself like he did back in May at the church social."

"I think one of these days you're not going to mind his attention quite as much," Cassie predicted with a smile. "I know he's younger than you, Marianna, but he's not as skinny as he used to be and he might not make a bad-looking fellow one of these days."

Marianna had a plump, big-boned frame and a round, friendly face which fell just short of being pretty. She and Cassie had been close friends for years, but Cassie knew that Marianna set her sights too high when it came to boyfriends. Today was a perfect example of that. Tine Brookshire was there for the taking and a perfectly ac-

119

ceptable young man, but Cassie suspected that Marianna would spend much of the evening pining for some handsome, charming fellow who was scarcely aware that she existed.

Beatrice Winger, the third member of their trio, was different in both looks and manner from Marianna. She was a slender, graceful girl with a sweet disposition and a quick, intelligent mind. At times she seemed to suffer from an almost paralyzing shyness around young men, but Cassie knew that deep within, Beatrice also possessed a capacity for deep affection which needed only the right male to bring it out. During the ride to the dance, Beatrice had timidly expressed her disappointment that Benjamin had decided not to come, and Cassie had made a mental note to somehow make her brother aware of that fact when he got home.

Once back in the yard, the three girls filled plates with food and sat down at one of the tables with some friends. Within a short time, they saw Tine Brookshire start across the grass toward where they sat, eliciting a low groan from Marianna.

But as he approached, Cassie realized that Tine was not coming over alone. Walking with him was a tall young man in his early twenties, dressed in simple work trousers and a clean white shirt. None of the girls at the table seemed to know him, and though he was not an overly handsome man, there was something striking about his features that caused several pairs of female eyes, Cassie's among them, to track his progress across the yard.

Tine greeted the young women at the table with awkward formality, then introduced his companion as his cousin, Mike Brookshire. Although he was courteous enough, the newcomer showed no special interest in any of his new acquaintances, and once the introductions were over, he stood quietly by while his cousin sought a promise of a dance from Marianna later in the evening.

After the pair were gone, one of the girls at the table who lived near the Brookshire farm told the others all about the stranger. For several years, Mike Brookshire had been employed as a teamster with the wagon trains which regularly made their way between Independence and Santa Fe. During that time he had saved a considerable portion of his wages, and now he was preparing to outfit a dozen or so wagons, load them with trade goods, and undertake the perilous journey to the gold fields in

Montana. His reasons for being in Clay County were twofold — to visit his relatives before the trip and to buy the necessary stock to pull his wagons.

"They say he has to take his goods to Montana because he can't go back to Santa Fe anymore," the girl who was relating the news explained. Her name was Pauline Blaise, and she was the friend that Cassie and her companions planned to spend the night with. It was obvious how much she was enjoying revealing the secrets of this interesting young man. "He's wanted there for killing a man, a Mexican don or something like that. The rumor is that there was some trouble over the Mexican's sister and that when he came looking for Mike Brookshire, Mike was forced to shoot the Mexican down. It wasn't so much a matter of trouble with the law because it was self-defense, but the Mexican had a large family and they swore to get revenge."

"What about the girl?" Cassie asked impulsively. "What did he do to her that caused her brother to want to kill him?" The question elicited a number of surprised looks from her friends, but she knew that all of them would be as interested in the answer as she was.

"They say," Pauline explained, lowering

her voice almost to a whisper, "that he was not a gentleman with her, if you know what I mean. Her family had promised her to another man, but when he found out what she had been up to with Mike Brookshire, he canceled the bargain. That's why the Mexican went after Mike, because he had dishonored his sister."

"He doesn't look like such a scoundrel," Cassie said pensively. Her gaze strayed across the yard to where Brookshire was leaning against the barn, lighting a cigarette. He did have a rugged sort of charm and an aura of intrigue which seemed to linger around him like the smoke from his cigarette. She could see how, in a moment of weakness a woman might. . . .

"Look, Cassie. Look!" Marianna exclaimed, nudging her urgently and pointing toward the corner of the house.

There stood William Bird. He was dressed in a tan suit which looked crisp and fresh despite the June heat and the long, dusty buggy ride which he had just completed. He looked every bit as handsome as she remembered, standing there smiling attentively at the two prattling, adoring young women who stood before him. Cassie felt a rush of unaccustomed jealousy which only began to drain away when she realized that

William was slowly trying to edge away from the two girls.

For the next few minutes Cassie remained patiently with her friends while William Bird spoke to other people at the party. She was determined not to flirt and fawn over him, as several other girls were already doing, and he seemed equally intent on not seeking her out right away. When at last she saw that his circuitous route was turning in her direction and would soon lead him to the table, Cassie rose impulsively and said to her friends, "Would anyone like to go inside with me? I bet Carrie Laclede has a place set up for us to freshen up in, and I'd like to run a brush through my hair."

"But he's *coming*," Marianna hissed urgently, staring at Cassie as if she had suddenly and inexplicably lost her mind. "He's finally started over this way!"

"He'll still be here when we come back out," Cassie replied flippantly though quietly. "After coming all this way, he's not likely to leave in the time it will take me to brush my hair."

Marianna and Beatrice went along, of course, not so much because their hair needed attention but because of the exciting girl-talk which was bound to go on indoors. As Cassie had predicted, their hostess had designated one of the back bed-rooms of her home for her female guests to use, and soon the three young women were cloistered within it.

As soon as they were alone, Cassie began taking off the cream-colored party dress which she had made for the occasion.

"What are you doing, Cassie?" Beatrice asked. "Is something wrong with your dress?"

"No, I just want to make one small adjust-ment," Cassie explained smiling conspirato-rially. Taking a small pair of sewing scissors which she found on a bureau, she began snipping at the threads inside the bodice of the dress. Moments later she pulled away a two-inch panel of material from the front neckline of the garment.

"Cassie Hartman, you brazen strumpet!" Marianna exclaimed with glee. "You had this planned all along, didn't you?"

"Well, I told you that my mother wouldn't let me make the dress the way I wanted, so I just decided that I would have to make some other sort of arrangements. I brought a needle and thread with me, and I'll just sew the piece back in before I go home tomorrow morning. No one will ever know."

"No one except every person here," Beatrice reminded her. She obviously had more reservations about the brazenness of Cassie's actions than Marianna did.

"But it's not like I was the only one," Cassie pointed out. "You saw the neckline on Elaine Porter's dress, and the ones on Marjorie Drew's and Sarah Will's dresses. It's the fashion now, and I'm not afraid to take my chances."

When all the necessary adjustments were made, she quickly began redressing. The difference in the dress was remarkable. Before it had been a fairly demure garment, attractive enough but hardly as striking as the gowns which Cassie had pored over so carefully in the magazines. Now, though, looking at herself in the mirror on the back of the door, she realized with satisfaction that she had achieved the effect she was after. Even a man like William Bird who seldom seemed to want for female attention would have to sit up and take notice of a woman in a dress like this.

Only in the past year had Cassie Hartman begun to mature into the beauty which she had now become. Her hair was blond like her Aunt Mollie's, but thicker and wavier than Mollie's had ever been. Her skin was fair, and her face was the sort that men found themselves staring at with unabashed appreciation. In her brashness, Cassie considered her eyes and her breasts to be her best attributes and she conspired frequently to use both to her own best advantage, flashing the former flirtatiously and proudly displaying the latter with straight shoulders and flawless posture.

She liked men very much, but was quickly bored with those who were too easy to conquer and manipulate. Although only eighteen, she had already received three proposals of marriage, but all three had come from local country boys who had little to offer except more of the same sort of rural existence which she had known all her life. The only difficult part about turning any of the three down was convincing the boys that she had given them any serious consideration at all.

Although her fantasies often carried her away to many exotic places with a variety of exciting, prosperous men, Cassie had, in truth, little notion of what the future held for her. The only fact of which she was absolutely sure was that she was not going to grow old keeping house and bearing children for some coarse, cornfed bumpkin.

"If it was me, I'd be mortified to show that much bosom to a pack of strangers," Beatrice said with more admiration than true disapproval in her voice. "But you have no shame at all, do you, Cassie?"

"I guess I don't!" Cassie exclaimed gaily. "As a matter of fact, I love the way I look right now."

Full darkness had arrived by the time they got back outside, but the area of the party was well lit by a multitude of kerosene lamps. The crowd had continued to grow until nearly two hundred people crowded the side yard, and more people were beginning to dance. Tine Brookshire descended on Marianna almost as soon as the three young women rejoined the crowd, and at last she agreed to let him lead her to the dance floor. A moment later, William Bird appeared at Cassie's side.

"Good evening, Miss Hartman," he said. "I was hoping to see you here tonight." In one sweeping glance, he surveyed her from head to foot, obviously approving of all he saw.

"It's good to see you too, William," Cassie said, putting on her best smile. "Let me introduce you to my friend, Beatrice Winger. Beatrice, this is William Bird from Liberty."

It hardly surprised Cassie that Beatrice was suddenly crippled with shyness. She managed to shake William's hand and mumble a greeting, but a moment later she excused herself and left, explaining that she wanted a drink of punch. Neither Cassie nor William tried to detain her.

"You really do look lovely tonight, Cassie," William said. It seemed that he was fighting to keep his eyes on her face, so she turned her head away for an instant to let him look where he might.

"Thank you, William," Cassie said. "And you're quite dapper yourself. Have you been here long?"

"A few minutes. I would have arrived earlier in the day, but a piece of last-minute banking business detained me. The responsibilities of running a bank can be very burdensome sometimes, but Mr. Morrison, the owner, counts on me quite heavily. I can't just leave when there are important matters to be attended to."

"Well, at least we're both here now," Cassie told him, "and that's the most important thing."

After another moment of conversation, William led her off to the dance floor, which was becoming crowded by this time. They danced their way through five songs in a row before stopping to cool off with glasses of punch. While they were sipping their refreshments, William took a long, slender cigar from his pocket and lit it.

"I have another sort of refreshment over in my rig," William told her. "There's an old man near Liberty who makes the most extraordinary boysenberry brandy I've ever tasted, and I brought a couple of bottles with me tonight."

"I see," Cassie answered, trying to sound intrigued but noncommittal.

"Perhaps later you might like to walk over with me and try some," he suggested. "I'd like for you to taste it, Cassie, because it's really quite good."

"Perhaps," Cassie said and smiled at him. "But right now I'd rather dance. Are you ready to go again, William?"

"Just try and stop me," he said, taking her hand and leading her into the throng once more.

After a few songs the band stopped for a break. By this time Cassie was winded and quite warm, and William suggested a walk in the night air to cool down. His intentions were obvious, and Cassie was not at all surprised when their meandering path took them around the house and back toward the field where the wagons and buggies were parked. When it became obvious that Cassie would voice no objections, William beaded straight toward his buggy. Once there, he fished around behind the seat for a moment, then produced a brown bottle with a cork protruding halfway out of its opening.

William had no cups to drink from, but Cassie raised the bottle to her lips without hesitation and took a healthy swallow. Having never drunk brandy before she was not sure what to expect, but the stuff was more smooth and mellow than she had anticipated. It had a rich, fruity taste which reminded her only remotely of boysenberries, but it slid down her throat in a surprisingly warm and comfortable way. She took a second, longer drink before handing the bottle back to William.

"Well, what do you think?" William asked, grinning. "Did I lie to you?"

"It's very good, William," Cassie said and then found herself giggling. "And even after you swallow it, it's almost like you can still feel it down in your stomach."

"Wait until it's been in you a few moments," he told her, "then you'll begin to feel it all over." He took a drink himself, then surrendered the bottle to Cassie once again.

"My oh my!" Cassie exclaimed after another swallow. "I bet I could get tipsy off that stuff without even knowing it!"

"Well don't do that," William told her. "At

least not yet. We still have a lot of party left to enjoy, and I don't want you thinking later that I spoiled it for you by letting you get drunk on brandy right off the bat."

After another swallow for himself, he recorded the bottle and put it back under the seat. "It'll be there," he said. "We can always come back later."

Cassie knew what was bound to happen next, even before William stepped closer to her and placed his hands lightly on either side of her waist. Ever since the moment they left the yard and entered the moonlit field there had been no question in her mind that William would try to steal a kiss. The tingling effects of the brandy only heightened the anticipation she felt. She surrendered her lips to him willingly, shivering with pleasure as he slid his arms around her and pulled her body close to his.

"On the way here," William told her, their faces only inches apart and their arms still around one another, "I was thinking that the whole evening would be a failure for me if I didn't get at least one kiss from you, Cassie."

"Well, I wouldn't want to be the one responsible for you not having a good time. And since I did have three swallows of your brandy, I think you deserve at least three kisses for your trouble."

William's hands began to roam as their lips met again, tracing the contours of her back and shoulders. He touched her as no admirer ever had before, and it felt surprisingly good. Cassie felt her pulse quicken, and she could not find it within herself to stop him even when one hand snaked up to sample the shape and fullness of one of her breasts. She drew back only when his fingers went to work on one of the buttons which held her dress together.

"Oh no you don't!" she said, drawing away from him just far enough to be out of reach of his exploring hands. "Your drink might be good, but it's not that good."

William smiled back at her, and though his grin was somewhat sheepish, his eyes still glistened with desire. "Honestly, I didn't really expect to get away with anything. But I just couldn't help but try."

"Well I won't blame you for trying," Cassie told him, laughing gaily, "if you won't blame me for stopping you. Now come on. The band should be starting back up soon, and I still have a lot of dancing to get in before the night is over."

The first of the revelers began to leave about midnight. As expected, there had been a couple of fights earlier in the evening. The second, involving six men, had threatened to erupt into a full-scale riot, but Matt Laclede had employed all the persuasive powers of an oak wagon wheel spoke to convince the drunken troublemakers to end their brawl. After that things had been fine.

Cassie had spent practically the entire evening with William Bird, dancing herself nearly to exhaustion and making three additional trips out to the buggy with her handsome young suitor. William's ardor had increased each time they disappeared into the darkness until his attentions had at last become more of a nuisance than a pleasure, but Cassie had no doubt that she could curb his fondlings whenever she chose to do so.

When the group she came with decided to leave, Cassie told them to go on without her. The Blaise farm where they were to spend the night was only a few miles away, and William had volunteered to deliver her there before he started back to Liberty. Before leaving, Beatrice had tried to get Cassie aside and talk her out of the idea, but Cassie had insisted that she was in good hands and so eventually the wagon left without her.

When the crowd finally began to thin, a pleasant sort of euphoria, spawned by the late hour and the rigorous exercise, began to settle over the final few hangers-on. Cassie and William danced the last dance together, a mercifully slow tune compared to some played earlier in the evening, then agreed at last that it was time to go. They bid goodnight to their host and hostess, then headed out toward William's buggy.

Cassie settled in close beside her companion as he grasped the reins in one hand and placed the other lightly around her shoulders. The two brandy bottles, one of them empty and the other nearly so, rattled around forlornly behind the seat as William's horse started forward. A warm, comfortable drowsiness overtook Cassie so unexpectedly and so completely that she was scarcely aware when William's hand slid down to touch one of her breasts. It felt warm and natural there, and she saw no real harm in it so she didn't even bother to make him take it away as she drifted off to sleep.

When she awoke, it was as if she had been asleep for hours, and it took her a moment to recall where she was and who she was with. The horse was stopped, and the ground nearby was illuminated by moonlight which filtered through the trees around them.

"Are we there?" Cassie asked, sitting up a

little straighter in the seat. She looked around in drowsy confusion, as she realized they were not in the front yard of the Blaise home.

"The house is just around the next bend," William told her. "I decided to stop for a minute because it's such a pretty night."

As she became more alert, Cassie realized that they had left the road and were in a small copse of trees. The whole situation was a little confusing to her until William put his arms around her, pulling her close for another kiss. It gave her no pleasure this time but only made her feel nervous and slightly afraid.

"I guess I let things go a little too far tonight because I was having such a good time with you, William," Cassie began tentatively.

"Maybe they haven't gone quite far enough yet," William suggested. With brash familiarity, he reached out and fondled the inside of her thigh through her dress, but she immediately shoved his hand away.

"I don't intend for this to go any farther than it already has," Cassie said. "We might as well just go on to Pauline's because you're not going to get what you want from me tonight."

"Just give it a few minutes, Cassie," William said, smiling. "You might change your mind." His hands were all over her now, and he was becoming rough and insistent. He tried to kiss her again, oblivious to her wishes.

"Stop it, William!" Cassie snapped at last, unable to curb his clumsy caresses. "Just stop it!" He withdrew his hands for a moment, but she could tell by the smirk on his face that he was far from giving up. "Do you think I'm such a tramp that I go around letting men have their way with me so easily?" she demanded angrily.

"I don't know about that," William replied haughtily, "but I do know that all night you've been just as much as promising me that this would happen. Why change your mind this late in the game? Why don't you just relax and enjoy it? I have a blanket in back, and while I'm spreading it over there on the grass, you can take your dress off."

"Are you crazy?" Cassie stormed.

"Look here, Cassie," William told her, his voice stem and impatient. "I could have had any girl at that dance tonight, but I picked you. There were plenty of girls there who would gladly trade places with you right now, ready to do whatever I want and more. So get off your high horse. If you're going to be my girl, you'll have to get used to doing things my way."

"My father or any one of my three brothers would gladly put a bullet in you if they heard what you just said," Cassie warned him.

"And I'm sure you're going to rush right home and tell them." William sneered at her. "Just don't leave out the parts about you getting drunk on my brandy, or how you insisted that your friends go on ahead so you could ride back alone with me."

"I won't be treated this way! I won't!"

"Then get out," William told her simply.

"What?"

"Get out of my buggy," he said. "If you're not going to make it worth my while to stay, then I might as well start for Liberty. But just keep in mind that you're not going to get another chance. If you mess this one up, it's your last."

Stunned by his audacity and trembling with rage, Cassie climbed down to the ground. Without even another glance at her, William Bird turned his rig around within the tight confines of the clearing and started toward the road.

Tears welled in her eyes as she realized that the most humiliating thing about the whole incident was the fact that she would have to let him get away with this. Just as

William pointed out, she couldn't tell her parents anything about it, and she wouldn't be able to tell any of her brothers either for fear that one or all of them might get in serious trouble defending her honor. She was powerless.

Cassie began walking only after the sound of William's buggy faded into the night. She had no real idea how far it was to the Blaise farm or whether she would be required to answer a host of embarrassing questions once she got there. All she knew was that she was nearly exhausted, and that the last few ugly minutes with William had completely negated all the fun she had enjoyed that night. All she wanted to do was to try to get into the Blaise house without rousing anyone.

Cassie had walked perhaps half a mile when she began to hear the distant sound of a horse's hooves on the road behind her. Her first thought was that William had probably had a change of heart and was coming back to apologize and deliver her to her destination. But then, as the sound grew nearer, she realized that it was made by a lone horseman rather than by a horse and buggy.

Common sense told her that at this late hour she would be wise to get off the road and hide until the rider had passed, but at this point she was so tired and drained that she just didn't have the energy left to worry about what some stranger on the road might do to her. Instead she walked on, stopping to look around only when the rider was quite near.

At first she didn't recognize the man, even when he stopped his horse beside her, but he apparently knew her and that reassured Cassie slightly. Taking off his hat so his face was clearly illuminated by the moonlight, he said, "There's no need to run. I'm not going to hurt you. Let's see. It's Miss Hartman, I believe."

"That's right, Cassie Hartman," she said in a shaky voice.

"I'm Mike Brookshire, ma'am. Tine Brookshire's cousin. We met earlier in the evening."

"Oh yes. I remember you now," Cassie sait with relief. Even though he seemed harmless enough, she wanted only for him to ride on, but he seemed in no great hurry to do so.

"Did your ride leave you behind at the party, ma'am?" Brookshire asked.

"Not exactly," Cassie said. "They did, but I told them to. I had a ride with someone else, but. . . . Look, I just don't want to go

140

into it right now."

"All right, ma'am," Brookshire answered, not seeming to be offended by her abruptness.

He said nothing else for a moment, but continued to sit there looking down at her. Finally Cassie was compelled to ask, "What is it, Mr. Brookshire? Is there something else you want to say?"

"Well not exactly. I'm just curious about whether you need any help. It seems mighty strange that a young lady should be walking the road at two-thiry in the morning, all alone."

"Two-thirty!" Cassie exclaimed. "Is it that late?"

"Thereabouts," Brookshire replied.

"Well at least I only have a short distance left to go. I'm staying the night, or at least what's left of it, with my friend Pauline Blaise."

"Well, ma'am, my horse is pretty stout and I'd be glad to take you the rest of the way. With that dress, you'd have to sit sideways in the saddle and I could climb up behind."

Her problems with William Bird made Cassie suspicious of the invitation, and the first words she spoke came out far harsher than she intended. "I'm quite all right, Mr. Brookshire, and I assure you that I don't

141

need any help whatsoever from anybody."

"Suit yourself," Brookshire said, still not seeming at all offended by her sharp tone of voice. "I know the Blaise place, and it's only another mile or so down the road. If you step out, you can make it in twenty or thirty more minutes. Good night to you, Miss Hartman." And with that he gave the reins a short shake which put his horse in motion.

"A mile did you say?" Cassie asked, causing him to stop once more and look back at her. "I thought I was almost there!" The idea of trudging along like this for another half-hour was almost unbearable to her.

"It's a good mile, but probably not a whole lot more than that."

"Listen, Mr. Brookshire," Cassie said. "I'm sorry if I was rude to you a moment ago. It's been a long and not-so-pleasant night for me. But if that offer of a ride is still open. . . ."

Smiling slightly, Mike Brookshire stepped to the ground and held his horse steady while Cassie climbed up into the saddle. Then he leaped up behind her, straddling the horse's rump behind the saddle. He ended up with his arms on both sides of her, holding the reins lightly, but there was no hint that he intended to plant either of his hands anyplace that it shouldn't be.

"All right, old horse," he said, speaking like a man who had spent plenty of time with no better companion than his mount to talk to. "This lady looks pretty tired and sleepy to me, so let's get a move on."

Her precarious seat on the horse prevented Cassie from drifting off to sleep again, something for which she was very glad. She had no intentions of letting down her guard with this unknown man.

Mike Brookshire seemed harmless enough on the surface . . . even nice, maybe, in a coarse and frontierish sort of way. He didn't have a whole lot to say during the ride to the Blaise house, however he did reveal, in response to a question from Cassie, that he would probably remain in Clay County for at least another month.

"Leaving that late in the season will mean that I'll probably hit a lot of bad weather about the time I reach the Rockies," Brookshire explained, "but I've decided to stay on here for a while longer anyway. Tine's mother and father are the closest thing to a family I've got left in the world, and I'm not sure when I might get back to these parts again. That's why I want to get in a good long visit while I'm here."

"Well after you sell your goods, won't you

be back for more?" Cassie asked.

"Not necessarily. When the goods are gone, I plan to sell the wagons and teams as well. And from then on, it's anybody's guess where my nose will lead me. For a smart fellow with some money to invest, there's profits to be made all up and down the Rockies, as well as on further west in Nevada and California."

They rode on for a while longer in silence. The only sounds that broke the stillness of the night were the clop of the horse's hooves and the creak of Brookshire's well-worn saddle.

Finally Cassie recognized a particularly sharp bend in the road and announced, "It's just up there. Back in those trees."

"Yes, I know," Brookshire replied. He steered his horse toward a wagon path at the edge of the road and into the trees which partially concealed a farmhouse. As they neared the front of the house a dog hidden somewhere under the porch growled deeply but didn't come out into the moonlight to get a closer look at them.

The house itself was dark and silent, its occupants apparently asleep. That pleased Cassie. If she was quiet enough, she thought, she could sneak through the front door and into Pauline's room without wak-

144

ing anybody. That might or might not save her from a scolding in the morning for coming in so late, but at least it would prevent Pauline's parents from knowing how truly late it was when she arrived.

Brookshire slid to the ground, then held out his hands and helped Cassie down. "Well, you made it, safe and sound." He smiled broadly at her.

"Yes I did, and thank you very much," Cassie said. "I want to apologize for being rude to you back there on the road, but it's late, and I'm very tired, and something happened just before that put me in an ugly mood."

"Well, ma'am, I don't mean to be nosing into your affairs," Brookshire replied, "but I have to tell you that I had that fellow you left with sized up for a swellheaded scoundrel the first minute I laid eyes on him. It didn't surprise me a whole lot to see that he ditched you on the road, and I guess I've got a pretty good idea why he must have done it."

His comment made Cassie angry, but she managed to swallow back the sharp words which sprang to mind. He had been kind to her, and during the short ride to the Blaise farm, she had started to like this quiet, easygoing man. "Thank you again for your

145

help, Mr. Brookshire," she said at last. "I have to go in now, but perhaps I'll see you again before you leave for parts unknown."

"It wouldn't surprise me a bit." Brookshire grinned as he stuck his foot in the stirrup and swung up into the saddle. "It wouldn't surprise me the least little bit."

Mollie Hartman lay in bed watching the nighttime breeze gently stir the curtains across the room. The softly moving air felt like feathers gliding across her bare flesh, and she considered with awe and wonder the incredible heights of pleasure which the human body was capable of experiencing.

The hour was late, and Mollie and Bedford Lee had finished making love only moments before. He had fallen asleep almost immediately after they were finished and now lay on the other side of the bed snoring lightly. But she didn't begrudge him the rest. Now, near the end of their third month together, the time was past when their long nights together were spent learning the joys of one another's bodies and sharing the innermost details of their lives and their hearts. Now they had passed into that phase in their relationship when being together was still a joy, but it was no longer a compulsion, and they felt comfortable enough with one another to speak and act in the most natural manner.

Soon she would be joining him in sleep, and she savored the thought of the delicious feeling of drifting slowly away, but she didn't want to let go, not just yet.

After the circumstances of their first encounter, there never was any true doubt in Mollie's mind that she and Bedford would have at least a brief affair. She had been attracted to him from the start, and the fact that he had saved her honor, and perhaps her life as well, in such a forceful and gallant manner only served to ingratiate her to him that much more. It wasn't so much that she felt she owed him anything as that she wanted to share that very special side of herself with him.

There were things about the man that bothered her, of course. His profession was one that was most often taken up by crooks and scallywags, and she had no true reassurance that he was not that type of man. Nor did he make any pretense of ever wanting to give it up. He was a gambler, he proclaimed proudly, and whatever other facets of his life could not be reconciled with that reality must either be changed or cast aside.

Bedford also made no secret of the fact

that he had spent most of the first half of the decade far to the west in order to avoid military service. Although his background remained somewhat a mystery to Mollie, he had alluded to being raised in Virginia and spoke openly and cynically about the foolishness of two of his brothers who had lost their lives in defense of the South, one at the First Battle of Bull Run and the other at Gettysburg. He was obviously not a cowardly man, but it bothered Mollie to think that he might be the type to choose his fights more on the basis of what could be personally gained than by what good cause could be served.

Bedford had no ambitions that could be easily detected, and he was almost totally irresponsible about money, spending his own with freedom and abandon and borrowing liberally from others without any means or intention of ever paying them back. He had an eye for the ladies which forced Mollie to keep her natural tendencies toward jealousy constantly in check, and occasionally he found pleasure in drinking himself into utter oblivion.

But there were plenty of points on the positive side as well. For one thing, he was a marvelous lover. He indulged Mollie's body with the worshipful attention of an artist appreciating a fine masterpiece. At first they had indulged in marathon bouts of lovemaking, and now, though their ardor had dimmed somewhat, Bedford still never failed to leave her satisfied and glowing with contentment.

He was also an excellent companion, both in public and in private. He was the sort of man that strangers of all kinds instinctively liked, and he performed extremely well at social functions where performance was far more important than whatever enjoyment might be derived from attending the affair. When the two of them were alone, they never seemed to lack for conversation, and Bedford's taste in music, art and literature were remarkably sophisticated.

And besides all that, Mollie thought with a rush of pleasure, Bedford Lee could always make her laugh, and such a talent was never to be taken lightly. After such a long time when there had been so little in her life to bring even a smile to her face, a man with the gift of laughter was a real treasure.

Mollie began to feel a chill as the heat of their lovemaking slowly dissipated from her body. She reached down at her feet and pulled the sheet up over her, then rolled over against her sleeping lover and shared the cover with him. His chest rose and fell gently with the rhythm of his breathing and the soft rumble of his snoring sounded to her almost like the contented purr of a tomcat sleeping in front of a fire.

She had a choice to make. Tonight at dinner Bedford Lee had produced a silver ring with a small diamond mounted on it, and he had invited Mollie to become Mrs. Lee.

She didn't accept the ring, but neither did she turn it and the offer down. His proposal came so unexpectedly that she pleaded for time to consider the matter more carefully.

Without seeming to be upset or angry, Bedford had agreed to wait, but later, after they returned to her house, he put the ring in its open box on the mantel of her parlor, explaining that she had only to either take it down and put it on, or leave it there for the next week, in order to give him his answer.

And although he never told her this in so many words, somehow Mollie sensed that if the ring didn't go onto her finger within that week, then shortly thereafter it and the man who had offered it would be gone from her life forever.

CHAPTER SEVEN

August, 1867

Although the hour was late and she was already in bed, Mollie Hartman was still wide awake. Bedford Lee had been here earlier and he hadn't been too happy about being sent home to sleep alone, but Mollie had insisted. In fact, she had been insisting all week that as long as her niece, Cassie, was visiting, there would be no other overnight guests in her house or her bed.

But what kept her awake was not the fact that Bedford was angry with her. Their relationship had become strong enough to survive a minor skirmish such as this one, and Mollie knew that once Cassie was gone and things were back to normal, Bedford would be all the more grateful for the liberties she allowed him to take with her.

The problem was that Cassie was still out somewhere with a man. The clock in the foyer downstairs had long since chimed out

151

the two o'clock hour, sending a shudder through Mollie as the deep gonging drifted up the stairs and into her room. Now she was beginning to imagine all the various tragedies which could so easily befall a young woman like Cassie in a place like Kansas City.

It had all seemed innocent enough at the start. Three days before, a young man who introduced himself as Mike Brookshire had showed up at the door asking to see Cassie. Cassie had feigned surprise at his appearance, but Mollie, remembering her own youthful connivances, imagined that the two of them had carefully orchestrated the encounter before either of them left Clay County. Mollie understood well enough that Cassie might enjoy spending some time with a new beau in an exciting place like this and away from the watchful eyes of her parents.

When Brookshire had come to dinner the following evening, all of Mollie's impressions of him had been good. He had been on his own since he was sixteen and had seen a good part of the Southwest during his years as a teamster. Luckily, he did not look or act like most teamsters, Mollie thought. He dressed nicely. He treated both Cassie and Mollie with courtesy and respect, and he had kept the whole table laughing most of the night with his tales of practical jokes and comic misfortune along the trail to Santa Fe. Later, when Cassie told Mollie that Brookshire had invited her to dinner and the theater, Mollie had voiced no objections.

But the theater let out at ten-thirty, and Mollie knew enough about the city she lived in to realize that even the restaurants which catered to the late-night crowd closed their doors around midnight. Barring some sort of disaster, Mollie could imagine only one place the young couple could be right now. Mike Brookshire had mentioned the night before that he had taken a room in the Grant Hotel.

Part of the trouble Mollie was having with the whole situation was that she felt like a hypocrite. If Cassie and Mike had indeed returned to his room after the show, Mollie could not find it in her heart to condone their actions, and yet she remembered clearly the way she had felt and the things she had done when she was eighteen. There had been an older man in her life at that time, a handsome adventurer named Kurt Rakestraw. Their affair had been as passionate and intense as anything that Cassie and Mike could possibly be experiencing right now, Mollie knew, and she recalled that in the midst of it all, no one on earth could have stopped her from being with Rakestraw nor could anyone have convinced her that what she was doing was wrong. Love wrote its own rules and dictated its own wrongs and rights.

Still, Mollie could not help but feel that she was betraying the trust Jason and Arethia placed in her. They no doubt knew that when their daughter came to Kansas City, Mollie permitted her to do things and savor experiences which were not available to her at home. But certainly they expected some restrictions to be placed on such adventures, and what was happening tonight went beyond all the limits of what they would consider reasonable and decent.

When the clock downstairs chimed once to signal the quarter-hour, Mollie rose and put on a light silk dressing gown over her nightgown. Since sleep was impossible, she decided that she might as well go downstairs and make herself a cup of tea. She was halfway to the door of her bedroom when she heard the faint, telltale click of the downstairs door opening and closing. A great sense of relief immediately flooded through her, but it was closely followed by another more confusing feeling. Something had to be said about this incident, and Mollie realized that if she was going to get any sleep at all before morning, it had to be said tonight.

Cassie moved softly through the house, hardly making a sound as she ascended the stairs to the second floor. But Mollie detected the light sound of her footsteps as the girl passed by in the hall. Mollie sat down on the edge of her bed to wait, trying to collect her thoughts as the minutes crept slowly by.

Finally, when she felt that sufficient time had passed, she went out into the hall. A light still shone under the closed door to Cassie's bedroom. Mollie knocked lightly on the door, then opened it and went in.

Cassie had already changed into her bedclothes and was sitting on the edge of the bed brushing her hair. She looked up as Mollie entered, but said nothing. The look on her face was a mix of guilt and defiance as she watched her aunt walk across the room and sit down in a chair a few feet away.

"I was worried about you, Cassie," Mollie told her. "I've been in bed for hours, but I haven't slept at all." She hated the accusatory tone of her words, but it was the truth.

"I was all right," Cassie replied. "Mike knows how to take care of himself, and he wouldn't let anything happen to me." A dim

155

light of defiance gleamed in her red-rimmed eyes, and it was obvious that she was not going to be forced by guilt into any sort of contrite apology for her tardiness.

"Judging from the life he's led, that's probably true enough. But that doesn't change the fact that it's very late and I didn't know where you were. Don't you think it's understandable that I should worry?"

"Well, nothing has happened to me, as you can see," Cassie said. "I'm here, aren't I? Alive and safe."

"You're here, but that doesn't mean that nothing happened to you. Both of us realize well enough that I'm not your mother, but —"

"That's right!" Cassie snapped. "I'm not a child and you aren't my mother!" She began raking the brush through her hair with harsh, and no doubt painful, strokes.

Mollie could feel her own temper rising as well. "All right then," she said icily. "If you want so badly to be treated as an adult, then I will treat you as one. I'll tell it to you straight just as I would with any other person. You are my guest here, and I refuse to be treated with this sort of rudeness and disrespect in my own home. I've done nothing to deserve it, and I won't accept it.

"You're eighteen now, Cassie. You are a woman, so what you do and who you choose to do it with is truly your own business. But don't try to convince yourself that your actions and irresponsibilities don't have an effect on the people around you who love you and want your life to go well."

"But I don't want that responsibility!" Cassie said. "I just want to be left alone to live my life as I please, to make my own decisions, and maybe my own mistakes as well. Why is it that everybody seems to feel the need to watch over me every minute?"

"Your parents do because that's their job and they'll never give it up. And I do because I'm your aunt and I care what happens to you. But my caring doesn't extend to the point where I'll simply accept any sort of headaches that you choose to hand me while you're here."

"I'll leave if you like," Cassie snapped. "I can go home early if you don't want me here any longer."

"We'll see about that later," Mollie said. "Perhaps tomorrow after I've had some rest and you've had a chance to lose that great big chip you're carrying around. But for now I'm content to let you know that tonight you caused me considerable worry and discomfort, and I don't like that. If you feel that you can't have your little dalliances without troubling me this way, then you probably should go."

Mollie rose and started to the door, thinking that if this conversation continued any longer, both of them would probably say things they would later regret. She was tired, and Cassie, from the look of her, was a little drunk. It was not a good time for either of them to be speaking their hearts or their minds.

For a moment it seemed that Cassie would be content to let her leave, but then, just as Mollie reached the open doorway, her niece stopped her.

"I just had to go with him, no matter what trouble it might get me into later," Cassie said, her voice meek and filled with a sudden unspoken plea for understanding. "Haven't you ever felt that, Aunt Mollie? Don't you know what it's like?"

Mollie stopped and slowly turned back to face her niece. "Yes, I know what that's like," she said quietly.

Cassie's head was bowed, and tears were beginning to flow gently down her cheeks. Mollie crossed the room and sat down on the edge of the bed, placing a consoling arm around the young woman's shoulder.

"I had tried to imagine what the first time

would be like," Cassie said. "What sort of fellow he would be, what it would be like to finally give in, and how I would feel afterward, but none of it was like I imagined . . . not even the man. It was frightening, and sometimes it hurt quite a bit, and when it was over I had this crazy thought that he would never like me again because I had let him do that to me. But I had to do it. Something inside me told me that I had to share this with him tonight because he's going away soon and I might never see him again!"

The memories which Cassie's words stirred in Mollie were so vivid and sharp that it was all she could do to keep from bursting into tears herself. Why was it, she wondered, that the ones you wanted the most always seemed to have one foot out the door already?

"How did he treat you afterward, Cassie?" Mollie asked. "Was he nice to you?"

"It was strange," Cassie said. "He wasn't at all bashful about trying to get me up to his hotel room, but afterward he seemed so shy about the whole thing. But he was very gentle, too. When he touched me, it was like I was made of porcelain and he was afraid he would break something."

159

"That's good. A gentle man is a real treasure."

"It's all so confusing, Aunt Mollie," Cassie admitted. "When I first met Mike a month ago at a party, I didn't see anything special about him. He wasn't the kind of man I wanted at all, and he was gone from my mind a minute after we were introduced. Even when he began to call on me at home, he just seemed like someone pleasant to pass the time with. It never crossed my mind to worry about the fact that he was leaving soon and that I probably wouldn't ever see him again.

"But then something started happening. I don't understand why, but he suddenly started mattering to me — what he thought, what he said, and how he felt about me. I would get this little tightness in my throat when he'd talk about Montana, and I kept dreaming that something would happen to keep him from going, that he'd lose his money or break a leg or something like that.

"After the theater we got in his buggy, and I saw right away that he wasn't heading back in this direction. Instead we drove up to a bluff somewhere to look at the river in the moonlight. While we were there he kissed me and he told me he wanted me to go back to his room with him. Just like that, he came out with it, and I said I would just the same way. Without even thinking."

At last Cassie raised her head and looked at her aunt, smiling past the tears in her eyes. "I'm sorry, Aunt Mollie, but you were the last thing on my mind after that. Until we left the hotel and started back here, it never even occurred to me to wonder what you might think or whether you might be awake worrying about me. But I am sorry now. I truly am."

"It's all right, Cassie," Mollie told her softly. By now she felt nothing but empathy for her niece.

"Thank you for not being too angry with me. I know I was rude and thoughtless, but this whole thing has just caught me so off guard. I didn't want this to happen. I didn't pick this man, but suddenly he's the only thing in the world that truly matters to me. I feel sad and happy and ashamed and fulfilled all at the same time. It's just so confusing! One minute you're fine and happy without anybody special in your life, and then suddenly there's somebody there, and the thought of simply going back to the way things were seems unbearable. I don't know what to do. What if he really does go? How can I stand it? How can I live?"

"The task you have ahead of you is probably one of the hardest ones you'll ever face," Mollie said slowly. "You're going to have to let life take its course. You've fallen in love with this man because of who he is, and now you'll have to accept him for that and nothing more. If he's the leaving kind, then you won't stop him from going. But if he does go, I have an idea that you'll find a way to bear it. Others have many times before."

Cassie looked at her aunt, realizing that there was more behind Mollie's words than simple advice meant to help her through a difficult time. Mollie was staring out the darkened window, her face intense as if some scene from the past had suddenly appeared, unbidden, to her. When she spoke again, her voice seemed distant.

"If you're strong and determined enough, you can put any heartbreak behind you. You can go on with your life, and be happy again, and even love again when the time comes. But it's never quite the same, and neither are you. It's never quite as exciting as it was that very first time."

It was nearly four in the morning before Mollie returned to her own room again. She felt drained and exhausted, and her eyes were gritty with sleepiness as she shed her robe and got into bed. She knew sleep would come quickly now. But the tears began even more quickly, and at last she submitted to her own bittersweet memories, giving them free reign over her thoughts and her heart until sleep worked its merciful magic at last.

CHAPTER EIGHT

Cole Younger paused on the board sidewalk long enough to light a long, dark cigar. He had just finished a leisurely breakfast in the restaurant of the nearby Berclair House, and now he seemed in no hurry to go anywhere or do anything. It was nine o'clock on a Thursday morning, and the streets of the small, central Missouri town of Berclair were still nearly empty.

A few yards down the sidewalk, John and Daniel Hartman emerged from the doorway of a general mercantile store. Like Cole, they were dressed in suits and bowler hats. They waited for Cole to approach them, then the three men started together down the street, talking casually as they walked. Nobody took much notice of them. There had been a big stock sale in Berclair just the day before so all the residents of the town were accustomed to seeing a number of strangers about.

164

Most of the businesses they passed were closed and locked. Such was the Thursday morning custom in small towns such as this. The merchants catered to the needs of the farming families who flocked into town to buy goods only on Saturday.

"Seems quiet enough," Cole commented to his friends as they stepped down into the street and started across to the row of buildings on the other side. "I didn't expect to see many folks out and about at this time of day, but this is even better than I'd hoped for."

"Still there's something about this place. . . ." Daniel Hartman began nervously.

"What's that, Dan?" Cole asked.

"I don't know what it is," Dan admitted. "I can't put my finger on it, but there's something."

"He's been saying that ever since we got here last night," John complained. "Hell, he wouldn't even go out for a drink after we checked in at the hotel, and as soon as we woke up this morning he started in on it again."

"I guess I'm a little nervous, too," Cole said, "but we did check this place out pretty closely, and not a one of us could find a single reason not to go through with it."

They stopped at their horses, which were tied side-by-side to a rail in front of a closed saloon, and each began checking his saddle cinch and other gear. Down the street to the east, Frank and Jesse James were coming into sight, riding side by side with no apparent objective in mind. The two groups of men seemed to pay no attention whatsoever to each other.

"We're set," Cole told his two companions. "Clell is in place in that alley across the street, and Bill and Bo are waiting at the west end of town."

"I still wish we had your brothers Bob and Jim along on this one instead of Bill Martin and Bo Henderson," Daniel told Cole. "None of us know them hardly at all, and we can't be sure how they'll act if there's trouble."

"Well, I guess if they were good enough to ride with Jo Shelby's outfit during the war, they're good enough to be with us," John pointed out.

"That's right," Cole agreed. "And besides, you know I don't want my kid brothers getting too used to this outlaw business. They're not like the rest of us. They didn't ride with the bushwhackers during the war, and as young as they are, I don't want them to start believing that all a man has to do to get whatever he wants in life is to take it at the point of a gun. So why don't you quit worrying about everybody else and just concentrate on your part in this thing. It's going to work out fine."

Before Daniel could say any more, Cole stepped up on the sidewalk and started walking east. At about the same time, Frank and Jesse turned their mounts aside to a hitching post and stepped to the ground. The three men came together directly in front of the entrance to the Farmer's Bank and Trust. The James brothers went in first, followed by Cole a few steps behind.

The cashier on duty inside took little notice of the three new arrivals other than to glance up from his work to give them a nod and a routine "good morning." A second employee who sat behind a desk off to the side didn't even go to that much trouble. Frank and Jesse walked straight up to the cashier, and Cole turned to the left toward the other man.

On a signal from Jesse, all three of them drew their guns. In an instant, the shocked bank employees were completely at their mercy. The teller immediately raised his arms in surrender, but the man at the desk remained seated, his hands down, out of sight.

"If you happen to have a gun down there somewhere," Cole told the man quietly, "I'm willing to bet my life against yours that you can't get it up and shoot me before I can pull this trigger. So what do you say? Do you want to try and find out if I'm right?"

"No sir," the man mumbled hastily, his courage disappearing. "No sir, I don't." He raised his hands slowly into view, and both were quite empty.

"Good, now move over there with your friend," Cole ordered. "If you two fellows keep behaving this well, we'll be finished and out of here before you can sneeze."

Jesse cleared the counter in one bound and began raking money out of the cashier's drawer into a cloth sack while Cole and Frank continued to cover the prisoners. When he was finished, he turned to the cashier and said, "So much for the small change. Now you can come with me back to the vault and show me where the real money is stashed."

"Most of what we have was right there," the clerk stammered out. "We're a small bank in a small town. We don't have much need to keep a lot of cash on hand."

"You're a lying bastard," Jesse replied. "We were here for the stock sale and we know the money was brought here afterward. Hell, I was standing right across the street watching while they carried the strongbox in."

The look of helplessness which the two bank employees exchanged was enough to confirm that the money was indeed on the premises.

"Show him where it is, Willy," the man from the desk instructed. "It's not our money, and even if it was, it wouldn't be worth dying over."

"He's got a point there, Willy old boy," Jesse said, sneering at the teller.

The vault was already unlocked, so it only remained for the cashier to pull the door open and lead Jesse in. "It's in there," the man said, pointing to a bank of drawers which lined one wall. "The third drawer down in the first row."

Jesse James gave a low whistle of pleasure when he pulled the drawer open and saw the stacks of cash inside. "I wish you fellows could see this," he called out to Frank and Cole. "It looks like at least twice as much as we'd hoped for. I bet there's thirty thousand dollars here."

"Fifty-one thousand nine hundred," the bank employee who had remained outside announced with measured calm. "It's the most cash this institution has ever kept at any one time."

"Then I guess you'll be setting two records in one day," Frank James commented. "One minute the most cash you ever had, and the next minute the least."

Seconds later, Jesse emerged from the vault carrying a bag bulging with money. His face was beaming as he held it up for the others to inspect. "Just look at it," he exclaimed. "Just look!"

"There'll be plenty of time for looking later," Cole told him. "Right now, let's just worry about getting out of town without collecting any bullet holes in us."

"Let's ride," Jesse said, rounding the counter and heading toward the door.

"We'd better take care of these two first," Cole said.

"Why bother?" Jesse asked. Then, turning to the man nearest him, he said, "You boys aren't going to give us a bit of trouble, are you?"

"Not one bit," the man rushed to assure him. "After you're out of here, I don't even think I'll be able to remember what you look like."

"Well, you're going in the vault anyway, mister," Cole said, prodding the prisoner across the room. After the two bankers were both inside the long, narrow chamber, he swung the heavy door closed and turned the lock.

"Hot damn, what a picnic!" Jesse exclaimed as he started toward the door once more. He holstered his revolver before going out, but the bag of money was simply too large to conceal. His only recourse was to carry it down at his side and to act as casual as possible.

Trying not to rush, Frank and Jesse went to their horses and Jesse began tying the bag of money to the back of his saddle. At the same time, Cole turned aside and started back toward where John and Daniel were waiting a dozen yards away. Neither of the Hartman brothers had a gun in sight, but each of them had a hand casually thrust inside his jacket, ready to draw a hidden revolver and fire in an instant.

As the five men in the street were mounting up, Clell Miller emerged from the alley across the street. He was already on his horse, and without a sign of recognition to any of the others, he turned and started toward the west end of town.

Suddenly the stillness in the street was shattered by the loud clanging of a bell. Although the sound was coming from somewhere quite close by, in that first confusing moment none of the outlaws could figure out where the bell was or what it meant.

Then, pointing up at the wooden facade above the bank building's entrance, Frank James shouted out to the others, "It's up there! They've rigged some kind of alarm behind the false front! Let's get out of here!"

The others were prepared to leave immediately, but Jesse James was not content to ride away without expressing his anger over the bell. He drew his revolver and fired six quick shots at the front of the bank, shattering the two large panes of glass along the front of the building.

"Come on, Jesse!" Frank shouted impatiently. "Those two bastards are probably ringing the bell from inside the vault. You're not going to hit anything!"

"I just want to leave them a little something to remember us by," Jesse replied. He had holstered his empty revolver and was reaching for another when Daniel reached his side.

Grabbing his friend's arm, Dan roared furiously in his ear, "Dammit, Jesse! You go ahead and throw your life away if you want to. Nobody's going to stop you. But if you plan to stick around here and do something stupid, at least give us the money so the rest of us can leave!"

Jesse James looked at his friend, his eyes blazing with anger. He seemed on the verge of shouting some taunt or insult, but instead he snatched his arm free of Daniel's grip and jerked his horse around savagely. In another few seconds all six horsemen were thundering away.

The first few random shots began to sing past them before they had gone another fifty feet. The buildings on both sides of the street were not uninhabited as they had seemed, and everyone in town apparently knew what the clanging of the bell meant.

Clell Miller, who was riding a full ten yards ahead of the others, was the first to get hit. The revolver he was holding leaped out of his hand as a bullet passed through his arm and penetrated his side, but he managed to stay in the saddle, and the pace of his horse hardly slackened.

Things were a mess at the west end of town. Bo Henderson was sprawled face down in the dirt at the edge of the livery stable corral, and Bill Martin was pinned down a few feet away behind a stack of planks. As the others drew closer, Martin shouted out something and pointed toward the front of the livery barn, where the fire from at least three rifles was pouring out into the street. Neither Martin's nor Henderson's horse was anywhere in sight.

Although their escape route lay clear before them and all six of the mounted men could probably gave gotten away without any further problems, there was no question about whether they would ride on and leave their comrades stranded.

"Clell, you take off and head straight for the rendezvous," Cole shouted to his injured friend. "You're hit and you won't be much good to us here anyway. Frank, you and Jesse gather up those two over there, and then follow Clell. John and Daniel and I will try to buy you a couple of minutes."

No one argued. There wasn't time, and all of them realized that it was probably as good a plan as any of the others might come up with anyway. Struggling desperately to remain in the saddle, Clell Miller, spurred his horse toward the edge of town while Frank and Jesse James charged across a dangerous expanse of open ground toward Henderson and Martin.

Neither John nor Daniel had to be told what "buying a couple of minutes" meant. With a pistol in one hand and their reins in the other, they dug their heels into the sides of their mounts and plunged forward toward the barn, riding close on Cole's heels.

Only the speed of their horses and the

audacity of their charge saved them from the deadly rifle fire of their opponents as they burst through the open front doors of the barn. The men inside had little time to escape or seek cover before being confronted by the three desperate horsemen. Cole felled one with his first shot, and John took another out a second later. The third, and apparently the last, of the barn's defenders made a frantic leap for a small door along the back wall of the building. Daniel was already leveling his revolver at the back of his victim when he saw the man cast his rifle aside in panic. The pressure of his finger on the trigger eased, and in another instant the man was gone.

"That's the lot of them, I guess," John announced.

"Then let's get out of here!" Cole shouted. "Every man in Berclair is going to be hot on our trail in another few minutes. We need to put some miles behind us now while we have the chance."

When they got back outside, they saw that Frank and Jesse had already taken care of their assignment. Frank had somehow managed to load the fallen Henderson onto the rump of his horse, and Martin was riding double with Jesse. With half a dozen gun-wielding townsmen running toward them from the center of town, the small band of outlaws put the spurs to their horses and thundered away amid a hail of bullets.

Even after they had passed safely out of gunshot range and the sound of shooting had died away behind them, the bloodied group of men galloped on for another mile before calling a brief halt to assess the damage. They stopped at their first preset rendezvous point, where the wounded Clell Miller awaited them.

Only Jesse James and the two Hartman brothers remained completely unscathed. With two bullet wounds in his chest and one in his neck, Bo Henderson was stone dead, and Clell Miller was beginning to suffer a lot of pain from the wound in his side. Bill Martin had been fine up to the point when he climbed onto the back of Jesse's horse, but one of the last shots fired by the townsmen had found his back and he was barely able to make it to the ground unassisted by the time they stopped. Frank James and Cole Younger had less severe wounds. Frank had a minor but painful bullet crease along one buttock, and Cole was carrying a bullet which was embedded in his left calf.

After hastily tying his neckerchief around his own injury, Cole fell to work helping

Bill Martin with his injury, and John and Daniel gave what aid they could to Clell Miller.

"All right, we're shot to pieces, we're two horses short, and we can feel pretty damn safe in assuming that we'll have a posse coming after us in less than an hour," Jesse James said. "Anybody have any ideas?"

"Well we know we can't just split up and head for home like we planned," Cole said. "It could be days before we shake them off our tails, and we can't risk leading them back toward our own home ground."

"There's not much chance of outrunning them, either," John said. "Not with wounded to take care of, and some of us having to ride double. They'd catch up to us before nightfall."

After finishing with the bandage which he had hastily tied around Clell Miller's waist, Daniel turned to face the others. "Well if we can't travel fast enough to lose them," he said, "then I guess our only other choice is to find some way to slow them down."

"What do you mean?" Jesse asked.

"I figure a town the size of Berclair might be able to put together a dozen or so men on short notice to come after us. Maybe as many as fifteen or twenty, but no more. But those men aren't going to be trackers and professional lawmen. They're going to be shopkeepers and hotel clerks and hayseeds, and a lot of them are already going to be scared to death wondering what will happen if they actually do catch up to a bunch of desperate characters like us.

"So what I'm thinking is, why don't we give them something to be afraid of? Remember the way we used to hit and run back during the war? Two or three good men with rifles and fast horses could make a twenty-man Federal patrol start jumping at their own shadows and shooting at boogerbears in the woods. And those were trained soldiers who had been chasing after the likes of us for years. Think what men like these will do if shots start coming at them from nowhere and their horses start dropping dead between their knees."

"We probably turned too many of their friends into corpses back there to stop them with something like that," Cole commented, "but it seems to me that it would make a man ride a little slower and look a little harder at every tree and bush he passes."

"So who's to do it, then?" Jesse asked.

"You and me, Jesse," Daniel said. "You're the best shot among us so you can do the most damage, and it was my idea so it's my right."

Daniel looked at John, and he could see that his brother wanted to object to the plan. When they fought with the bushwhackers during the war they had always done their best to stay together, knowing that in desperate situations brothers would watch over one another better than anyone else would or could. But back then it had not always been possible to stay together, and in this case it would not be possible either. Two men would be as effective a hit-and-run deterrent as three, and Cole and Frank would need all the help they could get to deal with the injured and dead. It had to be this way.

John and Daniel shook hands, and traded promises to take care and fight smart. The James brothers bid one another an equally solemn farewell, and within a couple of minutes everyone was back in the saddle and ready to ride.

The sun was nearly down, and at last the oppressive heat which had marked the afternoon was beginning to lose some of its fierceness. It would be dark in less than an hour.

Hunched behind a jumble of rocks on a bluff overlooking a small river, Daniel found himself wondering how much progress his brother and the others had made during the day and how well they were faring. Clell and Bill were probably in bad shape by now. He imagined them slumped forward in their saddles with their arms tied together around their horses' necks, their faces twisted into masks of agony as they jolted along mile after endless mile. It wasn't a pleasant experience to be badly wounded and on the run. Daniel remembered the feeling well, and he hoped never to go through such hell again. It could make the simple act of dying seem like an attractive alternative.

If they were able to travel through the night, though, they might find themselves in the clear by morning, Daniel thought.

It seemed unlikely that the posse would decide to continue their pursuit after darkness fell, not after the day they'd had. Daniel and Jesse had struck three times during the long day, and they were in position now to do so again if it seemed necessary. Although they were only a dozen or so miles from Berclair, the two young outlaws estimated that they had ridden at least twenty-five or thirty miles since leaving their companions that morning. Pushing the horses to their utmost limits, they had snaked and circled through the wooded countryside like a pair of jackrabbits, dividing their time between running for their lives and scouting out the most effective sites for their next sudden ambush.

In the first ambush, which had taken place no more than three or four miles outside the town, Daniel and Jesse had shot only horses, hoping that would be enough to discourage their pursuers. But the leaders of the posse had had the foresight to bring along extra mounts, and the brief skirmish had slowed them down only for the length of time that it took to switch four saddles from dead horses to live ones.

The next time, an hour or so later, it was human flesh which had been shot. Daniel and Jesse had been careful merely to wound their victims rather than to kill them, knowing that wounded men were a lot more bother to care for than dead ones. The nineteen-man posse had been diminished by five that time. Three had been shot and two left to help their wounded companions get back to town.

For a while after that, Daniel and Jesse had been too busy getting out of danger themselves to strike out again. But by four o'clock they had located another good site for an ambush. That time they killed the town marshal and wounded one other man. The will of the others seemed to falter then.

They continued the pursuit, but their pace was pathetically slow and they paused frequently to scout ahead and to their flanks in a clumsy imitation of military procedure.

The two outlaws were hidden now on a bluff overlooking the spot where the road from Berclair crossed the river below. From this vantage point, and with the weapons they had, Daniel could imagine how easy it would be to slaughter most of the remaining members of the posse. For practiced marksmen like him and Jesse, it would be as simple as shooting bottles off a fence.

But he hoped there would be no more fighting. During this one day, he had seen more action than he had at any time since the war ended, and now all the old feelings of guilt and fear were beginning to plague him again just as they had so many times during the worst years of the great rebellion. In his heart, he prayed that the final members of the posse would not attempt to cross the river before it became too dark to aim and fire a weapon.

"Look, Dan," Jesse said from his hiding place a few feet away. "Look over there to the southeast. It's smoke. They've built a fire."

"Thank God!" Daniel exclaimed. "That must mean they've stopped for the night."

"I hope so," Jesse said. "I'm getting tired of all this riding, and I'm getting so hungry that I think I can feel my backbone rubbing up against my ribs."

"It's the killing I'm tired of," Daniel admitted.

"Hell, Dan! It was them or us. Do you think one of those bastards down there would have hesitated an instant to put a bullet in you or me or Frank or John if they'd had the chance? It's a war, man, just like the old days."

Daniel looked over at his companion curiously. It seemed to him that his friend Jesse might be enjoying all of this just a little too much. He himself had no problems with the idea of killing a man if he felt the need was there. That was a part of the life they led and a part of the business they were in. But still he didn't delude himself to believe that it was like Jesse said.

The war was over. It wasn't like the old days, and it bothered him somewhat to think that Jesse might have convinced himself otherwise. They were just bank robbers, now, men who took money at the point of a gun.

"It will never be over, will it, Dan?" Jesse said, his voice throaty and odd. "Not for the likes of us, at least."

CHAPTER NINE

Cassie sat on the edge of her bed, the door closed and the lamp turned down low, trying to calm the nervous racing of her heart. She could hear the sounds of their voices in the front room: her father's and mother's, and her Aunt Mollie's, and though she could not make out the words being spoken, she knew that important decisions about her future were being made at this very moment.

"Damn you, Mike Brookshire!" she whispered under her breath. "Damn you for doing this to me . . . and damn you for leaving!"

She had been cursing him for weeks, ever since she realized she was pregnant. He was a convenient target for her anger, and hurling oaths at his elusive memory somehow seemed to help her handle the host of other feelings that barraged her.

But she knew that curses would not help

her deal with what she still must face in the weeks and months ahead. There would be scandal in the community, of course. An unmarried woman with a baby in her belly and no man around to take responsibility for it was a prime subject for universal scorn and condemnation.

But what bothered her more than the tongue-wagging and crude jests which would no doubt swirl around her wherever she went for months to come was the realization that the problems that lay ahead were not even something she could suffer alone. Her entire family would have to share her pain and her shame, and what would make it worse for her mother and father would be the nagging feeling that if they had done something differently, if somehow they had found a way to be better parents, this might not have happened.

It wasn't fair at all for fate to pull a trick like this on her, Cassie thought. Not simply after her first time with her first man. This was the sort of thing that was supposed to happen only to the white trash girls who gambled their reputations and their futures over and over with every randy suitor who came along with a bag of store-bought candy and a mouthful of sweet talk.

But fair or not, it had most definitely happened. The realization of that fact had come slowly to her over a span of about two months and now there was absolutely no denying it.

Back at the end of August when she missed her first monthly period, she had managed to effectively convince herself that nothing was wrong. She had heard women talk about such irregularities during times of great emotional stress, and the summer had been a confusing and not altogether happy one for Cassie.

A month of panic and irrational denial had begun when she'd missed her time again in late September. For a while she'd become obsessed, not with the fact that she was indeed pregnant, but with various devices and deceptions necessary to hide it from her parents. Although she'd cried almost constantly when she was alone in her room or working somewhere by herself, she was excessively cheerful and agreeable around the other members of the family. Making sure they didn't think that anything was wrong became the most important thing in the world to her.

But of course that hadn't worked, at least not for long.

Late one evening after both Jason and Benjamin had gone to bed, Arethia had come to Cassie's room unexpectedly. Her eyes had been rimmed with red but her voice had been calm when she'd sat down on the edge of her daughter's bed and asked her outright how long it had been since she'd had "the curse." Cassie's tearful outburst had been all Arethia needed to confirm her growing suspicions that her daughter had conceived a child.

When Cassie got to the breakfast table the next morning, she saw by the look on her father's face that he now knew as well. There had not been any anger or any solemn expressions of disappointment. There had been no speeches or firm demands that she reveal who the father was. Instead he had been quiet and introspective, and when he'd looked at her his eyes had been filled with love and pain.

It was a relief to Cassie to have the whole thing out in the open at last. Looking back on the torturous month of secrecy and deception she had just spent, she wondered how she could ever have believed that her parents would not accept this news with the same sympathy and compassion that they had always shown toward their children.

Whatever they might be thinking or feeling in their hearts, at least they spared her the pain of hearing it during those first critical days after the news was out.

It had been Cassie's idea to write her Aunt Mollie in Kansas City. She told her mother that it was simply her intention to let her aunt know that she was pregnant, but in the back of her mind another idea was already beginning to form. She was starting to consider the possibility of going to live with Mollie in Kansas City, at least until the child was born.

She knew there would be no way to keep the news of her pregnancy a secret from their friends and neighbors in Clay County, but if she left for a few months, at least she would not be around to remind people of her transgression. Then, after the child was in the world, she could decide whether she wanted to return to live with her parents or start a new life for herself somewhere else.

Although Cassie did not come right out and ask her aunt if she could come to Kansas City, she did end her letter with this thought: "It's going to be difficult for all of us around here. I just wish there was some-place where I could go to live at least until the baby is born."

In a family as close as the Hartmans, that simple suggestion was enough. Mollie started for Clay County almost immediately after receiving Cassie's letter. As soon as she arrived, she asked to talk with Jason and Arethia alone so that all of them could speak more freely about what had happened and what should be done now. That had been more than two hours ago, and now Cassie was growing more anxious and impatient with each passing minute.

At last there was a soft tap on the door to Cassie's room. Surprisingly enough, it was her father who entered instead of her mother or aunt. He seemed a little uncomfortable with the situation as he limped across the room and sat down on the edge of the bed by his daughter, but as soon as he was seated he put his arm around her and pulled her to him.

"I know you've been sitting here waiting to hear what we decided," Jason said, "so I won't keep you in suspense. Your mother and I have agreed to let you go and live with Mollie in Kansas City until the baby is born."

Tears filled Cassie's eyes as she turned to kiss her father's cheek and hug him. Although she was relieved that the decision was made and that she would be allowed to go, she was also filled with a sudden sadness and unexplainable sense of loss. It had not occurred to her until that instant that when she left to move to the city, she might never return home to live with her parents again.

That same realization already seemed to be weighing heavily on Jason's mind. When he spoke again, his voice was tight with emotion, and he had to clear his throat more than once as he continued. "At first your mother and I refused to even consider the idea of your leaving," he admitted, "and it took us awhile to realize that most of our reasons for not wanting you to go were selfish ones. In my heart, I still don't want you to go, but I know now that it probably would be the best thing for you."

"I think it would be best, Daddy," she agreed quietly. "I understand that you and Mama would rather I stay here, but in the long run it will be better for all of us if I go."

"You don't really understand what you're asking us to do," Jason said. "But when that baby you're carrying is born, then you'll understand it in your heart. Someday when you're holding your own child in your arms, you'll look back and think about today, and then you'll realize how hard it was for us to let you go. But it has to be. There's no denying it now. You should go with Mollie."

Cassie's tears were flowing freely down her cheeks now as the full impact of her father's words began to sink in. She realized suddenly that at this very moment her body was nurturing not just the inconvenient product of some man's desire, but a real human being, a child that she would soon grow to love more than anything else on earth, even more than her own life.

"Daddy, I'm so sorry to cause you and Mama all this pain," Cassie sobbed, her face buried against the coarse fabric of Jason's work shirt. "It seems like everything I do just hurts you more."

"But that's not something you should be worrying about right now," Jason counseled. "Right now you should be doing just what you're doing, and that is thinking about what is best for you and your baby. You mother and I have faced hard times before, some a lot more painful and difficult than this. We know how to get through them, and we know they don't last forever.

"Life throws one new thing at you after another. Some of those things are good and some are bad, but very seldom are they what you expected. It's kind of like a fistfight. You've got to stand with one foot cocked back so that no punch ever quite knocks you down. As long as you stay on your feet and keep fighting back, you'll survive."

They were quiet for a moment as Cassie

worked to gain control of her emotions again. Jason stroked her soft blond hair, managing somehow with that simple contact to make his daughter feel loved.

Then at last he went on. "Your aunt did use some trickery on us to finally convince us to let you go with her," he admitted, a grin slowly spreading across his face. "It seems she had another reason for wanting you to go with her, one that neither your mother or I expected."

"What was that?" Cassie asked.

"She told us she needs someone from the family with her in Kansas City to plan a wedding, and she nominated you for the job."

"A wedding?" Cassie exclaimed in surprise. "Her wedding?"

"I guess so. She said she and this fellow she's been seeing, this Bedford Lee, have set the date for around Thanksgiving. Just between us, I never was all that impressed with the man the one time I met him, but I guess part of that was because I'd always hoped that she and Cole would someday tie the knot." A few months back Jason had eaten dinner with Lee and his sister during a trip to Kansas City, and he remembered hoping at the time that this would be nothing more than a passing dalliance to Mollie.

"You'll like Bedford once you get to know him better," Cassie assured her father. "He's charming and funny, and very handsome."

"I'm sure I will in time," Jason said. "After all, Mollie is my sister, and if she sees enough in him to get married to him, then who am I to judge him?"

"A wedding!" Cassie exclaimed, leaping to her feet and hugging her father's neck enthusiastically. "I have to go now, Daddy. I have to go see Mama and Aunt Mollie. We have a thousand things to plan, and only a few short weeks to get it all done in. . . ." She raced from the room, eager to find Mollie and share the exciting moment with her.

But for a minute longer Jason remained seated on the bed, staring at the doorway his daughter had just passed through. It was going to be all right, he thought, suddenly feeling better than he had for days. The next few months would not be easy ones for any of them, but everything would eventually be all right.

Chapter Ten

December, 1867

Cole Younger charged the man head-on, seemingly unaware of the long bowie knife which the fellow had just drawn from the top of his right boot. The only thing which saved Cole from death was the fact that his opponent was at least as drunk as he was. At the last moment Cole managed to knock the man's right arm aside just as he was swinging the blade up into striking position.

When their bodies collided, the momentum of Cole's charge carried him and the man he was attacking back across a table, scattering chairs, whiskey bottles and bystanders in all directions. The man's knife went flying out of his grasp as his body struck the floor with a sickening impact, and the two of them wound up in a furious tangle on the floor.

The more experienced fighter of the two, Cole immediately began to lash out with his fists, but he and his opponent were too close for his blows to have much impact. The man he was fighting, a hulking keelboat deckhand, placed both hands in the middle of Cole's chest and gave a hard shove, hurling him back against the rough plank bar.

Both men managed to get back on their feet at about the same time. Cole moved in immediately, his fists flailing, but his repeated blows to the man's head and chest seemed to have little effect. It was a different story with the few lucky blows the other man managed to land, however. Each one struck Cole like a brick, making him stagger back and adding to the confused state of his already muddled senses.

Finally, with Cole backed up against a wall, the big man was able to wade in past his opponent's hail of blows. Instead of hitting him, he locked his massive arms around Cole's chest and began to squeeze with all his might, ignoring the ineffectual punches and gouges of his gagging attacker. Only when Cole managed to dig one thumb into the man's eye socket was he finally able to gain some relief from the deadly bear hug.

The man staggered back, roaring in pain and clawing at his damaged eye. Cole grabbed a whiskey bottle and shattered it against his opponent's head, then drew back his right fist and smashed it into the man's face with all his might. The big man went down.

With the end of the fight at last in sight, Cole stumbled forward to deliver the final blows. But just as the moment of victory was near, his feet tangled in the splintered remnants of a broken chair, and as he fell forward his head hit the side of an over-turned table.

Cole rolled aside, breathless and stunned, struggling to get his bearings once more. He choked back a wad of bitter, alcoholic bile which threatened to gush up into his mouth. His head reeled, partly from the blow against the table and the exertion of the brawl, but also from the formidable amount of alcohol he had consumed over the past twenty-four hours. He was aware of a hulking form beginning to rise up slowly beside him, snarling and cursing, but he couldn't find enough strength left in his body to fight back.

Men were gathered all around in a tight circle, taunting the two combatants to keep the fight going. Flat on his back, Cole stared up dully at their faces, trying to remember what it was the man had said that made his so mad. It was something about the war, he thought, or maybe something about the

South. He did recall that it had seemed important at the time.

By this time Cole's opponent had managed to rise up onto his hands and knees. There was a deep gash on the side of his head and a stream of blood was flowing down to the point of his nose and dripping onto the floor, but it was apparent that he still intended to go on fighting. Cole braced himself for the pain as he watched a huge fist rise up in the air directly over his head.

But the fist never descended. Instead there was a dull thumping sound, like the noise of a club striking a side of beef, and the big man crumpled unexpectedly over onto his side.

"Goddammit, you shoulda let 'em fight it out!"

"Shut up! He's a friend of ours."

"Well he started this thing. And over nothin', too. Over nothin' a'tall!"

"I don't care who started it. I'm not going to just let him lay there and get beaten to death."

"Then maybe you'd like some of the same?"

"I'm tired of talking with you, mister. If you've got anything else to say, tell it to this forty-five!"

Cole tried to help as two sets of hands

caught him under his arms and hoisted him to his feet. "John? Dan?" he mumbled. "What're you two doin' here?"

"We were supposed to meet you at the Brittany six hours ago, Cole," John Hartman told him. "Don't you remember?" John had a revolver in his free hand, as did his brother Daniel, and both of them were doing their best to cover all sides of the dank riverside tavern as they half led, half dragged Cole toward the front door.

"Yeah, the Brittany. Seems like I do recall somethin' now. . . ."

The cold night air hit Cole like a slap in the face. Once they were out of the tavern, he shrugged off the helping hands of his friends and staggered forward a couple of steps, feeling once more able to navigate on his own. But then, without warning, the contents of his stomach began to rush up into his throat. He tilted his head forward as the vomit spewed out in a disgusting, acrid flood, filling the air around them with the sickening stench of whiskey and half digested food.

"Christ almighty, Cole! What's got into you?" Daniel exclaimed. "What the hell are you doing in a dump like this fighting with gutter trash and begging somebody to put a knife in your back?"

"Felt . . . like . . . getting . . . drunk . . ." Cole choked, still barely able to catch his breath or stand up on his own.

"But what the hell for, Cole?" Daniel asked. "And why in a place like this? Are you doing this because of Mollie? Because she got married last week?"

"I thought you didn't mind about her marrying that fellow," John added. "You said you didn't. You said you were glad she did it, and you were fine at the wedding. But just look at you now."

Shaking his head, Cole finally managed to stand up straight again, and when he turned to face his friends his gaze was surprisingly direct and intense. "It's not 'cause of her!" he replied angrily. "She shoulda got married, an' it might as well have been with this Lee fellow as with somebody else. Can't a man jus' get drunk? Shit! Can't a man jus' go ahead an' get drunk when he takes a notion?"

"Sure, a man can," Daniel replied in a conciliatory tone. "There's no law against it."

"Look, Cole," John said. "We've got a room rented in the Savoy. Do you feel like heading up there with us?"

"I feel like drinkin'," Cole challenged.

"All right, if you want to drink, we'll drink

with you 'til none of us can stand up anymore," John said. "But why don't we go by the room for a minute first."

"What for?"

"So you can clean yourself up, for one thing," John told him. "You've thrown up all over your trousers and shoes, and you smell like something that died three or four days ago but never got buried. I've got an extra outfit that you can use, and after you've changed, we can head back out and drink 'til there's no more whiskey left to buy in Kansas City."

"A'right," Cole agreed reluctantly. "A'right, we'll go. Don't want to stink. . . ."

Cole began to lose consciousness about halfway to the Savoy, and when it finally became too much trouble for the brothers to keep him on his feet, John threw him over his shoulder and trudged on toward the hotel.

Cole was sprawled out across one of the double beds in the hotel room, lost in snoring, drooling oblivion. His friends had managed to wrestle him out of his ripped jacket and shoes, but undressing him any further seemed like too much trouble so they just piled him on the bed with the rest of his clothes on.

Daniel was reclining on the other bed, and John was stretched out on a long sofa on the other side of the room. Neither was asleep, although the hour was late and the day they had ahead of them promised to be a long one.

"I can't figure what's gotten into Cole," Daniel told his brother. "I can't remember ever seeing him like he was tonight, not even back during the war when everybody else in the outfit decided to cut loose and throw a good drunk. Hell, if we hadn't come across him when we did tonight, they'd have been hauling his carcass out of that place on a plank. It just isn't like him to get into scrapes like that for no good reason."

"I tell you it's her," John answered. "There's only one thing in the world that can make a man go crazy like that, and that's a woman."

"But he had his chance. He could have married her right after the war when he came back from California. Aunt Mollie told me so herself. So why should it hit him like this when she finally decided to marry somebody else two years after he turned down the chance himself?"

"Damned if I know why, Dan," John admitted. "But there's one thing I do know, and that is that we'd better stick with Cole

201

for the next day or so, just to make sure he doesn't go off and do something crazy again."

The brothers had originally come to the city on Cole's invitation, supposedly to sit in on a big private poker game which was to take place at one of the local hotels. The plan had been for John and Daniel to meet Cole for dinner at the Brittany at six the previous evening, and from there they were to have gone on to the game.

After it had become obvious that Cole was not going to show up at the appointed place and time, the Hartman brothers had started searching for him. First they'd checked a few local saloons which they had visited with Cole on other occasions, and then they'd both begun making the rounds of other drinking establishments.

Finally, at about ten o'clock they'd located a hostess in one saloon who knew Cole and remembered seeing him earlier that night. Her warning that he was already drunk and in an ugly mood had only made them search that much harder. The surly, obnoxious character that she had described to them hardly resembled their good friend.

Another conversation in another saloon had sent them toward the riverside district, where rows of cheap saloons competed with a variety of whorehouses, low-rent hotels, and warehouses for space along the streets near the Missouri River levee.

The fact that John and Daniel managed to save Cole in the tavern wasn't quite as much of an eleventh-hour coincidence as it seemed. They had actually spotted him in the place a few minutes earlier, and when Cole attacked the keelboat deckhand, they had been trying to decide whether to make him leave with them or to simply stay out of sight and give him whatever assistance he might need later in the night. Of course the fight settled that debate for them.

Cole rolled over heavily on the bed, turning his face away from the pool of spittle which had collected on the pillow under his head. He moaned something unintelligible in his sleep, coughed a couple of times, and then immediately resumed his loud, incessant snoring. Even if either of them had been in the mood, Daniel Hartman thought, it would have been difficult for him or his brother to have gotten any sleep in this room.

"After tonight, I'm not really sure we should even mention to Cole what we came here to discuss with him," John said. "With the mood he seems to be in, I don't know whether he'll even be interested in talking to us about it."

"Well we're going to have to decide pretty soon whether to bring it up," Daniel said. "Jesse said he wants to have our answer by next week so he'll know whether or not he has to round up somebody else to take our places. And of course if we talk Cole out of going, then Jesse and Frank will probably have to replace Jim and Bob Younger as well. I don't think they'd go that far from home to help with a robbery if Cole wasn't along." He took a sip from the glass of whiskey that sat on the table by the bed, then went on. "I just wish Jesse would back off from this business for a while. At least for another six months, or maybe even a year. You'd think he would have learned some sort of lesson after the way we got shot up down there in Berclair four months ago. They were ready for us, as sure as hell. We made a good haul, but it cost us two dead and four wounded, and all things considered, we were lucky to keep our losses to that."

"I guess that's the idea behind going clear over to Kentucky for the next holdup," John said. "Jesse thinks maybe they won't be quite as ready for us in another state as they seem to be here in Missouri."

"But why take the chance, John?" Daniel

asked. "Hell, we can't even risk spending much of the money we have now, not without causing a lot of suspicion. And what about that stranger that keeps drifting through this part of the state every few months, the one who keeps asking so many questions about all the men who used to ride with Quantrill? You were in Bourn's store that day when Harvey Bourn said there was somebody asking about the two of us by name. Somebody out there knows more about the lot of us than we'd like him to know, and every holdup we pull only adds to our chances of ending up in prison or with a hangman's noose around our necks."

"I know, Dan," John said. "I'm not the one you need to convince. It's the others. But it does seem to me that at this point, one more robbery probably isn't going to make much difference anyway. If somebody's after us, then they'll still be after us whether or not we go along to Kentucky."

"We're in too deep, John," Daniel said with a grim note of foreboding in his voice. "I've had this feeling for months now, and everything that's happened lately just makes it keep getting stronger. We've cut off a bigger plug than we can chew, and sooner or later there's going to be hell to pay."

"Well, I never was much on premonitions and the like," John admitted, "but after what you kept saying in Berclair and after the way things turned out there, I'm starting to wonder. I guess in the morning we'd better get Cole straightened out and try to have a talk with him."

"A man can only stretch his luck so far, and then it's going to snap," Daniel said. "No matter whether Cole's in the mood to hear it or not, we need to have a long, hard talk with him about Kentucky."

CHAPTER ELEVEN

June, 1868

Winfred Marks stood waiting patiently while Mollie reread the latest letter from Jack Marshall in Montana. The news that their gold mine was doing well was welcome, of course, but what worried her was the suggestion that she invest yet another large sum in equipment and supplies so the mining operation could be expanded.

Finally, laying the letter aside, Mollie looked up at her accountant and asked, "What do you think, Winfred? After two years, I still have yet to regain my original investment in this mine. Is it worth sinking another ten thousand into, or should I tell Marshall to do the best he can with the present equipment?"

"Well, he has made you quite a generous offer," Marks noted. "Owning an additional five percent of the property could be very lucrative if the vein he hopes to follow doesn't play out and if the equipment he wants to buy is sufficient to do the job."

"Those are two very big 'ifs,' though," Mollie said. "And with everything else that's going on right now, it's going to be a problem raising the kind of cash Marshall wants."

"You can get it if you have to, Mollie," Marks replied. "I don't know enough about the mine's prospects to risk advising you one way or the other, but your credit's excellent, and if you're willing to put the theater up for collateral, I'm sure any bank in the city would be glad to lend you twice that much."

Mollie leaned back in her chair and stared at the wall across the office, considering the matter. She had known she was taking a risk when she first agreed to back Marshall and his partners to the tune of four thousand dollars two years before. Her common sense had told her that she would probably never see any return on her investment. Even when, several months later, she received a letter from Marshall announcing that they had found colors and staked a claim, she still would not permit herself the luxury of being overly optimistic.

Since then Marshall had started sending her some actual profits a few hundred dollars at a time, and along the way Mollie and Marshall had bought out some of the other partners until now the income was being divided among only three people. As the original backer, Mollie received sixty percent, and Marshall and his remaining partner both claimed twenty percent each.

But even taking all that into consideration, the thought of investing an additional ten thousand dollars on such a risky venture made her nervous. She had learned enough about the mining business to realize that a gold-bearing quartz vein such as the one Marshall was following could play out at any time.

"Check around and see what interest rates are available, Winfred," Mollie said at last. "But don't tell anybody what the money's for, and don't indicate that I might be willing to put the theater up for collateral if necessary. I'm not going to commit myself to this business one way or the other until I've had some time to think about it some more, but it won't hurt to test the financial waters while I'm considering it. And in the meantime, I'll write Marshall and tell him I'm not sure I can raise that kind of cash. I don't want him to start thinking that I'm some kind of money river and that he can just dip his bucket in any time he wants."

"Yes, ma'am," Winfred said.

Mollie handed Marshall's letter over to be filed, then asked, "What's next?"

"This is, I suppose," Winfred said, passing another sheet of paper to her.

Mollie glanced the paper over quickly and a frown spread across her face. It was a bill from Cassandra's, an exclusive saloon, casino and brothel located a few blocks east of downtown Kansas City. The bill was for one hundred forty dollars, and across the bottom was the unmistakable signature of her husband of seven months, Bedford Lee.

"Pay it, Winfred," she said at last, passing the paper back to her accountant.

"Oh, I intended to, of course, but I just thought you might like to, uh, look it over first."

"Well, I've seen it. Thank you, Winfred. Now what else do you have?"

The pair remained in Mollie's small office in the back of the theater for the next two hours, going over various details relating to Mollie's ever expanding business enterprises. After a few more miscellaneous matters were taken care of, they spent the bulk of their time discussing Mollie's latest venture.

Early in the spring, she had bought a small twenty-acre farm on the southern edge of the city and had launched into one of her most ambitious projects to date. With the aide of a capable supervisor named Richard Hightower, she had instructed that the land be cleared and that a new street be laid out down the middle of it. Now, four months into the project, crews were just beginning to start the foundations on the first of twenty new houses which she intended to build on the land.

Since the end of the war, Mollie had been watching the rapid expansion of the Kansas City area and wondering what a wise investor might do to capitalize on that growth. With the aid of Winfred Marks she had investigated both the railroad and the meat packing businesses, but they eventually decided that such ventures would require far more capital than a woman could possibly raise.

The housing business had been third on Mollie's list of possibilities, and that idea proved to be more practical than either of the first two. With the influx of so many new people into the area, housing was a constant problem. Many of the people in search of accommodations earned enough to afford decent houses, but few homes were available and the scarcity made prices unreasonably high. So Mollie decided to build new homes.

At first the bankers Mollie approached for financing were skeptical about the enterprise, but now with four of the homes sold even before they were built, those same bankers were already encouraging her to expand onto available land to the south and west. Mollie was not yet convinced that she wanted to get that deeply involved in the construction business, but she was quite pleased with the progress she had made so far.

Mollie and Winfred were nearly finished with their morning's business when the office door opened and Bedford Lee strode in. As usual, he was immaculately dressed and groomed, but the redness of his eyes and the sallow cast of his complexion attested to his alcoholic excesses and the late hours he had kept the night before.

Mollie rose and went around the desk to give her husband a kiss in greeting, and Bedford and Marks exchanged routine nods. The two men cared very little for one another, but there had never been a reason or occasion for their mutual dislike to surface.

"I guess whatever is left can wait until later, Winfred," Mollie told her assistant.

"I think so," Marks agreed. "We've covered everything of any importance, and I had planned to ride out to check on the new construction in a little while anyway."

"That's good," Mollie said. "And be sure and let me know if that load of lumber has arrived yet. I'm going to raise hell with Jack Beasley if he doesn't deliver the full order sometime this week."

Marks was becoming such a key figure in the development of the new houses that Mollie was considering making him a full partner in the enterprise. She had yet to mention the matter to him, but she thought the fairest thing might be to let him buy in for half of her original costs.

After the accountant gathered up his paperwork and left, Bedford drew Mollie to him and gave her a longer, more intimate greeting. Standing enveloped in his arms, Mollie thought she could detect the faint scent of brandy beneath the odor of his cologne. Apparently he had felt the need for a little hair-of-the-dog before coming to see her this morning.

"How late were you out last night, Bedford?" Mollie asked, hating herself for the question even as it came from her lips.

"Quite late, I'm afraid," he answered. "The game broke up around one, but I met two gentlemen from Cincinnati whose acquaintance I wanted to develop, and I stayed out drinking brandy with them. They both have a taste for cards and the money to afford it, so I thought it might be a good idea to get to know them better. When I did finally get home, I just went straight to the spare bedroom because I didn't want to disturb you."

"But do you recall telling me you would be home at eight, Bedford?" Mollie said. "I waited to have dinner with you for nearly an hour."

"I remember telling you that I would try to make it home," Bedford said, "but as it happened, I couldn't make it after all. As I told you, there was a game last night." Mollie could tell by the tone of his voice that he was irritated by her questions, so she just let the matter drop. It was, after all, no great revelation at this point to realize that the man she married could not always be counted on to do what he said he would do, and she knew the best course was to just forget about the previous night.

But Bedford was not content to leave it at that. As Mollie started to turn away from him, he took her arm and pulled her back around.

"Look, Mollie, you knew what I did for a

living from the first day we met. I never lied to you about myself, and I never promised you I would change in any way. I'm a gambler. It's what I do and it's all that I want to do. It's my business, just like this theater and all these other things you're doing are your business."

"Well business isn't too good these days, is it, Bedford?" Mollie replied sharply. She didn't like being manhandled, and she didn't like the way Bedford was speaking to her either. "The latest of your bills from Cassandra's just arrived. This one was for one hundred and forty dollars."

"That was for Monday night," Bedford explained. "I rented a private room for a game, and then I paid for the drinks and companions for a couple of invited guests. But things didn't work out for me that night, and I didn't have enough cash left to pay the bill. I don't see why you're making a big stink about this thing, though. I've done it before and you haven't seemed to mind."

"I still don't mind paying the bill, Bedford," Mollie tried to explain. "I guess what bothers me about this whole thing is that you didn't even bother to mention it to me. It's come to the point that when you don't want to pay for something, or can't pay for

215

it, you simply assume that I will."

"Damn it, I'll get you the money," he growled back at her. "If things work out, I'll probably have it after tonight."

"But I told you, it isn't the money!" Mollie insisted. "It's being taken for granted that I dislike so much. We've only been married for seven months, but already I sleep in my bed alone four or five nights a week, and sometimes you don't come home for two or three days at a time. What am I to you, Bedford? Just the 'little woman' who's always there in case you need something or get the notion that it's time to take your pleasure?"

"No, damn it, it's not like that at all, and I want you to get those ideas out of your head right now!" Bedford told her. "You're my wife and I love you. I didn't marry you just so I could have a woman to walk all over. But I'm not like that Winfred Marks, your best boy, either. I could never be happy stuck in an office for ten hours a day, six days a week, or sitting at home every night reading the paper and watching you knit. It just isn't how I'm put together."

"I know it's not, Bedford, and I never tried to make myself believe that marriage would change you very much. But I just keep thinking that there is so much more that you could do with your life. Take the building project for instance. If you would just —"

"Damn it to hell, Mollie! Are you going to start in on that again? I thought we talked that idea to death a long time ago. That's your business, not mine!"

"You're right, we did talk about that," Mollie conceded, "and I'm sorry for bringing it up again. The project is going fine without you, so it would be a simple, condescending lie to tell you that I need your help at this point. But surely there's something . . . something that would get you involved, that would give you a sense of purpose and accomplishment."

"Damn it, Mollie, I've been hearing that all my life," Bedford complained, "but what nobody seems to understand about me is that I'm perfectly satisfied with my life the way it is!"

"But doesn't it bother you sometimes to realize that we're living in my house, and that most of the good things that we enjoy in life are bought with my money? Sometimes I can't help but think that surely you would be happier if you just had something of your own, a store perhaps, or some other kind of business, something that would give you an income of your own to do with as you please."

"And how do you suggest I acquire such a business? At this moment I hardly have enough money to buy you lunch."

"Arrangements could be made to get you started, Bedford," she said. "Winfred could take care of it for you."

"In other words, you'd give me the money," Bedford said.

"Yes, of course I would be glad to help. But it would be a loan, not a gift," Mollie insisted. "You wouldn't object to that, would you?"

"Hardly," Bedford chuckled. "After all, if I had an overabundance of pride, I'd scarcely be sending you my saloon bills, would I?"

Mollie didn't particularly like the note of sarcasm in his voice, but she did her best to ignore it. For the first time, it seemed that he might be honestly considering her suggestions, and she didn't want to say or do anything to discourage him at this point. "It would be a simple business arrangement between us," she said. "If you like, we could even have papers drawn up specifying the terms of repayment."

A smile slowly began to spread across Bedford Lee's handsome features. Mollie could tell by that look that he had something on his mind already, but an instinct also told her that it might not be an idea she would particularly like.

"What you've been saying has brought an idea to mind," Bedford said. "There is, in fact, a business that I would very much enjoy owning, and by coincidence, I heard recently that it's going to be on the market soon. About a week ago, Cassandra Steiner told me that she's about ready to retire and that she's been quietly looking around for a buyer for her place."

"You want to buy Cassandra's?!"

"Why not? It would be perfect for a man like me."

"But Bedford, it's a whorehouse, for God's sake! Would you honestly expect me to invest a cent of my money in a place like that?"

"You know as well as I do that the girls are only a small part of what goes on at Cassandra's," Bedford told her. "She has to keep them around, sort of like conveniences for her clients, but the real draw is the casino. *That's* where the money's made."

Mollie simply stared at her husband for a moment, amazed that he would come up with such a preposterous idea and then have the nerve to ask her to consider it seriously. From time to time it took all her inner strength not to be consumed with jealousy when she thought of the women who were so easily available to her husband each time he stepped through the front door of Cassandra's. She could only imagine how intolerable the situation would quickly become if he owned the place and the women that she so distrusted were at his beck and call every day.

"I just couldn't stand that," Mollie tried to explain. "I love you, Bedford, and you've never given me any reason to believe that you're not a faithful husband. But just the thought of you having women like that working for you, available to you. . . ."

"Just forget it, Mollie," Bedford snarled. His voice took on an icy tone which she rarely heard from him. "I guess I should have known better than to think you wanted to see me get ahead in my own way. All you really want is to find something that will occupy my time, something that will keep me out of places like Cassandra's and away from the people who entertain themselves in such places. But you can't have what you want. I plan to live my life the way I choose . . . with or without you!"

Mollie said nothing, not trusting the flood of feelings which was building up inside her. They had argued before, but never before had Bedford presented her with such a clear-cut ultimatum. It would have been easy to reply to him in kind — her anger was goading her to do so — but she knew what the consequences of that could easily be. One of them had to show some restraint at this critical moment.

"Bedford, I'm sorry I've gotten you so upset," Mollie found herself saying in a reasonable, controlled tone. She hated to apologize when she felt she had done nothing wrong, but it seemed necessary. "It's obvious that we're not going to agree on this, but my intentions were good and I don't want you to be angry with me."

"All right then," Bedford reluctantly said, "but from now on, just remember that I'm not the kind of man who can be dictated to. I don't need your help running my life. You're my wife and I love you, but even that doesn't give you the right to try to take charge of me."

"I'll remember," Mollie promised.

After he was gone, Mollie closed the door to her office and went over to stand by the open window. It was odd, she thought, that she didn't feel more upset about the harsh encounter with her husband. It had, without a doubt, been the worst fight they'd ever had, and it was strange that now she felt no anger, sadness or guilt. Searching into the deepest recesses of her heart, the only true feeling she could come up with was one of regret, but even that wasn't terribly strong.

Although she had not mentioned the fact to him, the dinner she had planned for them the previous night was to have been a special one. She had instructed the cook to prepare all of her husband's favorite dishes, and she had brought up one of the best bottles of burgundy from the small wine cellar in the basement of the house. Everything was perfect, right down to the polished silver table settings and the tall tapered candles which gave the dining room an air of pleasant intimacy. The entire meal was to have been a surprise, as was the announcement which she had planned to make at the end of it.

But now she had no clear idea when or how she would break the news to Bedford that he would be a father in a few more months. He had to be told, of course, but now the idea of doing it in any sort of romantic or intimate way had lost its charm.

If he came home tonight, she decided indifferently turning back to her desk and her work, she would tell him. If he didn't show up tonight, well, there was always tomorrow, or the next day, or the day after that. Eventually he would show up when he needed a good meal or a change of clothes or more money to support his indulgences. He would come back, and he would learn that he had fathered a child, and he would leave again. But nothing would be changed.

CHAPTER TWELVE

January, 1869

Sitting in a chair beside Mollie's bed, Cassie felt the grip of her Aunt Mollie's hand tighten and she knew that another contraction was about to start. Despite the chill in the room, Mollie's cheeks and forehead were beaded with perspiration, and her face slowly began to contort as the pain grew more intense. Finally, when she could resist no longer, she opened her mouth and cut loose with a harsh, prolonged moan which brought tears of empathy to Cassie's eyes.

Across the room Dr. Tuttle glanced down at the pocket watch in his hand and announced, "Two minutes apart. It shouldn't be long now." He was a tall, portly man in his late fifties with pince-nez glasses and a neat, full beard which gave him a thoughtful, wizened appearance. He was in a rather foul mood after being called away from his supper to deliver a baby, but there was something in his very gruffness that made Cassie feel reassured that everything was going as it should.

It promised to be a difficult delivery. Mollie had been in labor for nearly six hours, and though she had held up well at first, the repeated waves of racking pain now held complete sway over her. Each time another contraction approached, her face took on a look of absolute dread, and when the pain finally struck, her screams echoed through the house. But at least the doctor had arrived, Cassie thought, and though he was not an overly sympathetic fellow and had refused to administer any drug to ease Mollie's agony, his mere presence gave the situation an air of normality.

The door to the room opened and Amanda, Mollie's cook and housekeeper, came in with a great armload of towels, which she placed on a bureau near the bed. "I've got plenty of water heating downstairs," she told the doctor. "You just let me know when it's time to start bringing it up."

"Well, you might as well start up with a bucket or two right now," Dr. Tuttle instructed. "I've got a feeling we'll be able to put it to use before it has time to cool."

"Yes sir," the maid replied. She started out, but Cassie stopped her at the door by quietly speaking her name.

When she turned to face Cassie, Amanda simply shook her head, knowing the question before it was asked. "Walter got back a few minutes ago," she said quietly. "He looked everyplace he could think of, but he couldn't find hide nor hair of Mr. Lee anywhere."

They had sent Walter Perry, Mollie's gardener and handyman, out looking for Bedford Lee more than three hours ago, after it became certain that the labor was real. Mollie had not asked for her husband once during the long ordeal, but Cassie still felt that it was his obligation to be present and she had instructed Walter to inquire at every hotel, saloon and gaming parlor he could think of before coming back.

Another contraction hit just as Amanda was hurrying away on her errand. Mollie's back arched in agony, and she squeezed so hard on Cassie's hand that Cassie could scarcely stand the pain.

"We'd better get her ready," Dr. Tuttle announced. "It won't be long now." He drew a small table to the edge of the bed, spread a towel across the top, and laid out a few odd-looking instruments. Then he peeled back the covers from the bed and drew Mollie's gown above her waist. The bed was a mess already, but Cassie remembered from her own delivery that that was a normal part of things.

"All right, Mollie, you're going to have to help me with this," the doctor advised gruffly. "Every time I tell you, I want you to push down as hard as you can. The harder you push, the sooner we'll get this thing over with. Now push!"

The veins on Mollie's flushed face and neck bulged as she strained to comply with the doctor's instructions. Cassie could see how much pain the effort caused her aunt, but she also remembered from her own delivery that at this point, one was willing to endure almost any agony in order to end the whole ordeal.

"Good. Now do it again," Dr. Tuttle said. "Push as hard as you can, Mollie."

Four times they went through the same ritual, and then at last Cassie saw by the pleased expression on the doctor's face that something was starting to happen. Glancing down, she was utterly amazed to see a portion of the baby's head begin to appear.

"You're doing it," Cassie said excitedly. "It's happening, Mollie!"

Mollie was too absorbed in her own efforts to pay attention to anything else, but Cassie watched with absolute delight as her newborn cousin slid slowly from its mother's womb and into the world. Watching one human being emerge from the body of another was an experience quite unlike any she'd ever had, even during the delivery of her own son a year before.

"You've got yourself a boy here, Mollie," Dr. Tuttle announced as he reached for his instruments. At his elbow Amanda stood beaming like a grandmother, waiting to perform any service the doctor might require. The baby was already beginning to squall at the top of its lungs, but nobody minded. A basin of lukewarm water sat ready on a table nearby, and as soon as everything else was taken care of, the doctor and the housekeeper gently bathed the bawling, wriggling infant.

As the first sign of relief in hours, Mollie let a weak smile spread across her face. "A boy," she whispered softly to her niece. "I have a son."

"Yes you do, and quite a loud one, too." Cassie grinned. "I guess with a mouth like that, he'll fit right in with the Hartman family."

"He'll do fine," Mollie said and beamed as Amanda brought the baby over to her at last. "He's going to do just fine."

Cassie sat at the table in the kitchen drinking a cup of coffee and nibbling at the slice of apple pie Amanda had cut for her. It was nearly ten at night now and she hadn't eaten anything since noon, but still she was not hungry. The excitement and tension of the long afternoon and evening had robbed her of her appetite.

Mollie and the baby were asleep upstairs. The doctor had stayed around for an additional hour to make sure there were no complications following the birth, and when he finally left he promised to return in the morning to check on Mollie and her son. Cassie had looked in on her own son, Timothy only a short time before and saw that he too was sound asleep in her bedroom upstairs.

Amanda had been washing and putting away dishes, but when the chore was finished at last, she poured a cup of coffee and sat at the table with Cassie.

"I want to thank you for your help during all of this," Cassie told the housekeeper. "I don't know what I would have done if I'd had to handle everything myself."

"I wouldn't have missed it for the world,"

229

Amanda said wearily. "You know, I've worked for Mrs. Lee for over three years, and before that I was with the woman who used to own this house for six. All I did was what I was supposed to do."

"Well I still appreciate it, and I'm sure Mollie does too," Cassie said. "I only wish we could have had better luck at finding Bedford. The way he's been acting lately, it might be two or three more days before he finds out he's a father."

"That man! I don't understand him at all," Amanda complained. "Look at all he's got here. A fine home, a good wife, and now a baby son, and still he stays out all the time with that gambling, whiskey-drinking trash he likes to be with."

"Maybe things will be different now that he's a father," Cassie suggested. "Having that happen can change a man, if he wants to change."

"That's right. If he *wants* to change," Amanda added in a decidedly cynical tone.

The two of them were quiet for a moment, each sipping her coffee and thinking about the day's events. Then finally Amanda set her cup down and turned to face Cassie as if she had suddenly come to some important decision. "I guess there's something I need to tell you, Miss Cassie," she said hesitantly.

"I didn't want to say nothing to you earlier because of all that was going on, but it seems like you have a right to know."

"What is it, Amanda?" Cassie asked. The seriousness in the housekeeper's voice alarmed her, and she wondered if she was about to hear some startling revelation, perhaps about her aunt or about Bedford.

"You know when Walter went out this afternoon looking for Mr. Lee?" the house-keeper began seeming uncertain whether she should go on or not.

"Yes?"

"Well, it's like I said, he didn't find him, but he told me afterward that he saw some-body else that he recognized. A man who visited here at the house a long time ago."

"Was it Cole Younger?" Cassie asked.

"No, it wasn't him. It was . . . that young fellow that came to see you a long time back when you were down here visiting. His name was Brookshire, I believe."

"He saw Mike Brookshire?" Cassie exclaimed, nearly dropping her coffee cup. "Here in Kansas City?"

"That's right," Amanda said. "That's what Walter told me. He said it was late in the afternoon in one of those little saloon places over near the stockyards."

Cassie had always hoped that someday

231

Mike Brookshire might return. But she was not prepared for this announcement, not now, not yet, and she was startled by the profound effect it had on her.

"Did I do the right thing?" Amanda asked with concern. "Is it all right that I told you? I'm sorry if I did anything wrong."

"I'm glad you told me," Cassie assured her, trying to compose herself. "But it's just such a surprise. I wasn't prepared to hear this particular piece of news just now."

"Well, Walter just happened to mention it to me," the maid explained, "and I felt like it just wasn't my right to keep a thing like that to myself."

"Where exactly did he see him, and when was it?" Cassie asked urgently.

"He said something about a 'hog' or a 'pig' or something like that. I can't recall the name for sure, but it must have been about five o'clock."

"I remember seeing a place west of here called the Blue Boar," Cassie said. "Could that have been the name?"

"That sounds like it," Amanda said. "But you're not thinking of going over there are you? That's a bad part of town and it wouldn't be safe for you there after dark. And besides, it was hours ago. He's bound to be gone by now."

"I have to see him, Amanda." The pronouncement surprised her almost as much as it did the housekeeper, but the instant the words were out of her mouth she knew they were true.

"What on earth for?" Amanda asked. "He left you, didn't he? And when he came back, he never came around looking for you. Don't be foolish, girl. Put him and all that business behind you and get on with your life like you're supposed to."

"I have to see him," Cassie repeated. "I'm not sure why, but maybe doing that will help me put it in the past."

The Blue Boar saloon was located so near the Kansas City stockyards that the air was permanently saturated with the stench of livestock, manure, and meat processing. It was a dingy little place located on a narrow side street lined with small shops, boarding houses and brothels. The hour was late and the temperature had dropped well below the freezing point, but there was still some traffic in the area and Cassie did not feel particularly threatened as she paid her carriage, looked around carefully, and stepped down to the ground.

She was familiar with the location of the saloon because it was on the route which Walter sometimes took when he drove to a meat cutter's in the area. For special occasions Cassie sometimes went with him to pick out the choicest cuts of beef and pork.

She had put on the simplest clothing she had, knowing that in this area she would not want to appear either too affluent or too available. Concealed in the pocket of her long wool coat was a short-barreled, six-shot revolver, and she kept one hand constantly around its grip in case there was trouble.

Cassie paused outside the door of the place, steeling herself for what was to come. She still had little idea of what she would say to Mike Brookshire when she found him. Should she just blurt right out that she had borne him a son that she expected him to take some responsibility for, or should she be more subtle and take her cue from how he acted and what he said? It occurred to her suddenly that in a place like this, there was no way that the encounter could seem accidental. He would know the minute he saw her that she had come looking for him, and that knowledge would give him a decided advantage during their first meeting.

But it could not be helped. She hadn't come this far on such a dark, cold night only to turn around and go home again. Resolutely she reached out, opened the front door of the saloon and strode in.

The Blue Boar was almost empty, and Mike was nowhere in sight. It was a small, smelly place which was illuminated by two sooty kerosene lamps. A long bar constructed of simple pine planks dominated the back wall, and the remainder of the room was filled with an assortment of dilapidated tables and chairs which could, at most, accommodate twenty or twenty-five people. A tiny coal-fired stove along one wall was glowing red hot in its efforts to raise the temperature inside the saloon slightly above what it was out in the street.

Three men were sitting at a table in a dark corner off to the left, and two more were leaning on the bar, obviously drunk and near the point of collapse. The only person in the place who paid Cassie any attention at all was the husky, mean-eyed bartender.

"You sure you're in the right place, lady?" the bartender asked as Cassie stepped up to the bar. "You don't look like no whore, and that's about the only kind of woman we ever get in here."

"I'm here looking for somebody," Cassie explained.

"Wal, I ain't seen him," the bartender replied routinely. "And in case it's a 'her' instead of a 'him', I ain't seen her either."

"Look, I'm not some angry wife out in search of a wayward husband," Cassie said impatiently. "I'm looking for a man that I haven't seen in nearly two years, and I was told he was in here earlier. He's about twenty-four years old, a little taller than you, not quite as husky, with sandy-brown hair. His name is Mike Brookshire and he's probably just returned from a trip out to the frontier."

"Nope. I ain't seen him," the bartender repeated doggedly.

"Please," Cassie said. "I know he was here earlier and it's very important that I find him." Before leaving the house she had stuck several dollars down in the pocket of her coat, and it occurred to her suddenly that now the cash might come in handy. Producing a wad which contained half a dozen crumpled bills, she laid it on the bar and said, "I'll give you this if you'll help me. It's important."

The bartender eyed the money greedily. "Well ma'am," he stammered, "I think I do recall the fellow you're looking for, but you see, uh, he ain't exactly alone."

"Where is he?" Cassie asked.

Capitulating at last, the man reached out and claimed the cash, and when he spoke again, his voice became quietly conspiratorial. "We got these rooms in back, ma'am," he began, "for folks who want a little privacy. They go by the hour, and your friend paid me for one just a little while ago. But it's like I told you. He didn't go back there alone."

"Which room, and how do I get to it?"

The man tilted his head to the side, indicating a blanket-covered opening at one end of the bar. "Through there. Fourth room at the end of the hall. But if there's trouble, I never seen you or talked to you, and you never gave me nothing. You just came in here and found him on your own."

Without even bothering to reply, Cassie marched over to the blanket and pushed it aside. The hall before her was almost completely dark, lit only by the scant light which seeped out from under a couple of the doorways. She started forward cautiously, her hand once again gripping the small revolver in her coat pocket.

The sound of quiet conversation and a woman's laughter came from the first room as she walked past it, and out of the second came the harsh rumbling snores of a sleeping man. Finally, when she reached the fourth door, Cassie stopped once again. Suddenly she felt extremely foolish and afraid. From the way the bartender had talked, it was obvious that Mike was back here with a woman, and Cassie thought that there was probably no way she could emerge from this situation without looking ridiculous. But at the same time, she knew that if she let this opportunity pass, there was no telling when she might have the chance to see him again. She was ready to say what needed to be said right now, and she hated the thought of having to carry those words around inside her until another chance came along.

She tapped lightly on the door and waited. First she heard the sound of a woman's voice speaking quietly, and then a man asked, "What do you want?" It was Mike, all right. She recognized his voice as distinctly as if she had just heard it the day before. Her heart began to pound, and instead of answering, she raised the latch and pushed the door open.

The windowless eight-by-eight room contained a small table, four chairs, and a low cot along the far wall. Two candles standing in puddles of wax on the table lit the room. A little heat came from a small coal fireplace built into the wall to the left.

Brookshire was sitting in one of the chairs with a half-naked woman perched on his lap. Both of them had glasses of whiskey near at hand, and Mike held a cocked revolver pointed toward Cassie.

He burst out laughing the minute he saw who the unexpected visitor was. "Good God almighty, Cassie!" he exclaimed. "What in the world are you doing here?" As Cassie took a tentative step forward, Mike uncocked his gun and laid it on the table.

"I came to find you, Mike," Cassie told him, trying to maintain as much dignity as she could under the circumstances. "I have to talk to you."

"Well as you can see," Mike told her, "it's not a real good time. Me and Emma here were just about to strike a bargain when you came in." It was obvious that he was quite drunk, and he seemed completely unruffled by the circumstances under which Cassie had found him.

"It won't wait," Cassie replied icily. "You're going to have to get rid of her."

"Now just a minute here, little sister," Mike's companion protested. "I had him first, and I'm not going anywhere until I get damn good and ready." She looked to be in her late twenties, but already she had the jaded look of a used-up whore. Her dress lay across the back of another chair, but because of the coldness of the room, she had taken the blanket from the bed and draped it across her shoulders.

"You have to go," Cassie repeated resolutely.

"The hell I do," the woman replied. She rose to her feet, bristling for a fight, but before she could take two steps forward, Cassie had her revolver out and ready.

"Go," Cassie ordered. "Take your dress with you. You can put it on in the hall." She got no more arguments from the woman, who seemed to believe Cassie was perfectly capable of pulling the trigger if the need arose.

When the woman was gone, Cassie closed and latched the door, then turned her attention back to Mike Brookshire. He had observed the whole scene quietly, and still had a slight grin on his face as if he thought the incident was rather funny.

"All right, I give up," Mike said, glancing at the revolver which Cassie still had in her hand. "You got the drop on me fair and square, so now what are you going to do with me?"

"Damn you, Mike Brookshire!" Cassie shouted. "Damn you to hell!"

"Damn me for what?" Mike asked. "What are you so angry about? What did I ever do to you that was so terrible?"

"Why didn't you look me up when you came back?" she demanded. "Why didn't you even try to see me?"

"I thought about it," Mike admitted. "I honestly did, Cassie. But all that, it happened nearly two years ago, and I figured a woman like you who was so prime for plucking two years ago was sure to be married off by now. In a few more days I was planning to go see my people up in Clay County, and I planned to ask them about you then."

"Well, it's too bad you didn't go through Clay County first," she replied, "because you sure would have gotten an earful about me up there."

"Look, Cassie," Mike said. "I still don't know why you're here or what you're so wrought up about, but let me tell you this. I never forgot about you. All the way to Montana, just about the only thing I could think about was how crazy I probably was to leave you like I did just when something good had gotten started. But I had to go. Every cent I had was tied up in that freight and those wagons, and it looked to me like my one chance to make good."

"But you could have at least written me a letter, or tried to find me when you returned."

"I could have," he agreed. "But I never promised you that I would, did I? In fact, I never made you any promises about anything, did I?"

"No, but you left me something that I think you should own up to just the same as if it was a promise."

"What did I leave?" Mike asked. "I don't remember anything of the sort."

"Mike, I had a baby just about a year ago," Cassie blurted out at last. "That's why I live here in Kansas City now instead of with my parents in Clay County. The folks in the country don't think too highly of a woman without a husband bringing a child into the world."

An odd look of skepticism clouded Mike's features. He picked up his glass of whiskey and took a swig, then said, "And this baby that you had, you think it might be —"

"It's yours, Mike," Cassie told him.

"But there was only that one time!" he protested. "You can never be exactly certain when these things start, and as flirty and friendly as you were back then, surely there were other men who —"

"Damn you, Mike Brookshire!" Cassie exploded. "Will you listen to me! There was only one man and one time, and it's your baby! You're not going to weasel out of this by trying to make me seem like some kind of white trash whore that took a roll in the hay with every man she met."

"All right, all right!" Mike exclaimed. "But what do you expect me to do about it now? It's already done and I can't go back and change anything."

"I expect you to face up to your responsibility," she told him. "You have a son now."

"Okay, Cassie. That's a reasonable enough request, and I'm an honorable man as much of the time as possible. I have some money, a few thousand dollars, and I guess I could —"

"To hell with your money! With my aunt's help, I haven't had any trouble providing for our son's needs, but what I haven't been able to give him is a name and a father. That's what he needs from you." The notion sounded incredible even to Cassie, but as soon as the words were out of her mouth she realized that they were the ones she had come here to speak. This was the message that had compelled her to find Mike Brookshire, even if it meant coming to a place like this to talk to him.

Brookshire himself was struck dumb by her pronouncement. For a minute he just sat there staring at her, trying to comprehend all that had happened during the last few moments. Finally he picked up his glass and drained the remaining two fingers of whiskey from it in one big gulp. Then at last he asked, "So you want me to marry you, Cassie? Is that it?"

"That's it," she replied. "I won't have my son growing up a bastard. Not when his father is alive and well and perfectly able to give him a proper name."

"And if I say no?"

"I . . . I haven't really thought about that," Cassie admitted. "I might just kill you right now if you do that."

"Well, what's to stop me from telling you anything you want to hear right now, and then just getting on my horse and leaving the first chance I get? Surely you don't intend to keep me under armed guard until we find a preacher who'll tie the knot."

"I don't know, Mike. What *is* to stop you? If your own heart wouldn't prevent you from doing something like that, then maybe the thought of a little boy named Timothy Michael Hartman might." She could feel the tears begin to fill her eyes, but there seemed to be nothing she could do to stop them.

"Oh, Mike!" she said. "Don't you want to see him? Aren't you curious at all about what your son looks like, whether he's got your eyes or my mouth, what color his hair is, and how it feels when you pick him up and hold him in your arms?

"I wasn't lying to you before," she went on. "You were the only one ever, and you still are. And that night, the only reason I allowed it all to happen was because I thought you were kind and strong. We only knew each other a little while and I wouldn't even let myself start to think about loving you because I knew you were leaving soon. But when we were together, I thought you were the kind of man that I could love. Was I wrong? Don't you care at all about your son . . . or about me?"

"Yes, of course I do, Cassie," Mike answered quietly, his eyes lowered toward the table. "But I just don't know what to do about this. You hit me with too much too fast, and it doesn't fit in with any of my plans for my life."

"It didn't fit with mine either, Mike," Cassie told him angrily. "But it happened all the same, and now I don't feel any guilt or any regrets."

She had long ago lowered the revolver toward the floor, and now she uncocked it and put it in her pocket as she turned toward the door. She felt drained and exhausted, but she also felt an odd sense of peace in her heart now that she had accomplished the task that she had yearned for so long to complete. She paused with her hand on the door latch and turned for one final look at Mike Brookshire. He still sat with his head lowered and his eyes downcast as if lost in some deep thought.

"Forget about what I said about marriage, Mike," Cassie told him. "I was angry, but I'm not foolish enough to think that I could actually force you into something like that. And it's not like Timmie will never have a father for his whole life. I'm only twenty years old, for heaven's sake, and once in a while I can still turn a man's head if I work hard enough at it. I just really wanted you to know. . . ."

Mike spoke her name just as she was opening the door to leave. She paused in the doorway and turned back to him once again.

"I can't come tonight," he said, "not like this. I'm drunk, and I'm filthy, and I've still got the stench of another woman's cheap toilet water all over me. I'd be too ashamed to come the way I am now. But tomorrow . . . if you'll allow me. . . ."

PART TWO

CHAPTER THIRTEEN

January, 1874

John Hartman sat with his head against the window and his hat tipped down over his eyes, lightly dozing as the train swayed and clattered along. Beside him his brother was leafing through a two-day-old issue of the St. Louis *Dispatch* that some previous occupant of his seat had left behind.

The brothers were sitting in the last two seats on the left in the rear of the passenger car. The car was about one-third full, as was the second passenger car behind it, but no one was sitting in any of the seats directly in front of or beside John and Daniel, so they were able to speak freely to each other as long as they kept their voices low.

They had been on the train less than half an hour, having boarded it a few miles to the north in a small hamlet called Des Arcs. Although they knew that their ride would actually be quite short, both had purchased tickets all the way to Little Rock to avoid suspicion, and they had paid extra to have their horses brought along in a cattle car.

John's head thumped against the window as the train swung into a wide arc to the right, and he awoke from his nap. Daniel, seeing his brother stir and straighten in his seat, said, "Listen to this, John. It's from the St. Louis paper from two days ago." John pushed his hat back higher on his head and turned to look at Daniel.

" 'A gang of hooligans believed to be followers of the notorious Jesse James,' " Daniel read, " 'stopped the stagecoach between Hot Springs and Malvern, Arkansas last week, robbing its passengers of cash and jewelry.

" 'According to reports from the local authorities, the five heavily-armed desperadoes threatened the lives of all aboard before taking an estimated four hundred dollars in ill-gotten booty.

" 'It is said, however, that a man believed to be the infamous Jesse James himself returned the watch and wedding ring of one Rutherford Lawrence after questioning the male passengers about their affiliation with the Lost Cause and learning that Lawrence once served under Confederate General Ben McCulloch during the War of the

Rebellion.' "

"I'm still not sure whether I believed that fellow," John commented. "His accent wasn't right for an Arkansan, and he had a shifty look in his eye. I believe he was just telling us what he thought we wanted to hear."

"Well, Jesse believed him," Daniel said, "and it makes good reading in the newspaper. But I just wish we'd stopped the right coach that day and got our hands on the express shipment we thought we were going to find. Split five ways, the little bit of cash we ended up with sure wasn't worth taking any risks for."

"Maybe today will be different, Dan," John suggested. "Jesse swears that he knows for a fact there will be money on this train."

"I sure hope he's right," John said. "We've been gone from home nearly three weeks now, and after expenses, we still have less than five hundred per man to show for all our efforts. And I don't like leaving a trail of little stick-ups behind us like we've done, either. Five or six years ago, it wouldn't have ever occurred to Jesse and Frank to steal nickels and dimes from country stores or to stop hicktown stagecoaches and steal the stick-pins from the passengers. Stuff like that makes me feel like nothing more than a two-bit thief."

"Well, I guess it's a habit they picked up during their trip out west," John said. "A couple of nights ago I heard Jesse tell a story about stealing two eggs from an old man in a mining camp who kept a setting hen. He said that because eggs were so scarce, the old man could sell them for up to two dollars apiece during the winter. He bragged about how he slipped in, tied the old fellow up, and then cooked and ate the eggs right in front of him."

"That's really something for a man to be proud of," Dan said sarcastically.

The door at the front of the car slid open and a heavyset, blue-clad conductor entered. As he made his way down the aisle, he announced to the passengers, "Gads Hill! Next stop is Gads Hill!"

As the conductor neared the rear of the car, John delayed him to ask, "Does the train always stop at Gads Hill?"

"Not unless there're passengers or freight to take on," the man explained. "Gads Hill is just a little burg, and nine times out of ten we just pass right on by it without even slowing up. It all depends on whether or not the engineer sees the signal flag on the track."

"Are we still on schedule?" John asked.

Checking his pocket watch, the conductor replied, "Let's see, it's five-forty-five now, and the schedule has us reaching Gads Hill at five-forty. I guess we're a few minutes late."

After answering their questions, the conductor slid open the door at the rear of the car, stepped through to the connecting platform outside, and closed the door again.

"I guess I'll follow along after him," Daniel said. "We'll just about be there by the time he gets to the back of the next car"

"All right, but don't show any hardware until the train's stopped. Two or three of those men in the car behind looked like they could handle themselves, and we can't risk giving them any warning before we have some help on board."

"I'll be careful," Daniel promised.

As he followed the conductor onto the platform and into the second passenger car, John rose from his seat and started forward, as if on his way to the lavatory. He could hear the screech of brakes and feel the train begin to slow down. He smiled to himself, knowing that Frank, Jesse, and the others must have reached the Gads Hill station in time and that things were going according to plan.

The train was nearly stopped by the time

he reached the front of the car and stepped outside onto the platform, and he could see the train station sliding into view about fifty yards ahead. In front of him was a flatcar loaded with farm implements, and beyond that was the coal car and the locomotive. John's task at the start of the robbery was to be ready in case the train's engineer suspected something about the Gads Hill station and tried to pass on through without stopping. If that happened, John would be near enough to scramble over the two cars ahead and get to the locomotive before the engineer could get his speed built up again.

But the station and platform appeared to be deserted, and the engineer apparently suspected nothing because he finally brought the train to a complete stop. Steam hissed from valves on either side of the locomotive, and five men, all neatly dressed in trousers, jackets and ties emerged from the station as if to board. They began to separate as they neared the train, one toward the locomotive and the other four toward the two passenger cars.

John opened his suit jacket, drew a revolver from a concealed holster under his left arm, and turned to re-enter the car he had just come out of.

The robbery was officially in progress.

Jim Younger entered the car from the opposite end only a second or two after John. He too was carrying a pistol in his right hand, but at first none of the twenty or so passengers in the car seemed to notice that they were being threatened by a pair of armed men.

"Everybody, just be calm," John announced loudly. "We're robbing this train, but if you all behave yourselves, there's no reason why anybody should get hurt." As he spoke those words, he kept a particularly close eye on two men who sat midway back in the car on the left side. Both were dressed in worn western garb, and earlier he had sized them up as the ones most likely to cause trouble.

"I want everybody to stand up slowly and put your hands up in the air," John went on. "My friend back there is going to come through once collecting weapons, and then he'll make a second pass to gather up any contributions you good people care to make to our cause."

Every passenger in the place complied immediately, including the two men John was watching most closely. As they rose he saw that both of them were wearing sidearms under their long, heavy coats, but neither seemed to want to risk a confrontation.

Frisking each man in turn, Jim Younger collected an assortment of pistols and knives, which he dropped into a burlap sack which he had brought along for that purpose. When he was finished, he deposited the sack on the floor at John's feet, then drew a second, smaller cotton sack out of his pocket.

"We want wallets, jewelry and watches from all the men," John announced as Jim started his second collection. "You ladies can keep your jewelry and other personal effects, but I must ask that you turn over whatever cash you have to us." Then he added in a more threatening tone, "And you folks better not try to hold out on us. My friend's going to be checking, and God help you if he finds out you've held back anything."

It took Jim three or four minutes to complete his assigned task, and when he was through the sack bulged with the booty he had collected. "I guess that's about it," he announced as he watched the last wallet drop into the sack. "We do thank you kindly, folks, and we appreciate your cooperation."

The plan called for Jim to leave the car at this point, taking the sacks of weapons and loot with him. John was to stay behind to guard the passengers until the rest of the robbers had completed their work, and then he too would go out on a signal from Jesse James.

But before Jim could get outside, Jesse came strolling into the passenger car through the rear door. He had a broad smile on his face, and he swaggered up the aisle as if somebody just signed the deed to the whole railroad over to him.

"Just a minute, Jim," Jesse said. "Don't leave with that stuff yet."

Jim Younger stopped and looked at Jesse, confused by the order.

"Are there any men of the South in this car?" Jesse called out loudly. "Do we have any Confederate comrades in arms here?"

For a moment no one moved, then finally one of the male passengers, a man of about forty in ordinary working clothes and a dark felt hat, spoke up. "I was at Vicksburg," he volunteered. "And after it fell, I spent thirteen months in a damn Yankee prison camp in Kentucky."

Jesse James stepped forward and eagerly shook the man's hand. "The name's Howard, sir, Thomas Howard, and it's a pleasure to meet you," he said. "Tell me, brother. What has my companion taken from you?"

"He got eight dollars from me," the man

257

replied, "and a silver-plated watch and chain. The watch ain't worth much, maybe three or four dollars if you was to sell it, but it means a lot to me because my wife gave it to me before she died."

"Give him back his belongings," Jesse instructed Jim Younger. "And give him twenty dollars instead of eight."

The man beamed as Jim stepped forward to comply with his instructions, and when he had received his watch and cash, he told Jesse, "I'm much obliged to you, Mr. Howard."

"We don't harm ladies, and we don't rob men of the South," Jesse explained magnanimously. "We may be thieves, but we're honorable men as well, and we can make all the profits we need to by taking what we want from the plug-hat scallywags. The only difference between them and us is that they use business to steal from people because they lack the backbone to do it at the point of a gun the way we do."

John quickly began to tire of Jesse's theatrics. He had heard it all before, and he knew that their leader employed his high-sounding principles only in the most convenient or public situations.

But still John had to admire the strategy that Jesse had developed over the past few years. When word of this robbery spread, as it certainly would over the next few days and weeks, what would remain most in people's thoughts would not be that they had stolen the life savings of one man or the mortgage money of another. What would come to mind when the Gads Hill train robbery was mentioned would be that the robbers were daring former Confederates who had too much nobility to steal from their fellow Southern veterans.

Suddenly the muffled sound of a pistol shot roared out from the direction of the second passenger car. It was followed almost immediately by two more shots fired in quick succession.

In an instant, the congenial smile disappeared from Jesse James' face and he was all business again. "Jim, you stay here and watch these folks," he ordered quickly. "John, you come with me to see what's going on."

With guns ready, the two outlaws rushed out of the first passenger car and into the second, but Frank James and Clell Miller had already handled the problem by the time they got there. Both were near the center of the car with their guns pointed down at a man sprawled out on the floor between them. The man was still conscious, but he was writhing in pain as he desperately tried to stem the flow of blood from a leg wound.

"What happened in here?" Jesse asked.

"The son of a bitch had a derringer hidden in the waistband of his trousers," Frank explained. "He tried to plug Clell with it, but I guess he was nervous and his shot went wild."

"I wonder why in the hell would he try a stupid thing like that?" Jesse said. Then, looking at the downed man, he asked, "Are you out of your damned mind, mister? Did you really think you could shoot it out with us when all you had was a little bitty popgun like that?"

The man didn't answer. He was in too much pain for that.

"He could be a lawman, Jesse," Clell speculated.

"Yeah, but he's not wearing a badge," Frank pointed out. "Maybe he's a Pink."

"I bet that's what it is!" Jesse James exclaimed. "I bet he's a goddamned Pinkerton agent!"

"But if that was true, what would he be doing on a two-bit railroad like this one?" John asked. "It seems to me if they were putting agents on the trains, they would be riding on the bigger railroads like the

Northern Pacific and the Santa Fe."

"Hell, they're all in it together," Jesse explained bitterly. "All the railroads, and all the banks. They're all putting up a piece of money to hunt us down." He delivered a hard kick to the stomach of the man at his feet, doubling his victim up with pain. Then he told John and Clell, "I want you two to take this fellow back to one of the other cars and search him. Find out if he's got anything on him that proves he's a Pink, and if he does, kill him. They should have the express car secured by now, so you can take him there."

John Hartman and Clell Miller hauled the injured man, squalling and sobbing, out of the passenger car and into the express car behind. There they found Daniel and Cole Younger rifling the contents of the express safe, tossing worthless papers and documents aside and shoveling the stacks of cash they found into a sack.

"What the hell happened up there?" Cole demanded. "We started to come up and check, but since there were only three shots we figured the rest of you must have handled it."

"This fellow tried to put a bullet in me," Clell Miller explained, "but he missed and Frank shot him. We think maybe he's a

Pinkerton, so we brought him back to search him." The man was almost unconscious now, and when John and Clell released their grip on him, he slumped limply onto a pile of mail bags.

"Listen to me, you fellows, there's no Pinkerton agents on this train," the conductor told the robbers. He and the express agent were sitting off to one side of the car. Their hands and feet were bound with leather thongs, but Cole and Daniel had not seen any need to gag them as well. "The Iron Mountain Railroad is just a little local line. They don't have the money for any kind of foolishness like private detectives. And besides, I know that man. He works as a butcher down in Piedmont. He's been up in St. Louis seeing his sister, and he's on his way home now."

"Well if he's a butcher," John replied. "What's he doing carrying around a little pocket derringer in his belt? Is he afraid some gang of desperadoes is going to come in his shop someday and steal a pork chop or a handful of ground beef?" He and Clell were already beginning to search through the man's clothing, looking for anything that might confirm their suspicions about him.

"He's the constable in Piedmont, too," the conductor answered. "The people in town pay him fifteen dollars a month to haul in drunks and serve warrants for the county court. I guess he just got carried away."

John and Clell finished their inspection of the prisoner, but found nothing to indicate that he might be an agent for the Chicago detective firm which had, for the last few years, been plaguing them after every robbery they committed, as well as some they hadn't. At about the same time, Cole and Daniel finished with the express safe.

"I guess that's it," Cole said. "You two find anything on him?"

"Nothing," Clell admitted, "but I've half a mind to shoot him anyway." His hand rested on the grip of his holstered revolver, but he hadn't drawn the weapon yet.

"Why waste a bullet on a butcher, Clell?" Daniel asked quickly, not wanting to see a man die for no good reason. "We've made a decent haul here, so let's just leave."

"All right, let's get out of here," Miller agreed.

By the time the four of them got outside, Jesse was up near the locomotive. John and Daniel Hartman hurried back to get their horses out of the cattle car. A moment later, Frank James and Jim Younger emerged from the passenger cars, each carrying sacks of loot and weapons. Frank waved a signal to Jesse, and Jesse gave some instructions to the engineer which none of the rest of them could hear. In response to his orders, the drive wheels of the locomotive began to turn slowly.

John and Daniel stepped into their saddles and rode around the side of the depot where the other men had left their mounts tied. The rest of the gang followed and mounted up, all except Jesse, who stepped into the depot briefly.

"What's he doing in there?" Cole asked. Now that their work was done, he didn't like waiting around in the open like this. The train was already beginning to pick up speed as it moved slowly away from the station, but it still wasn't so far away that another fool with another hidden gun couldn't get off a shot at them.

"I expect he's dropping off that damn newspaper thing he wrote," Frank said. "He'll be along in a minute." As a lark the night before, Jesse had written up a full account of the robbery beforehand, and things had gone so well that the details he put down were surprisingly accurate. He had even thought to leave a blank on the paper where the amount of money taken from the express safe could be filled in.

They all knew that Jesse James had a fascination with reading newspaper accounts of the robberies they committed. Sometimes after he or other members of the gang were mentioned in connection with a particular hold-up, Jesse would write an open letter to one of the major newspapers in the state proclaiming their innocence and passionately protesting the smear on their reputations as honest, law-abiding citizens.

By this time few people believed these denials, but the letters still rated him front-page coverage any time he saw fit to submit one.

Frank James had his brother's horse waiting when Jesse hurried out of the station, and he leaped right off the edge of the platform into the saddle. Then the seven men turned their horses west and went thundering out of town. No shots were fired in their wake, and they saw no sign that anyone in Gads Hill was interested in pursuing them.

After they had ridden about a mile, the group came to a stop again at a crossroads just west of Gads Hill. "It doesn't look like we're going to have to worry about a posse coming after us," Jesse said. "By the time the train gets to Piedmont, even if they do put together a posse our trail will be too cold for them to follow. But just in case, I still think we should split up according to plan. Cole, you and Jim can take one sack of loot with you, and Frank and I will take the other. John, you and Daniel can carry the express money, and Clell, you can strike out on your own or ride along with whoever you want to. Unless there's trouble, we'll meet in a week at my mama's farm in Clay County, and we can split everything up then."

John and Daniel chose the road due west, while the rest headed off in various other directions. But before starting off again, Daniel took a minute to stash all the money from the express safe into his saddlebags, knowing it would be safer and less obvious there than in a cloth sack tied to his saddle horn. He and Cole had estimated the take to be something over twenty-thousand dollars, which would break down to about three thousand per man after the split was made.

Once they were back on their own, the Hartman brothers pushed their horses at a steady gallop for more than an hour before finally slowing the pace. They had been at this business long enough by now to know when haste was necessary and when it wasn't, and they realized that there would be no effective pursuit after this robbery. The road home was free and clear ahead.

CHAPTER FOURTEEN

February, 1875

John Hartman was up on the roof of the house replacing a patch of shingles that had blown off during the snowstorm the night before. The day was bitter cold and each gust of wind bit through his trousers like icy needles. It was hardly the best time to be taking care of a chore like this, but the snow was filtering through into the attic, melting, and leaking down into his aunt's bedroom, so the repairs could not wait even another day.

Over a foot of the white stuff was already on the ground and more was still coming down, but it seemed that the worst of the storm was over now. The snow that had already fallen was causing a lot of problems, though, and the roof was only one of them. Soon they would have to start hauling hay from the barn to the pasture so their cattle and horses would not starve, and there was some storm damage to both the barn and the chicken house. John and Daniel Hartman faced a long, hard day exposed to the elements.

Daniel remained on the ground below his brother, passing him shingles as John needed them, but his main job was to break John's fall in case he lost his footing on the steep, icy roof.

"Aren't you almost through up there?" Daniel asked at last.

"Just about," John told him. "It's a pretty sloppy job, but it should do 'til the snow melts and I can do it right."

"When you're through, let's go inside and get a cup of coffee," Daniel suggested. "I'm so damned cold my teeth are starting to rattle."

"I'm about to freeze up here myself. I guess we're just getting old, little brother," John said. "Hell, I can remember back when we were bushwhackers we'd lay down on the bare ground in weather like this and sleep the night through."

"Sure, but that was more than a dozen years ago, John, back when we were young and crazy. And even then, we weren't so crazy that we wouldn't still find ourselves a warm place indoors to bed down whenever we got the chance."

John put the last shingle in position, hammered a couple of nails home to keep it in place, then called down for the tar paper. Daniel cut three six-foot strips from the roll and passed them up one by one while John tacked them in place over the hole. Then he began his careful descent down the slick roof to where the twelve-foot ladder leaned against the eave of the house.

But before starting down, John paused and gazed off into the distance. Daniel turned to look in the same direction, but he wasn't high enough to see whatever his brother had spotted.

"Riders coming about a quarter-mile down the road," John announced at last.

"How many?"

"I just see two on the road, but that doesn't mean there couldn't be more hereabouts."

"Then we'd better get in the house and get ready," Daniel said urgently. "I can't think of many good reasons why anybody would be out riding around in weather like this . . . unless they think we might not be expecting them on such a day."

John descended the ladder quickly, then the two brothers turned and slogged through the deep drifts toward the back door of the house. The kitchen was warm and cheery when they got inside and their aunt Sarah had a fresh pot of coffee brewing on the stove, but a dark expression of concern immediately crossed her features when she saw the intent looks on her nephews' faces. Normally the two brothers would have removed their boots and knocked the snow off their clothes before coming in beyond the back doorway, but this time they didn't bother. Instead they headed straight across the kitchen and into the front room. Both had revolvers in their hands by the time they reached the front windows.

"I can't see them yet," John said. "Break out the rifles, Dan, while I keep watch."

Daniel headed to a gun case along one wall and withdrew four repeating rifles. Out of habit he quickly checked each of them to make sure it was loaded, but that wasn't really necessary. Every gun in the house was always kept clean, well-oiled, and loaded at all times. Daniel carried two of the rifles across the room and leaned them against the wall near his brother. He kept the other two for his own use.

By that time Sarah Parkman had come to the doorway which separated the kitchen from the front room, and was watching her nephews with trepidation. She didn't even bother to ask what was going on. This sort of drill had happened too many times before for her not to realize that her nephews had seen something suspicious outside.

Life was like this for them now, ever since it had become commonly known that the Pinkerton Detective Agency in Chicago had been employed by the railroads to track down Frank and Jesse James and the members of the gang they led. The Hartman brothers still didn't know for sure whether their names were known by the Pinkertons, but after the numerous robberies they had participated in, they had to assume that they were targets just as much as their long-time friends were.

Until recently, though, they had still felt reasonably safe, even when they were here at home sleeping in their own beds. On the whole, the people of Clay County were a clannish lot, still bitter about the war, and still fiercely defensive of the local men who, more than a decade before, had fought for the lost Confederate cause. All strangers, and especially those from the Northern states like the Pinkertons, were soundly distrusted, and even a number of local law enforcement officers were reluctant to provide any information which might lead to the capture of the James brothers or any of their cohorts.

Less than a year before, two Pinkerton agents had been killed in a roadside shoot-out with three members of the Younger clan, and other strangers suspected of being detectives had either fled the area in fear of their lives or had disappeared mysteriously. It wasn't a safe place to go bandit hunting in, nor was it wise for even the casual stranger to show too much curiosity about the county's most notorious residents.

After the loss of several men, the Pinkertons finally seemed to have learned their lesson, however, and the previous month they had changed their strategy from stealth to brute force.

On the night of January 26, 1875, a large band of armed men had surrounded the home of Frank and Jesse's mother and stepfather, Zerelda and Reuben Samuels. They demanded that the brothers surrender themselves and promised that if they gave up peacefully, they would not be harmed and would be taken in for trial. No one was quite sure how the men were able to get there without being seen by any of the gang's network of spies across the county, but the rumor was that one of the railroads provided a special train which transported the group to within a short distance of the

Samuels' home.

Of course the James brothers were not the surrendering type, and they didn't go out. Instead they hid under a special false floor they had built in one of the upstairs bedrooms of the house, figuring that if the strangers searched the place and didn't find them, they would go away peacefully.

But after the loss of so many of their own, the Pinkertons had been in no mood to take chances. Instead of trying to enter the darkened house, they pitched something through the window which later newspaper accounts explained was a cylindrical metal flare but which the James brothers suspected was a bomb. Whatever the thing was, it exploded with disastrous results. The blast killed Frank and Jesse's nine-year-old half-brother Archie, and their mother's right hand was so mangled that later it had to be amputated.

Although Frank and Jesse had not been caught that night, their hatred for the Pinkerton Detective Agency became even deeper and more bitter than before, and their cries of unjust treatment and persecution were rehashed and debated on the front pages of newspapers across the state. The Pinkertons were soundly condemned for their harsh and brutal act, but editorial opinion remained divided about whether the James brothers' lawlessness was the cause of this senseless tragedy, and if, in fact, they were truly the untamed desperadoes that the banks, railroads, and Pinkertons accused them of being.

For the Hartman brothers, however, the most telling result of the raid on the Samuels home was that they learned they could no longer afford to be complacent about their safety or that of their aunt when they were at home in Clay County. It was evident now that a lot of money was being spent to capture the members of the gang, and that the Pinkertons were prepared to do just about anything required, legal or otherwise, to earn their fee and avenge their comrades.

Over three weeks had passed since the raid on the Samuels' farm and no more serious incidents had occurred since then, but few days passed without an alarm similar to the one they were now experiencing. Now anyone who approached the house had a bead drawn on his chest until he was recognized, and sometimes it took as little as a branch scraping the roof at night to bring the brothers up out of bed.

Several long, tense moments passed before the two approaching horsemen finally appeared around a tall hedgerow and approached the house. As soon as he got a good look at them, John reholstered his revolver and turned to face the others, a broad smile of relief on his face. "It's just Daddy," he announced. "He's got some other fellow with him, but he's so bundled up that I couldn't make out his face."

"Well, whoever it is, he must be okay or Daddy wouldn't have brought him over here," Daniel said. "Here, I'll put these rifles up before they get inside." He put the rifles back in the cabinet, then the two went into the kitchen to shed their coats and wet boots.

Sarah already had five cups of coffee poured by the time the two new arrivals reached the back porch and started stamping the snow off their boots. She turned as John opened the back door to let their visitors in, but she was hardly prepared for whom she saw standing there in the doorway. For a moment she stood motionless, staring across the room as tears of joy gathered in her eyes.

"Ridge?" Sarah whispered, her voice husky with emotion.

"Hi, Mama," Ridge Parkman said. A characteristic grin was spread across his features as he unpeeled the muffler from around the lower half of his face and laid it and his hat aside on the table.

Sarah Parkman rushed across the room and threw her arms around her son, ignoring the snow which still clung to his heavy coat. "Why didn't you write and tell me you were coming?" she scolded lovingly. "Why must you always surprise me like this by just appearing out of nowhere?"

"Well, it was another last-minute thing, Mama," Ridge explained. "It's like I told you in my last letter, I didn't plan to come back this way until spring. But then a sudden piece of business came up, and next thing I knew, I was on a train bound for Kansas City."

"He showed up at my house about midnight last night looking more like an icicle than a human being," Jason explained. He had come into the house behind his nephew, and was now busy shedding his coat and boots. "The storm caught him about midway along during the ride up from Kansas City, but I guess he didn't have sense enough to stop for the night along the way. After he warmed up at my place, he wanted to ride on over here last night, but Arethia and I talked him out of it."

"I was just in a hurry to see this lady here. That's all," Ridge told his uncle. "But I admit now that you were right. If I'd had to ride much farther last night in that storm, I think my fingers and toes would have started breaking off."

"Well, you're here now, and that's the main thing," Sarah told them. "Get your things off and come on over to the table. I've already got coffee poured for everybody."

Ridge shed his snowy garments, shook hands with his two cousins, and took a seat at the table with the others.

"So what brings you over our way this time, Ridge?" John asked. "More desperadoes to deliver into the hands of justice?"

"Well, in a manner of speaking," Ridge said. The question brought a strange look to his face, and the quick glance that he and Jason exchanged indicated that the two men had already discussed the reason for his trip back east. "I'm here on what I guess you'd call a 'special assignment.' " Then he added, with a casual wave of his hand, "But there'll be plenty of time to talk about all that later. Right now I'd just like to relax and enjoy the feeling of being back with my family again after such a long time."

It had indeed been a long time. Nearly two years had passed since Ridge Parkman's last trip to Missouri in the summer of 1873. During that time, his letters to his mother had been sent from everywhere from Oregon to California. It seemed that in recent years as a U.S. Marshal he had become something of a troubleshooter for the government, traveling to remote areas where little or no law existed and performing special assignments.

He didn't talk much about his work, either in his letters or in person, but from what his family could gather, he did a lot of undercover work, often operating without a badge and without any sort of back-up to support him in case of trouble.

In the light of all that had happened lately, Ridge Parkman's mere presence in Clay County was cause enough for John and Daniel to be concerned, but they tried to hide their apprehension for their aunt's sake, knowing that if the two of them were the reason he was here, they would find out about it soon enough.

After a few minutes of visiting, Sarah Parkman got up and began preparing lunch. Jason and Ridge remained at the kitchen table, catching up on everything that had gone on in their lives since they were last together, but John and Daniel had to return to their chores. Starving livestock would not wait, company or no company, but they promised to hurry through their work and return to the house as quickly as possible. Within a few minutes they were back in their heavy coats and boots and were trekking through the deep snow on their way to the barn.

In a way, the brothers were somewhat grateful for the opportunity to get out of the house so they could discuss the unexpected appearance of their lawman cousin. Ridge's reaction to John's question about why he had come to visit had been too obvious for either of them to miss, and his ambiguous answer had done nothing to erase their worries. The recent raid on the Samuels farm had made the brothers skittish and overly-cautious, and now Ridge's sudden arrival here seemed almost too much of a coincidence to be ignored.

Ridge Parkman was their cousin by birth, but he had been a lawman for these past fifteen years, and they were not absolutely sure which of his loyalties might come first.

John and Daniel hitched their two stout mules to a wagon and drove it to the front of the barn. Then they climbed up in the loft, opened the access door on the front, and began pitching down forkfuls of hay into the back of the wagon.

The pair worked in silence for a while, but finally Daniel broached the topic which had been on both their minds for the past several minutes. "I was none too fond of Ridge's answer when you asked him what had brought him back east," he commented.

"He sure wasn't very anxious to talk about it, was he?" John replied. "I guess it could have been because it's something dangerous and he didn't want to say anything about it in front of Aunt Sarah, but still, that look he gave Daddy. . . ."

"I saw it too," Daniel said. "Whatever it is, Daddy already knows about it."

"He knows," John agreed.

The pile of hay on the back of the wagon grew steadily as the two mules waited patiently to haul their burden out to the fields. This was a chore which the men and beasts would repeat time and again over the next few days until the snow melted away and the livestock could begin to graze on the winter grass in the pasture again.

"I've heard talk about the state bringing in outside lawmen because the locals aren't willing to do anything in Clay County that would likely get them killed," Daniel commented. "But it never occurred to me that they might bring in the federals. Are they that desperate to get us?"

"They might be," John said, "and yet I still can't see Cousin Ridge getting involved in something like that. And besides, if it's like we think, and if Daddy knows why he's come back, he wouldn't have any part in letting Ridge arrest us. No matter what he might think of our riding with Frank and Jesse, he'd take up a gun and side with us before he'd let anybody take us in, cousin or not."

"It still makes me nervous having Ridge here, though," Daniel admitted. "I don't like it, and after I hear the real reason why he's come, I have a feeling that I'll like it even less."

"I feel the same way, but it looks like we're just going to have to bide our time and wait until he's ready to talk."

It took the brothers nearly an hour to load the wagon and drive it to the fields where the hungry livestock waited to be fed. They spread it on the ground just at the edge of a patch of trees. The snow was not deep there and the horses and cows would have some shelter from the cold, stiff wind while they ate. Sarah was used to delaying meals for the working men in a family, and she didn't begin putting the bowls of preserved vegetables and the platter of fried pork on the table until John and Daniel had returned to the house.

Ridge ate ravenously, as he always did during his trips home. He was a man accustomed to living on his own simple trailside cooking much of the time, so sitting down to the kind of spread that his mother prepared was a rare treat which he enjoyed to the fullest.

His conversation during the meal provided no more clues about why he had been sent back to Kansas City. He told a number of anecdotes about his work, most of them quite amusing, but he carefully avoided all allusions to the more deadly side of law enforcement. Sarah soaked it all in like the proud mother she was, knowing as well as anyone at the table that there were many dangerous aspects to his life which her son avoided mentioning in her presence.

After the meal the five of them moved into the front room, and Daniel added two large armloads of wood to the fire in the fireplace. Soon the room was filled with a cheery warmth. While Jason stoked up his pipe, the other three men rolled cigarettes and Sarah settled into her accustomed seat near the fireplace.

"You still haven't told us what sort of business it is that brings you back this way, Ridge," John said to his cousin. He tried to keep his tone of voice casual, but he wasn't sure he succeeded.

"No, I guess I haven't, have I?" Ridge replied. It appeared that he still wasn't ready to discuss the matter, but then his uncle stepped in to lend a hand.

"Now is as good a time as any, Ridge," Jason said. Then, turning to his sons, he explained, "I had asked Ridge to let me talk to the two of you first and prepare you for what you are going to hear, but I can see that you have an idea of what's going on already, so we might as well bring everything out in the open right now." He paused to pull on his pipe, sending a cloud of smoke drifting into the air near his head. "The fact is," he continued, "Ridge is here because I wrote him a letter asking him to come."

"Why did you do that, Daddy?" Daniel asked coldly.

"Ridge is a lawman, and he's also a member of our family," Jason explained. "I figured that made him the ideal person to try and help the two of you get out of the mess you're getting yourselves in. Look, boys, this business about the James brothers and the Pinkertons is getting all out of control, and I don't want us to —"

"Daniel and I don't want to talk about that," John snapped. His tone was stern and abrupt, and it was obvious that he thought his father was completely out of line in bringing up such a subject in front of Ridge.

But Jason was determined to say what was on his mind. "Well, if you don't want to talk about it, then just listen for a while because I *do* want to talk about it. There's some pretty serious trouble shaping up around here, and the two of you are sadly mistaken if you think it's just your business and nobody else's. What's going on affects the lives of every member of your family, and it's time that the two of you faced up to that fact."

"How much have you told Ridge, Daddy?" Daniel asked.

"He's told me that you ride with Frank and Jesse James, and that you rob banks and trains," Ridge said bluntly. "The only way I would agree to help is if he told me everything he knew, and he gave me his word that he has."

Both John and Daniel were thunderstruck by what seemed to be such a stark betrayal by their father. They realized, of course, that he had never approved of their outlaw activities but it never occurred to either of them that he might go so far as to reveal their secrets to any man with a badge on his chest, relative or not. They sat silent and tense as their cousin continued.

"I'm not here to arrest either of you,

though," Ridge explained. "For one thing, I don't have any real evidence that what Jason has said is true, and for another, the crimes you've committed don't fall within my jurisdiction. But that doesn't mean that I'm not going to wade right into the middle of this mess and do what I can to straighten it out. You're my kin and I'm concerned about what happens to you, but even more important is the fact that whatever danger the two of you face here, my mother is also facing. I heard about what happened at the Samuels' farm last month, and I won't sit by and see my mother crippled or killed just because she happens to be living with two nephews who are wanted men."

"Who says we're wanted men?" John asked. "Have you ever seen any warrants out on us? Have you talked to the county sheriff or any of the constables hereabouts to ask them if they want to arrest us?"

"I don't have to, because your father has told me enough about what's going on for me to realize that no local lawman is likely to try to bring you in. But it's a different story with these Pinkertons. At this point they're not going to give up until all of you are either dead or behind bars."

"So what do you think you can do?" John asked. "If you aren't going to try to arrest

286

us, what other options do you have? Do you want to make us quit living here so your mother will be safe from the Pinkertons?" His voice had become cold, and he was staring across the room at his cousin as if the man were a threatening stranger.

"Believe me, I've thought about that, but I decided that it wasn't the answer."

"So what is the answer?" Daniel demanded.

"We've been discussing the possibility of amnesty," Jason said. "Ever since the tragedy at the Samuels' farm, the papers have been full of talk about amnesty for Frank and Jesse, and sometimes even for Cole Younger. Some say the governor is considering it, and I've also heard that a bill might be introduced in the state legislature. If any of that's true, there's no reason why the two of you shouldn't be included in whatever amnesties are handed out."

"And you think Ridge might be able to help out with that?" John asked.

"He's been in law enforcement for nearly half his life, and he's a well-respected man," Jason said. "I can see how his advice might carry some weight with the elected officials of this state."

"I think the whole idea is crazy," John replied. "As far as Dan and I know, our names have never been connected with any of the robberies the James brothers are blamed for. We've never been told that the Pinkertons are after us either, so why should we want to do something like this?"

"I agree," Daniel said. "It would be like admitting to crimes that nobody has ever accused us of committing."

"You're fooling yourselves if you don't think they know who you are," Ridge said. "From time to time, I've worked with these Pinkerton agents out west, so I know how thorough they can be. My guess is that they're just letting you alone while they go after bigger fish, but sooner or later. . . ." He glanced at his mother, who had been listening intently to every word.

"You know, I've spent my life hunting down men who do the same things that you two do," Ridge went on. "I've hauled them off to jail, and when I thought it was necessary, I've gunned them down like animals without feeling any sort of guilt or remorse.

"That's what makes it so hard for me now not to despise the pair of you for what you've become and the grief you've caused your family over the years. You two are criminals. You're common thieves, and maybe murderers as well. The war was over ten years ago, and that's too long a time for you to keep hiding behind the image of the bushwhacker or the rebel. You know the difference between right and wrong as well as any of the rest of us do, and you know that what you're doing is wrong."

"That's enough, Ridge," John said threateningly. "That's just about enough."

Daniel looked at his brother and realized that John was close to some sort of violent eruption. His fists were clenched tightly, the muscles of his shoulders and neck were tensed, and his face was red. It occurred to Daniel that his brother might be so angry because he knew, deep inside, that what Ridge was saying was true. He reached out and placed a restraining hand on John's arm, knowing how disastrous it might be for all of them if the situation erupted into a fight.

"I've taken a leave of absence from my work to come here and do what I can," Ridge went on. "I haven't come to get your consent about anything. I'm here because your father asked me to come, and because anything of this sort that involves my mother involves me, too. Tomorrow I'm leaving for Jefferson City and I'll do what I can for you. If it looks like any sort of amnesty is possible, I'll do my best to see that it includes the two of you.

"But let me tell you this as well. Amnesty or not, you can't go on living the way you've been living for these past ten years. You'd better put an end to it, or somebody will be putting an end to you before much longer."

"Boys, you can't keep chasing the devil like you've been doing," Jason told them. "One of these days, he's going to stop running and turn on you, and when that happens, it'll to be too late for anything except maybe a final regret or two."

CHAPTER FIFTEEN

"They stayed at the Clinton, ma'am. It's a small hotel near the waterfront. They usually didn't get out and about until mid-morning. Most days they'd have lunch, and then maybe go shopping, or rent a rig and go riding in the country. It's really pretty around there. Lots of trees and rolling hills, and then, of course, there's the rivers to look at."

"I know, Mr. Daly," Mollie said, trying to sound impersonal. "I've been to St. Louis."

"Yes, ma'am. Then in the evenings they usually went to the theater or to some saloon that featured entertainment. They generally ate supper about ten, and then stayed out quite late, sometimes until three or four in the morning."

"And you are certain that they slept in the same room?" Mollie asked.

"Yes ma'am. In the same room, in the same bed. I paid a maid to let me in one day while they were out, and I checked the place over completely. There was only one bed in their room."

"Well if you got into their room, then perhaps you found out her name," Mollie suggested.

"I did. Her name is Gertie Talbot and she's about thirty years old. She came from back East somewhere, and she's been in St. Louis about eight years. At first she worked in a bordello near the waterfront, but about three years ago she started singing in a saloon. That's where your husband met her last year, ma'am."

"I see," Mollie said. She hated all of this — the spying, the deceit, and of course the sordid details of her husband's tryst with a whore in St. Louis. It made her feel cheap and unclean even to be associated with anything so despicable, but at this point she felt that she no longer had any alternative. She had to know what went on when Bedford took his so-called "business trips" out of town, and she knew of no good way to find out except to hire a private detective and have her husband followed.

There was a lot more to the detective's report. Harry Daly was a thorough man. His little notebook was crammed with details about Bedford Lee's recent week-long rendezvous in St. Louis. But it was all in the written report which he had provided her as well, and Mollie was tiring now of hearing all of it. The details mattered little. She had the evidence she needed, and that was what counted most.

After another minute or two, Mollie finally told the detective that she had heard enough and promised to read his report carefully. Then she opened the checkbook which lay on the desk in front of her and began writing.

"I believe this was the sum we agreed on, Mr. Daly," she said, handing the check to the detective.

"It is," Daly said, examining the check. "But if you recall, Mrs. Lee, I explained that court appearances are extra. If that becomes necessary, my fee is forty dollars per day."

"I remember," Mollie told him. "But believe me, this matter will never be taken to court. I'll handle it in my own way, and your report will be all I need to do what I must do."

"All right then, ma'am," Daly said. "I guess if that's all, then I'll be going."

"Thank you very much, Mr. Daly," Mollie replied. "You've done a good job and I appreciate it."

Daly was on his way out, but he paused in

the doorway to look back across the office at Mollie one last time. When he spoke again, there was a look of true compassion on his face and a note of sympathy in his voice. "If you don't mind me saying so, Mrs. Lee," he told her, "I think your husband is an addle-headed idiot for pulling a trick like this. This woman, this Gertie Talbot, is just a painted-up floozy. Only a blamed fool would risk what he has with a lady like you by going off to chase a piece of trash like that."

"Well, there's no explaining people's tastes, is there?" Mollie said, smiling gently to show her appreciation of the compliment. "My husband and I have been married for almost seven years now, and I guess the romance wears a little thin after so much time."

"But still, Mrs. Lee, she couldn't hold a candle to you. There's just no comparison. . . ."

After the detective was gone, Mollie remained in her small office in the back of the theater for a long time, thinking about all that had gone on up until now, and what still remained to be done.

Surprisingly enough, she felt little animosity toward Bedford, even in the face of the damning evidence she now possessed. The man was a worthless scoundrel, an incurable gambler, a liar, a rogue and a dandy, but in truth, he had never pretended to be anything else. From the very start, he had proclaimed his right to continue the decadent lifestyle that he so enjoyed, and if Mollie ever fostered any hopes of him changing and becoming a responsible husband and father, those hopes had not been based on any signs of change in Bedford.

Mollie had hung on this long only for the sake of their two children. But over the past couple of years, ever since Bedford had become so blatant about his philandering, he had been no more of a father to his children than he was a husband to Mollie. Days, and sometimes weeks, passed when he paid them little or no attention, and Mollie now thought that her children would feel little sense of loss if their father disappeared from their lives forever.

That was the major deciding factor for the move she was about to make. It was time for a change, time to end a marriage that should have been put out of its misery a long time ago. Now that the decision was made, she was determined to take action as soon as possible.

The telegram Bedford had sent her the day before lay on the desk beside Harry

Daly's report. In it he explained that his luck had not been good in the big game he had supposedly traveled to St. Louis to participate in, and he told her that he would be arriving back in Kansas City on the train early in the evening.

"That's fine. You just come on back, buster," Mollie said calmly, looking at the telegram. "I've got one hell of a reception planned for you when you get home."

The dining table was set exquisitely. Mollie had instructed her housekeeper to prepare a special meal for the occasion and to use the best china and silverware. A silver candelabra graced the center of the table, and all the food was to be served on the silver-plated platters and bowls which Mollie usually reserved for special occasions and holidays.

Mollie had not told her children that their father was coming home, and she had put them to bed early. After they were settled in, she carefully dressed in one of her favorite gowns, a sleeveless, white satin affair with a low-cut neckline and an abundance of delicate lace across the bodice. Her silky blond hair was arranged in an elaborate pile on top of her head, and the diamond-studded clips which held it in place were a perfect match to the diamond necklace, bracelet, and ring which she wore.

"Not bad for a forty-one-year-old woman," Mollie said confidently as she surveyed herself in a full-length mirror. In fact, all the years that she had made such careful efforts to take care of herself were now paying off. At an age when most women were finally resigning themselves to the lines and pounds of their middle years, Mollie still had a figure that many women half her age would have been proud to claim. And although the passage of time had matured her, the full essence of her beauty remained intact, and was as powerful and intriguing as ever.

When she was finished preparing herself, Mollie went downstairs to check the dining room over one more time. The table was prepared and Amanda was holding the food in the kitchen so it could be served piping hot as soon as Bedford arrived. Everything was ready.

Mollie only began to feel a little nervous when she finally heard a carriage arrive. She had sent Walter, the handyman, to the station to meet Bedford's train, and she knew that what she heard must be the sound of her husband arriving home at last.

She was at the door when Bedford entered

the house. She waited for him to set his valise down, then gave him a warm, lingering kiss on the lips.

"You look stunning tonight, Mollie," Bedford said with a noticeable measure of surprise in his voice. "What's the occasion? Have I forgotten another birthday or anniversary?"

"No, it's no special occasion." Mollie smiled. "I just decided to do something special for your homecoming this time. I decided to make this an evening you would remember for a long, long time to come."

"That's great," Bedford said. She could tell by the look in his eyes that he was still confused by all of this, but she acted as if she didn't notice. It was important for the effect she wanted that he not expect a thing, right up until the last moment when the axe finally fell.

"I've asked Amanda to cook a special dinner for us tonight, and everything's ready," Mollie told him.

"It smells delicious. What is it?"

"A standing rib roast with all the trimmings. And I have a bottle of wine too, a special burgundy that I've been saving for an occasion like this. It'll be wonderful . . . just the two of us eating a candlelight dinner together like we used to. And then after dinner. . . ." Mollie let her voice trail away in an unspoken promise as she took Bedford's arm and led him away toward the dining room.

Amanda began to bring the food in on cue, and within a few minutes the two of them were well into their delicious meal. While they ate Mollie kept her husband talking about his trip. He seemed to have thought out his story beforehand, she realized, because his account was filled with many details and amusing anecdotes designed to convince her that the trip consisted of little more than a long week of marathon gambling.

"Well I'm sorry the trip wasn't more profitable for you, Bedford," Mollie said. "It must have been a disappointment to go all that way only to have things turn out so badly."

"Well, it's the nature of the game," Bedford replied philosophically, "and anybody who can't accept that has no business playing." He paused to nibble on a bite of beef, then looked across the table at Mollie and said, "But my bad luck in St. Louis has left me with a problem. I lost several hundred dollars in all, and the trip itself was a fairly expensive one. I'm afraid I'm just about tapped out, Mollie, and I was hoping. . . ."

"You don't have to say any more," Mollie said reassuringly. "I'll have a talk with Winfred in the morning, and he'll take care of it for you."

"Thanks," Bedford said. "A few hundred, or maybe a thousand, ought to be stake enough. I figured for the next few weeks I'd work the small games around town and build my seed money back up slowly. The stakes aren't as high, but my chances of winning are better, and within perhaps a month I should be able to pay you everything back and still have cash left over."

"That's fine, Bedford," she replied quietly. It amazed her that after all these years, he was still promising to pay back the money he got from her. He never did, of course, but it seemed to satisfy the mandates of his male pride just to tell her that he intended to.

When they finished eating, Amanda brought in a bottle of brandy, and Mollie poured some for both of them. Carrying his, Bedford rose from the table and started into the parlor, but Mollie had a different destination in mind for them.

"We might be more comfortable upstairs," she said softly, taking his hand and leading him toward the stairs. They had been together long enough and knew each other well enough that she didn't have to explain what was on her mind. The look on her face and the tone of her voice was enough. Bedford responded with an eager smile.

You bastard, Mollie thought. You really think you've got it made, don't you? You'd leave her bed this morning and crawl into mine tonight, and never feel even a twinge of guilt over any of it.

But she never let a hint of her feelings show even after they arrived at their bedroom. The covers on the big bed were already turned back. The air was scented with lilac, and two candles provided the only light in the room.

Bedford took Mollie in his arms as soon as they were safely behind closed doors. His breath started to quicken as he kissed her, and his hands began their first tentative explorations of her body. The row of buttons on the back of her gown was halfway open before she gently drew away from him.

"I've been thinking a lot about our marriage lately, Bedford," she said softly. "All along, it's never been perfect, but then what in life is?"

"Nothing is," Bedford mumbled. She could hardly hear his words because he was nipping lightly at the flesh of her neck. Once, she thought, this would have driven her delirious with desire. But tonight she hardly noticed.

"During these last two years it seems like we've grown farther and farther apart, though," Mollie continued, "and I think the time has finally arrived when we have to make a new start. Everything has to change, beginning today . . . right now."

"Look, I know I neglect you sometimes," Bedford said. "I'm sorry if I hurt you because that's not my intention. I just get caught up in things, but I'll try to do better. I promise you I will."

Mollie could feel his desire for her growing, which is just what she intended, and she knew that at this minute he would probably have said or promised just about anything if it would bring an end to the talking and a start to the lovemaking.

"Do you still love me, Bedford?" she asked.

"Of course I do," he replied. "More than ever." He had snaked his hands inside the open back of her dress and was caressing the soft skin on her back. She could hear his husky breathing near her ear and felt his heart pounding in his chest. It was the perfect moment for the coup.

"Well, that's really quite sad," she went on, never changing the soft tone of her voice, "because I no longer feel anything for you except perhaps a little pity. That's why I'm throwing you out of here tonight."

It took a moment for the full impact of her words to hit him. At first he simply quit kissing and caressing her, and then drew away so he could look at her face. He looked stunned, as if somebody had caught him off guard with a sneaky punch.

"What in the hell are you talking about?" he asked. "Is this some kind of silly joke?"

"It's no joke, Bedford," Mollie told him. At last she began to let the coldness in her heart begin to creep into her voice. Looking her husband straight in the eye, she explained, "That's the new start I was talking about a minute ago. I'm throwing you out . . . out of my house and out of my life."

"The hell you are!" Bedford stormed.

"Yes, the hell I am," Mollie replied. "As a matter of fact, all your belongings are already packed into a trunk, and while we were eating dinner, Walter was loading the trunk into a wagon. He'll take you anywhere in town that you want to go to spend the night, and I never want to see you back here again."

Bedford stomped across the room to the closet and flung the doors open. Then for the next moment he simply stood there staring in disbelief. The left side of the closet where his wardrobe had once hung was now vacant. Even the shoes on the floor and the hats which he had kept on the shelf above were gone. Mollie had purposely left his side of the closet empty of her belongings so she could enjoy this moment more fully.

"You can't do this," Bedford warned her. "You're my wife, and I won't let you."

"You can't stop me from doing it," she answered. "And as far as my being your wife, that's what you haven't let me be in a long, long time. I might have been your bed-mate once in a while when you took a notion to come home, but even that ceased to have any meaning years ago."

She watched as Bedford's surprise and frustration slowly transformed into seething anger. He began to clench and unclench his fists, and his eyes seemed to become dark pits of fury. She stood waiting, unafraid, as he started to approach her.

"After he loaded your trunk," Mollie told Bedford, "Walter got his rifle and came upstairs. He's waiting outside the door right now, and his instructions are that if I call out to him, he's to come in here and shoot you."

"You're lying," Bedford sneered. "You think if you tell me that, I won't beat the hell out of you for trying to pull this on me."

"He's there, Bedford," Mollie warned. "As a matter of fact, we've already made up a story to keep him out of trouble in case he has to kill you. It seems you came home drunk after a big time with one of your whores and started demanding money from me. You began to beat me up, and Walter had to kill you to save my life."

"What's this talk about a big time with one of my whores?" Bedford demanded. "I just got back from a trip out of town. People saw me get off the train. Nobody would believe that!"

"I mean your whore in St. Louis," Mollie explained.

"You're crazy, woman!" he yelled. "I told you I went there —"

"I mean Gertie Talbot," she stated coldly.

The name caught Bedford so much by surprise that he had to turn away to hide his shock. He strode to the nearby window and stood staring out into the night through the sheer curtains, silent and brooding, as she continued.

"I hired a private detective to follow you, Bedford, and he's delivered a report with all the spicy little details about your trip to St. Louis in it. I've prepared everything before-hand so all of this should go as easily as possible. As I told you, all your belongings are already packed, and there's an envelope with a thousand dollars in cash inside the trunk to get you started somewhere away from here. The easiest thing for both of us would be if you simply disappeared so I could file for divorce on the grounds of abandonment. But in any case, I intend to obtain a divorce from you as soon as possible, whether you're here in the city or gone away."

When Bedford turned back to face her at last, she could see that he had regained his composure and was ready now to fight back. He had a rakish smile of amusement on his face, and before speaking he took a slender cigar from his pocket and lit it.

"Let me see if I understand correctly," he said. "You expect me to simply leave with a trunk of clothes and a thousand dollars and call it even after seven years of marriage. And you think because a detective says I slept with another woman in St. Louis that I'll go along with anything you say. Is that correct?"

"Well, it's not quite that simple, but you've got the basic facts straight," Mollie replied.

"And what about my children?" he asked. "Is it part of your plan for me to simply leave them behind as well?"

"We can make arrangements if you want to see Edward and Melinda, but it would surprise me if you keep that up for long. Let's face it, Bedford, you haven't exactly been the most devoted daddy, have you? My handyman has been more of a father to them over the years than you have."

"We'll just have to see about that, I guess," Bedford said. "But there's also the matter of all the property, and all the money in the bank. Do you honestly expect me to accept a paltry thousand dollars and leave all the rest behind?"

In recent weeks, Mollie had started taking measures to protect her property and businesses from Bedford, but she decided not to show her hand just yet. Instead, she was curious about what her husband might have in mind.

"I figure it should be worth something for me to agree not to stay here and contest the divorce," Bedford said. "In the end you would probably get almost everything you wanted, but it could be a long, drawn-out process, and it certainly wouldn't be easy for the children to suffer through such an ordeal. That's why you want me out of town. But why should I leave? What's in it for me?"

"I don't know," Mollie replied. "What would convince you to leave?"

"A piece of property perhaps," he suggested slyly. "Something far away from here that I would need to go investigate and manage firsthand."

Mollie realized immediately that he must be referring to her Montana mining property because that was the only property she owned outside this immediate area. "Are you crazy?" she exclaimed, purposefully injecting a note of hysteria into her voice. "Do you think I would deliberately give you my share in the gold mine just to get rid of you? Do I seem that desperate to you?"

"You might," Bedford answered confidently.

"But there's no telling what that property is worth," Mollie said.

"Look, Mollie. It's not like you need the income from that mine to keep you going," Bedford told her calmly. "You have all that you need and more right here in Kansas City. You have the theater, the new houses you built, and heaven only knows how many more investments scattered all over.

"Right now I know you think you've been pretty clever with your private detective and this little ruse you played tonight just to make me look ridiculous before you ordered me to leave. But we both know that I could cause plenty of trouble for you if I wanted to. Scandal doesn't bother me, and if I chose to do so, I could sling plenty of muck around before I turned my back on this part of the country."

The idea of giving Bedford the gold mine had never really occurred to Mollie, but she decided to let him seem to convince her, by degrees, that it was a good idea. "I would like to have this thing over as quickly and smoothly as possible," she said tentatively.

"And so would I," Bedford replied. "But I refuse to leave like a whipped dog. I might not have been the best husband in the world, but I did put seven years into this marriage, and I want something to show for my investment."

"I'm not saying I'll do it," Mollie told him, "but if I did decide to give you my share in the mine in Montana, what would I get from you in return?"

"I'll sign whatever you want," he explained. "You have your lawyer draw up whatever papers you think you need to get your divorce and protect your property, and I'll sign everything. It won't matter to me because I'll be gone the day after you put that deed in my hands."

"You know that if I do this and then you

come back here again, there will be big trouble," Mollie warned him. "There'll be no returning a year or two from now and wanting more from me. I won't abide it, and I'll do whatever it takes to stop you."

"I understand that, Mollie," Bedford said. "But why should I want to come back?"

Mollie walked across the room and opened the bedroom door. Immediately outside Walter Perry waited with a rifle in his hands. He seemed tense at first, but relaxed when he saw that things were apparently peaceful between Mollie and Bedford.

"You really meant it, didn't you?" Bedford said staring in amazement at the handyman.

"Absolutely," Mollie replied. Then, turning to Walter, she asked, "Is Mr. Lee's trunk loaded?"

"It's loaded, and the team is hitched up," Walter replied.

"Good, then take him wherever he wants to go tonight," Mollie instructed. "And tomorrow afternoon, say about two o'clock, I want you to pick him up again and bring him to my office in the theater. We have some business to transact. That should give me time enough to have the necessary paperwork drawn up."

Mollie permitted her husband a kiss in

parting, but her body was stiff and her lips were cold as he brushed his briefly against them. When he looked into her eyes, all he saw there was her unyielding determination to have this marriage over as soon as possible.

"No matter how terrible you think I am," Bedford said softly as he left, "I do have feelings and I'm going to miss you, Mollie."

"I know," she replied. "I used to miss you too, but I got over it a long time ago."

After the two men had gone, Mollie went back into her room and locked the door behind her. She picked up her glass of brandy with a trembling hand and sat down to consider what had just taken place.

The business about the gold mine had to be the ultimate irony, she thought. It would never have occurred to her to offer it to him, but when he suggested it, she had to admit that it was precisely what he deserved.

If her husband had been at all involved in her life or bad paid even passing attention to her business interests, he would have known that her gold mine, along with several others in the district where it was located, had closed down nearly a year before. When Bedford Lee got to Montana with his deed in his pocket, he would discover that he was the owner of a worth-

less hole in the ground on the edge of a
ghost town.

CHAPTER SIXTEEN

August, 1876

Kite Lundgren slid the last of the planks on top of the frame of the stock shed he was building, then pulled his handkerchief out of his pocket and mopped the sweat off his forehead. He figured this last load of lumber should complete the shed. Next would come the task of fencing in a forty-foot-square area behind it. Then his feed lot would be completed, and he could think about buying half a dozen yearling steers to fatten up, some for sale later in the fall, and some to provide meat for his table during the long winter months.

Building a place up from scratch was a long, difficult process, especially for a man like Lundgren who worked ten hours a day, six days a week at the sawmill in Grain Valley and could only devote a handful of hours each week to his own property. But he remained encouraged by the steady progress he was making week by week, month by month. He had finished the house three months before, and now the stock shed was well underway. By this time next year, he hoped to have a decent-sized barn up as well.

Kite Lundgren was a stolid, patient man. He had headed west after the war like many of his fellow Missouri veterans, hoping to put the fighting behind him and make a new start on the frontier. He drifted for years, looking for a place and a reason to settle down, but neither ever seemed to present itself to him. Then finally one day it occurred to him that where he really wanted to be was back home, back in Missouri among the people he knew and understood.

His goals were simple now . . . a farm, a wife, and some children to brighten his days and care for him in his old age . . . and he knew that hard work was the only way to get the things he wanted. He figured the farm had to come first, because he would never persuade any woman to marry him if all he had to offer was a tent and a garden patch on forty acres of uncleared land. But with a solid house and barn already standing, a few head of stock, and a decent crop in the making . . . well, they said the war had left the state short of men, and Lundgren figured he'd be able to find some woman willing to marry him.

It was almost nighttime now, and Lundgren figured it wasn't worth the effort to climb up on the roof of the shed just to put in another fifteen or twenty minutes before it became too dark to work. Instead he pulled his ragged cotton shirt over his hairy, strong torso and started for the house.

It was Saturday, which meant that his evening would be spent hauling water for the wash tub, scrubbing the week's accumulated grime off his body, shaving, ironing a shirt, and generally preparing himself for the six-mile ride to Grain Valley for church in the morning.

Maybe if he was lucky, he thought, someone in the congregation would invite him to Sunday dinner as they occasionally did, and he could spend a pleasant, lazy afternoon in the company of other people. It got pretty lonely sometimes, living out in the woods as he did, spending all his daytime hours in backbreaking labor and all his nights in an empty house and an empty bed. But at least he was actually living on his own place now. He had a home at last. And it wouldn't be too long before the barn was up.

The sound of hoofbeats on the narrow wagon road leading to his house made Kite

Lundgren stop and strain his eyes to see in the growing darkness. He figured it was probably Tom Preston, coming over with a jug of corn whiskey to share with his old wartime comrade. Preston, like Lundgren, lived alone on an isolated farm, and it had become his habit once or twice a month to ride over on a Saturday night to spend an evening drinking, playing cards, and swapping yarns about their days with Quantrill.

But as the rider drew closer, Kite Lundgren realized that it was not his friend. The horse was wrong. Tom rode a chestnut mare, and this animal was much larger and darker. And the rider sat too tall in the saddle as well. Tom was much shorter than this man. But still it would be good to have any sort of company for a while, Lundgren thought as he strode forward to greet his visitor.

When the man drew to within a dozen feet of Lundgren he stopped his horse and dismounted. By then Lundgren realized he didn't know his visitor, but he still greeted him without fear.

"Is your name Lundgren?" the stranger asked. "Kite Lundgren?" Seeing him standing on the ground, Lundgren could see that he was indeed a tall fellow, an inch or two over six feet at least. He was dressed in black trousers, a gray shirt, and a black leather vest with fancy silver studs adorning the front. He wore a revolver in a holster at his side, and a second weapon, a rifle, hung in a scabbard at the front of his saddle.

"That's me," Lundgren replied. "And who might you be, friend?"

"Morgan Hartman," the man replied, his voice stern and deep. The name sounded familiar to Lundgren, but at first he couldn't place it. "I am an operative for the Pinkerton Detective Agency, and I've come here to ask you some questions about some robberies which have taken place in this area in the last few months."

In a flash it came to Lundgren who this man was. This was the Morgan Hartman of Kansas Jayhawker fame, the man whose name had ranked up there with Jennison and Lane as one of the most vicious and brutal executioners ever to ride across the state line to wreak havoc in Missouri back during the war. Legend had it, in fact, that this Morgan Hartman, the very same man who now stood here demanding information, had once gunned down *his own grandfather* after the old man resisted a raiding party which came to his Missouri farm. Now he was a Pinkerton, which made him more despicable than ever to Lundgren.

"I've got nothin' to say to you," Lundgren said venomously. "Get off my place and count yourself lucky that I didn't have a gun in my hand when you told me who you were." He turned to start away toward his house, but the click of a revolver cocking stopped him dead in his tracks.

"I noticed that you weren't armed, Lundgren," Hartman told him, "and I'm sure you noticed that I am. Since you seem to know who I am, then you must know that I won't flinch from doing whatever it takes to get the information I came for."

Lundgren turned slowly. By the time he faced the intruder again, his eyes were ablaze with a hatred so intense that Hartman could not overlook it even in the fading light.

"I ain't telling you nothin', mister," the former bushwhacker growled, "so you might as well just kill me now if that's the only other choice I got!"

"You've got no choice at all, Lundgren!" Hartman announced firmly. "Before this business is over with, you'll be answering every question I ask and begging me to ask you more."

"The day I beg you for anything, you Jayhawker bastard," Lundgren snarled, "will be the day I —"

His exclamation was interrupted by a sharp report from Hartman's gun. Kite Lundgren's right had leaped away from his body, as if of its own accord, and a sharp stab of pain raced up his arm from the bullet wound in his palm. Through clenched teeth he managed to say, "That was a plumb bad shot, Hartman. Another inch or two and you would have missed me completely!"

"I hit what I aimed at," Hartman assured him. "Now turn around and head for the house. Unless you decide to change your mind pretty soon, we've got a long night ahead of us."

Morgan Hartman sat at the crude plank table in the front room of Kite Lundgren's house, sipping a cup of coffee and staring absently at his scraped and bleeding knuckles. Across the room Lundgren lay in a mangled heap on the floor. His hands and feet were still tied, as they had been all night, but by this time the bonds were hardly necessary. All the fight had been drained out of him hours ago.

The first signs of daylight were just beginning to filter through the trees outside. There had been some rain during the night, but the day was dawning bright and clear. Hartman was glad about that because he

319

didn't relish the thought of having to ride for hours in the rain after his business was finished here.

On the table in front of him was a single blood-splotched sheet of paper with the names of several men written on it. The two top names on the list, "Frank James" and "Jesse James," were hardly a surprise to Hartman, but some of the others were. Two names in particular near the bottom of the list — "John Hartman" and "Daniel Hartman" — brought a terrible grin to the Pinkerton agent's face when he thought of tracking them down and killing them.

On the floor, Kite Lundgren moaned dully, bringing Morgan Hartman's attention back to his hapless victim. He had been a tough one to break, Hartman thought. The former bushwhacker had amazing stamina, and for the first two or three hours his sheer hatred for Hartman and for everything Kansan in general had helped him survive an incredible amount of physical abuse. But every man had his breaking point and eventually Hartman had found Lundgren's.

As it turned out, Kite Lundgren had participated in only one robbery with the James Gang. His share of the take from a Missouri Pacific train robbery had paid for this land, his team of plow mules, and the lumber in this house.

It was impossible to tell whether Kite Lundgren was conscious or not. His eyes had been swollen shut almost since the beginning, and by now his entire face was so mangled that it scarcely resembled anything human. His body and limbs bore a number of gunshot wounds, all carefully placed by Hartman so they would not be prematurely fatal, and his breath hissed harshly and raggedly from his chest after the hours of incessant beating and kicking.

Draining the last of the coffee from his cup, Morgan Hartman decided at last that it was time. At this point even if Lundgren did have more information to offer, Hartman doubted that he would be able to give it, and the start of the new day increased the possibility of someone coming along before Hartman's work here was finished.

Rising to his feet, Hartman folded the paper and put it in his pocket, then drew his revolver and checked the load. He crossed the room and stooped beside his victim, prodding him with the muzzle of the weapon in search of signs of consciousness. His gesture elicited only a throaty gurgle from Lundgren.

"I don't even know whether you can hear

me or not," Hartman said, "but I sure as hell hope you can. Before you die, I want you to know that as bad as things have been for you, I still don't think it's payback enough for what you and your kind did during the war." His eyes took on an even more hateful gleam as the words spilled out of him.

"If I had the time to spare, I'd gladly keep you like this for days," he continued. "I'd take you to the point where you'd be convinced that there couldn't be any pain or suffering worse than what you were feeling, and then I'd show that there was worse. But since I've got to go, I'll have to settle for you dying with the knowledge that you betrayed your friends. I want you to start the trip to hell knowing that every man you named is going to die ugly, even worse than this I hope, and it was all your doing."

Then, rising and moving back slightly so he would not be splattered with blood, Hartman shot Lundgren twice in the head.

After reloading and holstering his revolver, Morgan Hartman found a two-gallon can of kerosene, and splashed the stuff liberally around the room. When the can was empty he tossed it aside, then struck a match and dropped it in a pool of kerosene on the floor at his feet.

Flames were already beginning to lap out the open windows and door of the house by the time he reached his horse. An hour or two from now, nothing would be left of Kite Lundgren and his home but a pile of smoldering ashes, and no one else would ever know what happened here . . . no one, that is except the men Hartman would tell just before he killed them.

Stepping up into the saddle, Morgan Hartman headed his horse west toward Tom Preston's house, following the directions he had forced from Kite Lundgren.

Morgan Hartman had hated Missourians for as long as he could remember. In the 1850s he and his father, Charles Hartman, had fought alongside John Brown and other great abolitionists of the period in their struggle to make Kansas a free state, and he had seen his father perish for the cause. During the Civil War, when Kansans more often than not had the upper hand over their pro-slavery neighbors, Morgan had been an ardent Jayhawker and had participated in some of the more famous atrocities of the era, most of which were committed against the helpless residents of the Missouri counties closest to Kansas.

Later, as the war finally drew to a close, he drifted westward, putting his talent with a gun to good use as a town tamer and lawman-for-hire in the wild and woolly frontier towns in western Kansas, northern Texas and eastern Colorado. By the mid-1870s he had developed a considerable reputation for efficiently dispatching thieves, rustlers, murderers and sundry other types of frontier rabble in the name of peace and justice, or at least for the benefit of whoever was paying his salary at the time.

When the Pinkerton Detective Agency invited Morgan Hartman to return to Missouri and help track down the members of the James Gang, he recognized the opportunity to settle some old scores which had been left unresolved from during and even before the war. And chief among his surviving enemies were some members of his own family, whom he hated with a passion as deep and abiding as any he had ever felt in his life.

CHAPTER SEVENTEEN

The house was located on a quiet side-street in one of the older neighborhoods of Nashville. It was much like all the other neat, two-and three-bedroom frame homes nearby. A white picket fence enclosed a twenty-by-thirty foot plot of grass which served as a front yard, and a drive around the side led to the back yard and the stables. The house itself had a covered front porch which stretched the full width of the structure. There was a single door near the center of the porch with a lace-curtained window on either side.

The name on the mailbox read "Howard," and the neighbors knew the residents of the house to be a reclusive but not unfriendly couple in their early thirties. Thomas Howard, who was known to be a trader and livestock speculator, was away from home a lot, frequently for days or weeks at a time, and usually his pretty young wife Zee traveled with him. Even after the birth of their son late the previous year, the family usually traveled together except in the most severe winter weather.

No one asked many questions about the young family, and, considering the business he was in, no one seemed to think much about Thomas Howard's irregular comings and goings. Because the couple lived such quiet lives, no one in the vicinity had any reason whatsoever to suspect that Thomas Howard, their neighbor was, in fact the notorious desperado, Jesse James.

Using the name B. J. Woodson, Jesse's brother Frank lived nearby. He and his wife Annie had a small farm on the edge of town where Frank raised a cotton crop and indulged his passion for horse trading. Jesse also had a string of fine blooded mounts which he kept on his brother's farm.

Few people back in Clay County, Missouri knew of the new homes the James brothers had established in Tennessee. Even the families of their wives were kept in the dark for fear that a casual comment at the wrong time to the wrong person might destroy the veil of secrecy under which they managed to live fairly normal lives.

Rumors about their supposed whereabouts circulated constantly, though. Most often people thought they were in Texas, but occasionally stories also drifted in about Frank and Jesse being seen in St. Louis, New York, Denver, Kansas, and even California. The death of one or both of them had been reported on several occasions, and they were still blamed for widely-scattered and diverse crimes ranging from bank robbery and murder to rape, arson, and petty theft.

The truth was that the James brothers and their gang had only committed two robberies in the past year. On both occasions, Jesse was responsible for planning the crime while Frank traveled back to Missouri to enlist the necessary manpower for its execution. Cole Younger had gone along on both robberies, but John and Daniel Hartman had only participated in one of them, the robbery of a Missouri Pacific train near Otterville, Missouri.

After the visit from their cousin Ridge, the Hartman brothers had waited over a year before resuming their criminal careers. But eventually the talk of amnesty for the former bushwhackers faded again, as it always had before, and all Ridge Parkman's efforts on behalf of his cousins went for nothing.

In fact, much to his deep regret, the only tangible result of Ridge's attempt to gain pardons for his cousins was that John and Daniel's names were now definitely associated in the minds of the powers-that-be with those of Jesse James, Frank James, Cole Younger and several other members of the gang.

The fact that Frank and Jesse James had so carefully isolated themselves from their home state and county made Jesse's summons in August, 1876 all the more surprising. John and Daniel had known for a few months that their friends were living somewhere in Tennessee, but they had never visited them there. Cole Younger and his brother Bob had made one trip to Nashville to see their friends, but they were very closed-mouthed about the trip and provided few details about Frank and Jesse's lives after they returned to Missouri.

But then, without warning, several of the most trusted members of the gang were invited to Nashville for what all expected would be a planning session for a major robbery of some sort. John and Daniel Hartman made the three-day trip from Kansas City to Nashville in the company of their friends, Cole, Jim, and Bob Younger. After arriving in Nashville late on the third day, they spent the night in a hotel near the depot and rose early the next morning to go to Jesse's house.

As planned, John and Daniel left the hotel half an hour later than the Youngers, and now they were the last to arrive at the meeting place. They rode their rented mounts around the side of the house to the stable, where a young black stable boy met them at the door and accepted the reins from them. Jesse himself was waiting at the back door as the Hartmans mounted the back steps, and he greeted them with a handshake and a warm welcome.

"Come on in," Jesse invited. "Everybody else is already in the front room sampling some Tennessee corn squeezings that Frank managed to get his hands on. It's almost like a reunion of our old bushwhacker outfit."

"Who else is here besides the Youngers and us?" John asked.

"Well, we've got Bill Chadwell and Charles Pitts," Jesse answered. "And of course, Clell Miller is here. Then there's Tom Hatfield and Price Stevenson and Mike Wildemann. We invited a couple of others from the old bunch as well, but they sent word that they didn't want to do this one."

"Thirteen men. That's quite a group," Daniel commented. "You must have a pretty big job in mind to need so many guns along."

"It could be the biggest thing we've ever tried, Dan," Jesse replied. "But let's hold off talking about it for a little while. I'd rather explain it when everybody's together."

"That's fine, Jesse," Daniel said. "It's your show. You run it however you like."

After crossing the kitchen, they were met at the doorway to the front room of the house by Frank James, who shook their hands and handed each of them a glass of corn whiskey.

"It's good to see you two again," Frank said. "I guess you know everybody else here, don't you?"

"I think we do," John said, looking around the room and nodding to a number of the other men assembled there. Every face in the room was familiar to him, although it had been awhile since he and his brother had seen some of them. During that first moment, one fact became immediately apparent to John. For this job, whatever it might be, Frank and Jesse had gathered together some of the best talent available. Every man there had proven his courage and his competence with a gun beyond any reasonable doubt, and as a group they would constitute a formidable and highly dangerous fighting unit. During the war, John and Daniel had ridden with outfits such as this against enemy units three and four times their size, and they were well aware of what a small, determined band of men could accomplish when they shared the same motives and fought as one.

Most of the men in the room were talking among themselves and the Hartman brothers soon drifted to the nearest cluster to listen in on the conversation. Not surprisingly, Cole Younger, Clell Miller, and Price Stevenson were discussing the mysterious deaths of two of their friends only a couple of weeks before.

"To tell the truth, I can easily see Kite Lundgren getting drunk and burning himself up in his house by accident," Stevenson was saying. "Even before the war started and we joined up with Quantrill, I can remember him getting so drunk that he couldn't tell you his own name. But this business about Tom Preston dying at almost exactly the same time is just a little too much of a coincidence for me."

"It was strange," Miller agreed, "and I guess by the time they found him, Tom was so chewed up that nobody could even tell exactly how he died. I heard that his own hogs got to his body while it was laying out in the barnyard and that some whole pieces of him were missing."

"It makes cold shivers go down my spine just to think about it," Stevenson admitted. "But the thing that keeps going through my mind is that the hogs aren't what killed Tom. Something, or somebody, had to have killed him first, and then later the hogs probably got out and started chewing him up."

The fact that made the deaths of the two men so important to every man there was that both Tom Preston and Kite Lundgren had, in the past, ridden with the James gang. Kite had only been invited along once. After that Frank and Jesse had decided that he was a little too plodding and dull-witted to be reliable, but Tom Preston had gone along on two separate robberies and had shown himself to be a valuable man.

Although no one in the room had yet said it out loud, after hearing about the deaths of their two comrades, every man there found himself wondering whether he might be the next one to die in a similar horrible manner. If in fact these were killings instead of accidents, whoever was doing them was operating savagely and striking fear and dread in the hearts of the outlaws who remained at large.

After another few minutes of scattered conversations, Jesse at last called the assembly to order.

"I guess sine everybody's talking about the deaths of Kite Lundgren and Tom Preston anyway, we might as well deal with that first and get it out of the way," Jesse began.

"Now Frank and I don't know anything more about what happened than anybody else, but my guess is that this is the Pinkertons' doing. Hell, they've been trying to get at us for years, and they even stooped low enough once to try and burn our mama's house down on top of her. I don't think they'd bat an eye at shooting Kite and setting fire to his cabin or killing Tom and then turning his hogs loose to eat him.

"But whatever did happen," Jesse continued, "my brother and I have talked about it and we've decided that we can't let it change anything for us. We had this job in the works before all that came up, and we're still going ahead with it. Now if any of you have your doubts about whether you want to go along, now is the time to speak up. There'll be no hard feelings, but we'll be asking you to leave before we start talking about the details of the job we have planned."

There was a moment of uncomfortable

silence in the room, then Price Stevenson finally spoke up. "Look Jesse, you and Frank have known me long enough to know that I'm no coward, but I got to talking with Mike Wildemann on the way down here, and I started having second thoughts about this whole thing. I'm a family man now, so for me it can't be like it was in the old days. I can't take the kind of risks I used to, not and call myself a good father and husband."

"Several of us here have families, Price," Frank James pointed out.

"I know that, Frank," Stevenson said. "I guess it's every man's decision how many risks he should take after he's married. But for me, I just decided that I've got too much to lose. I'm afraid I'm going to have to back away from this one and leave it alone."

"And how about you, Mike?" Jesse asked Mike Wildemann. "Have you reached the same conclusion Price has?"

"I reckon I have, Jesse," Wildemann said. "I've got a good home and my store in Liberty is doing all right. It's not like I need the money anymore like I did in the old days."

"All right, then, I guess we'll be bidding you two fellows good-bye," Jesse told them. "Sorry you had to come all this way for nothing, but it was good seeing you again."

Somewhat self-consciously, Stevenson and Wildemann walked across the room toward the kitchen door. They shook hands with a couple of their friends before leaving, but it was obvious that they suddenly felt like outsiders and that they were in a hurry to leave.

After the two were gone, Jesse turned back to the others and said, "Anybody else?"

No one else spoke up. The band was complete, and the planning of the job could finally begin.

"This time I decided that it might be best to stay clear the hell out of Missouri and hit someplace that no one would ever suspect," Jesse said. "It took me awhile to find the right town and the right bank, but I finally did. It's a place called Northfield, Minnesota, and if my guess is right, it could be a score like none we've ever made before."

They raced across the open pasture, riding at breakneck speed toward the distant tree line. Cole's horse was larger and more powerful than Mollie's but for short sprints such as this, nothing could beat a well-trained quarterhorse like the one she was riding. When the contest was over, Mollie was the winner by at least a half a length.

Once into the trees, they both stepped to

the ground and let their mounts walk on a few feet ahead to get a drink from the small creek nearby.

It was a lovely day, bright and clear and unseasonably warm for early September. Drifting white clouds looked like paper cutouts on the pale blue sky, and the small clearing they were standing in was covered with a thick carpet of green grass. A faint breeze drifted through the treetops around them, tugging loose the first of the yellowing leaves and carrying them gently toward the ground.

"Do you remember this place, Cole?" Mollie asked.

"Are you kidding?" Cole said, grinning. "Is a man likely to forget the time and the place when he quit being a boy and finally became a man?"

"Well, to my way of thinking, you were quite a man even before that day," Mollie said, "but I guess that's the way a male would think."

They were standing in the place where they had first made love nearly twenty years before. Today the four-year difference in their ages was unnoticeable, but back then when Cole was still a gangling, rawboned teenager and Mollie was an experienced "older woman" in her early twenties, the four-year span had been significant. But even then the attraction between them had been strong and undeniable, and after more than a year of close friendship, Mollie had at last decided to do something about the strong feelings which she had secretly harbored for Cole for so long. Of course, being a young man eager to sample all of life's experiences, Cole had needed little persuasion.

They were here today so Mollie could try out a horse that she was thinking about buying from her nephew John. Her son Edward was eight years old now, old enough to have a horse of his own, but she wanted to make sure the animal she selected was both well-trained and manageable. John himself had broken and trained the bright-eyed, agile quarterhorse that she rode today, and the results of his efforts were clearly evident. It would be a perfect first horse for her son.

"Has anyone heard from Cassie lately?" Cole asked as the two of them followed their horses down to the edge of the creek. He had only arrived at Jason's house about two hours before, just in time for lunch, and he still had a lot of news to catch up on.

"I got a letter from her about a week ago," Mollie answered. "She's in San Francisco now, waiting to have her fourth baby in another couple of months. She said the stage line Mike got into is making a good profit, but he's already thinking about investing in railroads instead."

"I'm glad to hear she's doing so well," Cole said. "There was a time a few years back when it didn't look quite so good for her."

"I know, but I guess Mike has made a good husband after all. From all that Cassie writes, it looks like he's on his way to being a very successful man, and the two of them still seem very much in love."

"And how about you, Mollie?" Cole asked. "Have you had any news about Bedford lately?"

"Well, of course I heard from him after he got to Montana and found out that all he wheedled me out of when we separated was a worthless hole in the ground. The letter he sent was full of all kinds of threats and demands, but I didn't take any of them too seriously."

"What's to stop him from coming back here and making more trouble for you?"

"Just one thing," Mollie said. "I told him that I would have him killed if he ever came back and tried to bother me or the children. Whatever else Bedford Lee might be, he's not a stupid man, and I'm sure he knows I meant what I said."

"Don't the children miss him?" Cole asked.

"Not much. After all, he wasn't around very much when we were married, so it wasn't like he left any great void in their lives when he went away. It's funny, but now they sometimes talk about him almost as if he was dead, and I think they have no problem accepting the fact that they probably won't ever see him again."

"How about you, Mollie? Do you have a problem accepting that fact?"

On its face the question seemed ridiculous, but it caught Mollie off guard and it took her a moment to formulate a truthful reply.

"I don't think so, Cole," she replied at last. "Not like I might have once. There are still times, I guess, when I miss some things, like the days when I was still in love with him and things were good between us. I'd like to have that again someday with somebody . . . but not with Bedford."

"You will, Mollie," Cole assured her. "You being the woman you are, all you'll ever have to do to bag the man you want is to set your sights on him and squeeze the trigger. What man could resist you for long?"

"I know one who has for years and years,"

Mollie said and smiled. Cole looked deep in her eyes and smiled back, but made no reply. "But the truth is," she went on, "at my age what I want and need in a man is much different from what it used to be. All my life I've gone for true love, and that never has seemed to work out very well.

"You know, when I first married Bedford I was ridiculously in love with him, but it didn't take me long to realize that I didn't like him very much. He wasn't a friend or a companion. He was just somebody who thrilled me when he touched me, but he was never there when I needed him, and it would never have occurred to him to put my needs or desires ahead of his own even occasionally."

"But he was just one man, Mollie," Cole said. "There are plenty of others out there. There are lots of good men still available for the choosing."

"I know, Cole," Mollie said. "And maybe the next time I'll finally have the sense to pick a man who will be good for me instead of one who's simply too much of a challenge to resist. I hope I've learned at least that much out of all this."

They settled on the soft grass at the edge of the creek, sitting side by side as they watched the ripple of the shallow water lowing over its rocky bed. The horses had finished with their drink and were now grazing contentedly a few feet away.

"It's been so long since we've been together like this, Cole," Mollie said. "You know, you're still my best friend in the world, and I still miss you terribly sometimes."

"I feel the same way, Mollie," Cole answered quietly.

"Is there any way that I could persuade you to come and stay awhile in Kansas City?" she asked. Even she was surprised by the note of yearning which seemed to creep unbidden into her voice. "We could spend some real time together for the first time in years. We could share ourselves with each other like we used to a long time ago. I'd like that very much, Cole. It would make me very happy to have you close again."

"I'd like it too, Mollie," Cole said, "but I can't . . . at least not now."

"I understand," Mollie replied sadly, although she knew in her heart that she really didn't understand anything.

"I want to come," Cole said. "As a matter of fact, I've been thinking the same thing for quite some time now, ever since I heard that you and your husband couldn't make your marriage work anymore. But before

we could ever be together, I'd have to b
able to stand on my own two feet and pay
my own way. I could never use you like your
husband did.

"What I've been thinking is that maybe I
could start a little business of some kind in
Kansas City, a gun shop, maybe, or a livery
business. But it takes money, and I haven't
got enough, not quite yet."

"Well if that's the only problem, Cole, I
could arrange . . ." Mollie began, but he
interrupted her with a raised hand.

"I'd have to do it on my own," he insisted.
"That's the only way it would ever work for
me. It wouldn't bother me if I was never as
successful as you are, but whatever it was
that I put together, I'd have to know that I
had done it myself. You of all people should
know enough about me by now to realize
that's the way it would have to be."

"You're right, Cole," Mollie replied. "But
when . . . how long do you think it might
be before you . . . ?"

"Some of us are taking a little trip next
week," Cole told her, "and when I get back,
I might have enough to give it a try."

The announcement sent a cold chill
through Mollie. She knew that Cole would
never admit to her or anyone else that he
sometimes rode with Frank and Jesse James,

but she knew about it nonetheless. His participation in the James Gang holdups, along with John and Daniel's, had been common knowledge for years among the members of the Hartman family, although it was a subject they rarely discussed. And this "little trip" he mentioned had all the markings of yet another James Gang holdup.

"Are my nephews going with you on this trip?" Mollie asked.

"They are, along with several others," Cole replied vaguely.

"My God, Cole!" she exclaimed. "When are you going to learn? When are you and John and Daniel going to give this up? Will it take one or all of you dying before you're finally through with this awful business?"

"This is the last time, Mollie," Cole told her. "I had already decided even before we got together today that this will be my last trip. But I just couldn't turn this one down. Jesse says it will be a good haul, and like I told you a minute ago, I need a stake so I can get started in something different, something honest."

Mollie knew it was no use arguing with him about this. Despite their closeness, neither one of them could talk the other out of anything important, and seldom either of them tried. But knowing that she couldn't

343

change his mind didn't necessarily mean she couldn't express her disapproval of his decision.

"What if it doesn't work out the way you plan, Cole?" she asked. "What if you can't steal all the money you think you need? Does that mean that we can't be together until there is another holdup, and then maybe another one after that?"

"This is the last time," Cole repeated. "I swear it is. I'm getting tired, Mollie. It seems like for most of my life I've been on the move, fighting somebody, facing some kind of danger. But a man can't do that forever. I've got to give it up sometime, and I've decided that it will be after this trip.

"And as far as the money is concerned," he went on, "if I don't get all that I need, we can talk about it when I get back. Maybe a man's pride isn't always worth all that he thinks it is if it costs him too much to hang onto it."

Mollie didn't say anything else. Her answer was a kiss.

CHAPTER EIGHTEEN

The camp was quiet the night before the robbery. Each of the eleven men in the band was caught up in his own thoughts, and none seemed particularly inclined to share his reflections with his fellows. Most of them were drinking, some fairly steadily, but even the liquor induced no lighthearted camaraderie among them as it might have under other circumstances.

No matter how many times a man did this sort of thing, he could never completely free himself from the nervousness of waiting for it to begin. All of them had been at this business long enough to realize, however, that waiting to face danger was much more difficult than actually facing it.

The camp was in a deep patch of woods about a mile off the main road and five miles south of their objective, Northfield, Minnesota. During the day several of the men had ridden into town in twos and threes to get a feel for the place, and earlier in the evening Jesse had carefully gone over a sketch of the town with the entire band. By now each man had memorized the part he was to play in the robbery — where he would be while it was taking place, which directions he should cover in case of trouble, and what route he should take out of town after it was all over.

The stillness of the camp was broken when Cole Younger rose and tossed an armload of deadfall on the campfire. "This far north, I guess the nights get a little chillier than we're used to for September," he commented to nobody in particular. "I think I'm going to appreciate that extra blanket I decided to bring along."

"Yeah, we probably need to gather up some more firewood before we turn in," John Hartman said. "About two or three in the morning it sure will be nice to have some handy to knock the chill off."

After the flames from the fire began to light the area once again, John rose and went to the edge of the trees nearby to begin gathering up some extra wood. A minute later a couple of the others did the same. Soon they had a respectable pile of fuel stockpiled near the blaze.

Jesse James watched them at their work,

but made no effort to help. He had a glassy, intense look in his eye which Daniel Hartman, who sat nearby, thought was probably caused more by the bottle of whiskey he had drunk than by the tension of planning an event of this sort.

It wasn't like Jesse to drink that much, Daniel thought. In the past he might take a swallow or two to ward off the nighttime chill, but never before had he even approached becoming drunk. Tonight he clearly had had much too much. It must be the trouble with Zee, Daniel decided. A couple of days earlier, Jim Younger told John and Daniel in confidence that Jesse's wife had staunchly opposed this trip and that when the couple parted, it had been under the most strained of circumstances.

The fact of Jesse's drunkenness wouldn't have worried his friend quite so much, if this had been the light-hearted, comfortable sort of binge that many men occasionally engage in. Instead, it was serious drinking, and with each swallow of liquor Jesse's mood seemed to become more pensive and foul.

"Pass that bottle over here, Tom," Jesse mumbled to Tom Hatfield, who sat about a dozen feet away. "Mine's empty."

"Hell, I ain't got much left myself, Jesse,"

347

Hatfield complained. "Why didn't you bring along enough liquor for yourself like everybody else did?" He had put away about as much liquor as Jesse or any of the others during the evening, and even cold sober he was not known as a man with any great reservoir of patience or tact.

"Are you so damn greedy that you won't even share a damn swallow of whiskey with a friend, Hatfield?" Jesse growled.

"Ease up, Jesse," Frank advised. "It's Tom's whiskey, so it's his decision whether or not he wants to share it with anybody. And you've probably had more than enough to drink for one night anyway."

"I think I've got sense enough to decide that for myself, brother," Jesse replied sharply. "But the thing is, I just wonder what kind of man won't even give a friend a drink if he asks for one."

"Well maybe if you were a friend yourself, you wouldn't ask a man for a drink knowing that he didn't have but a little bit left for himself," Hatfield replied with equal vindictiveness. "Damn you, Jesse, do you think just because you're the one that plans these little get-togethers that you can run over anybody in the outfit any time you want?"

Surprised at the sharpness of the words,

Daniel Hartman glanced over at Jesse just in time to see him shift his position slightly. It was a small movement, but it was significant because it placed Jesse James' hand inches closer to the holstered revolver at his side. What alarmed Daniel even more than that, however, was the look on the outlaw leader's face. The expression was almost like a grin, but it was entirely too sharp and piercing to be interpreted as anything friendly or good-natured.

Daniel knew that look well, and he knew the dangerous mood which usually accompanied it.

Some of the others also seemed to realize that the whole situation was getting out of hand, but they all kept quiet. It was a part of their code, a carry-over from their old bushwhacker days, that when men reached this point in a dispute, drunk or sober, it was their obligation and their right to work it out any way they decided was appropriate. Even Frank James, after his initial effort to calm his brother, remained silent.

Hatfield himself was the only one who did not seem to realize how much trouble he was stirring up for himself. He uncorked his bottle and took another slug, purposely draining the last of the whiskey from it. Then he tossed it over on the ground at

Jesse's feet.

"There you go, Jesse," he said harshly. "Have at it!"

Jesse's grin grew until his features were contorted into a fearsome grimace. Every other man in the group knew that Hatfield's actions would serve as a challenge which Jesse could not ignore. The only question that remained was what form the fight would take.

And then Tom Hatfield spoke the words that sealed his doom. "You think you're such a goddamned big-shot badman, don't you Mister Jesse James? But I say you ain't shit!"

Hatfield put a hand on the ground beside him and began to turn. He could have been reaching for a weapon, but more likely he was simply shifting his position so he could face Jesse more directly. No one would ever know for sure, because an instant later he lay dead.

They all sat silently for a moment as the sound of the gunshot echoed through the empty forest. No one had actually seen Jesse draw, but it surprised none of them to see the smoking revolver which he now held in his hand. Drunk or sober, he was amazingly fast and accurate with a handgun.

"Damn it, Jesse," Frank exclaimed. "What

did you do that for? Hell! Tom was our friend, and now you've killed him!"

"Friend or not, no man ever cussed me like that and got away with it," Jesse said. "And besides, he was getting ready to draw on me. I just beat him to the shot."

Tom Hatfield lay toppled over on his left side as if he had simply fallen asleep and slumped over. The small round wound in the middle of his forehead was so well placed and so immediately fatal that it hardly even bled. For a little while they all just sat there staring at him in disbelief, wondering, at the fragile nature of life and the sudden permanence of death.

"There was no call to kill him, Jesse," Daniel Hartman found himself saying. "If you didn't like him cussing you, you could have beat him up or run him off."

"I told you, he was trying to draw on me," Jesse replied angrily.

"Look, damn it!" Daniel insisted. "The flap is still down over his holster! He wasn't trying to draw. He was just turning, and you killed him for that! What the hell's got into you, Jesse?"

They all looked over and saw that the leather flap which protected Tom Hatfield's sidearm was indeed still buttoned down over the handle and hammer of his revolver.

If he had been reaching for it when Jesse shot him then his action was tantamount to suicide, but the men who knew him well knew that he wasn't the type to do anything so foolish in the midst of a fight. He wouldn't have tried to draw his gun under such a disadvantage.

But Jesse James was still not willing to admit that the killing might not have been necessary.

"Look, Dan," he exclaimed, staring intently at his friend, his eyes ablaze. "You sat right there and listened to Tom cussing me like I was some kind of dog. Would you take that kind of treatment from any man, friend or foe? Would you just swallow it all down and then tell him, 'Thank you. Can I have some more, Mister Hatfield?' "

"I wouldn't have started the goddamned fight in the first place, Jesse!" Daniel replied heatedly. "I wouldn't have gotten drunk on the night before a big job, and I wouldn't have let such a stupid argument get so far, and I wouldn't have killed a man I've known for fifteen years over the last swallow of rotgut whiskey in a bottle."

All the other men there were beginning to watch Daniel apprehensively, wondering whether he would anger Jesse as Tom Hatfield had done. But some were also agreeing with every word he said. Jesse had gone too far this time, and somebody needed to tell him.

"I've heard just about enough out of you," Jesse James warned. He still held the revolver he had used to kill Hatfield. "Even you can push me too far if you aren't careful."

"What do you mean by that?" Daniel demanded. "What are you going to do? Wait until I reach around to scratch my ass and then put a bullet between my eyes like you did to Tom? And then who will you plug after that? My brother John? And then Cole, and then his brothers after him?

"Christ almighty, Jesse! You and I have been friends since we were kids. I saved your life when we were fourteen years old, and we've ridden side by side through every kind of crossfire and ambush a man can imagine. I know you about as well as any man on earth, including your own brother Frank. But I still can't figure out what's happened to you lately. It's like nothing and nobody matters to you any more . . . not your friends, or your honor, or maybe even your own family.

"I don't know you anymore, Jesse. Not really. And seeing you the way you are now, I'm not sure you're the kind of man I want to know."

The stillness around the campfire was so complete that every nighttime sound seemed magnified. Crickets chirruped in the bush nearby, oblivious to the deadly doings of the men around the fire, and somewhere deep in the woods a hoot owl moaned out its plaintive call as it swooped smoothly through the forest in search of prey. Daniel Hartman knew that at that moment his life hung by a thread.

"Don't do it, Jesse," Frank pleaded with his brother, his voice low and even. "There's not a man here who will let you get away with killing Dan. Not even me."

Jesse James remained absolutely still, his finger on the trigger of his pistol and his eyes dark with deadly menace. "Then get him out of here, Frank," he spat. "Just get him clear the hell away from me."

Daniel needed no other encouragement to leave. Without another word, he rose and began gathering up his bedroll and other gear. John hesitated only a moment before doing the same. The others watched quietly as they assembled their belongings. Then when they turned and started over to where the horses were tethered, Cole Younger got up and followed after them.

John and Daniel started saddling their

horses while Cole stood nearby watching. The three of them were far enough away from the others that they could speak freely without being overheard as long as they kept their voices quiet.

"It needed saying, Dan," Cole offered. "You did the right thing, and I doubt that a single one of the other men would have argued with anything you said."

"Well, I guess I could have chosen a better time," Daniel admitted. "But it's done now, and I'm not sorry. I've seen Jesse do some pretty mean things in his day, but tonight this had to be about the lowest he's ever stooped."

"By the way, Cole," John Hartman spoke up. "I saw what you were doing over there to the side, and I appreciate it."

"Well, do you think I would just sit by and let Jesse shoot either one of you in cold blood?" Cole replied.

Daniel paused from his efforts and turned to them. "What are you two talking about?" he asked.

"Cole had Jesse covered the whole time. I saw it, and some of the others did too. Even Frank, I think."

"If he'd even flinched that trigger finger," Cole vowed, "I would have killed him. But I'm glad it didn't come to that because I hate to think what would have happened afterward. Frank would probably have felt bound by honor to do something about it, and he and I are too good friends to be snapping off rounds at each other."

"Thanks, Cole," Daniel said. "I'd say I owed you one, but John and I already owe you our lives so many times that I guess one more doesn't make much difference."

"It's balanced out over the years," Cole assured him. "I guess not one of us would be around today if it weren't for the others." He paused for a moment, obviously uncomfortable with what he wanted to say next, but finally he made an attempt to get it out. "Listen, you two, about your leaving . . ." he began. "If it was any other time and any other robbery, I'd be saddling up right now too. . . ."

"It's okay, Cole," Daniel told him. "I don't expect that of you. What you did was enough."

"It's just that I need the money so bad this time," Cole went on. "I'd already made up my mind that this was going to be the last time for me, and this thing tonight has made me feel more strongly about that than ever. But I need a good stake and I need it bad. Mollie and I have made some plans. . . ."

"There's still eight of you left, and that's plenty for this job," John said. "You stick around and get your stake. Dan and I don't mind. Honestly we don't."

"All right, then," Cole said. "You two take care on the way back home, and I guess I'll be seeing you a few days from now."

"You're the ones that had better take care," Daniel reminded his friend. "And just remember that here it's not like it is back home. This is Yankeeland, Cole, and if you get in a jam, you won't be able to trust anybody in these parts. No matter what happens, all you'll have is each other."

"Isn't that pretty much the way it's always been?" Cole asked, grinning as he reached out to shake the hands of his two friends before they left. "Most times, all we've ever had was each other, but that's always been enough . . . up to now."

"Up to now it has," Daniel agreed.

Cole Younger and the two James brothers entered the First National Bank with the same cool confidence which they always displayed in situations such as this. As usual, Jesse's plan was a fairly simple one, relying more on the skill and daring of its participants than on any complex strategy.

Just outside the door Bill Chadwell and

357

Clell Miller waited, their guns concealed under the flaps of their jackets. The other three members of the band, Charlie Pitts and Jim and Bob Younger, were stationed a couple of blocks away on the edge of town, ready to ride in and lend a hand if their guns were needed.

Only two employees were in the bank when the outlaws entered. One was seated behind a small desk at the rear of the building near the vault, and the other was standing in a teller's cage counting money into a small cash drawer built into the counter in front of him.

All three of the bank robbers drew their guns as soon as they were inside the building. As planned, Cole remained near the door to keep anyone else from coming in the bank while Frank and Jesse moved around behind the counter to gather their loot. Before the startled teller could even open his mouth to complain, Frank jammed a revolver into his ribs and suggested that he keep his mouth shut and cooperate if he wanted to live through the rest of the day. Jesse moved straight back to the man behind the desk and uttered a similar threat.

"All we want is to take what's in that safe over there," Jesse explained to his captive. "We can have this over with and be out of here in five minutes flat if you'll just open the door to the vault and let us get what we came for."

"I'm not going to open the safe for you," the prisoner replied abruptly. He seemed almost insulted by the mere suggestion that he would do such a thing.

As could be expected, Jesse responded to the man's words suddenly and violently. Holstering his gun, he grabbed the man by both lapels, dragged him over the desk and slammed his back against the closed door of the vault. His victim cried out in pain as the lever on the front of the door smashed into the small of his back.

"Now are you going to open it?" Jesse demanded furiously.

"No!" the man replied through teeth clenched in pain.

Jesse James slammed the man against the vault door three more times in rapid succession, then drew a long knife from a sheath on the back of his belt. Holding the blade close against his victim's throat, he snarled, "If you don't open that damn door right now, I'm going to kill you! Don't you understand that, you lame-brained idiot?"

"Then do what you must," the man responded, "and damn you for it."

"No, Jesse! Don't!" Frank called out

urgently from a few feet away, but it was already too late.

The man against the vault door instinctively raised both hands to his neck, but of course there was no way to stem the sudden crimson flood from his severed throat. A look of terrified disbelief flashed over his features as he slumped slowly toward the floor, but his executioner ignored it as he released his victim's lapel and turned away toward the second captive bank employee.

"Dammit, Jesse, he's not dead yet!" Frank James exclaimed furiously, pointing toward the vault. The man whose throat Jesse had cut seemed to have gone into some sort of feeble convulsion, and a stream of pathetic gurglings were coming from his severed windpipe. "You can't leave him like that!"

"He won't cause us any trouble," Jesse replied. "Now let's go to work on this other fellow and see if he's ready to die the same way."

"I said you can't leave him like that!" Frank repeated angrily. And with that, he shoved past his brother and stormed across the room to where the mortally injured man lay. He raised his revolver and fired one quick shot into the man's temple, which brought an immediate end to his torment.

Jesse whirled again to curse his brother

for the noise he had made, and in an instant they were nose to nose, so lividly angry at one another that they seemed to have forgotten all about where they were and what they were doing.

Then from the front door a second shot rang out only seconds after Frank had fired the first one.

"You two idiots have just let the damned teller escape!" Cole Younger roared, pointing to a side door which the man had flung open to get out of the building. "I think I might have winged him, but he didn't go down."

"I'll get him," Jesse said starting for the door.

"No. Forget it. He's long gone by now, and we've got to get out of here. I'll bet half the town heard those shots, and in a couple of minutes they're going to be on this place like flies on a dead horse."

As if to fulfill his prediction, a third shot sounded from somewhere outside the bank followed by at least half a dozen more. Cole looked around in time to see Clell Miller spin and fall, clawing at his left shoulder as he went down. He tried to rise again, but then a second shot found its mark and he crumpled face-down in the dirt. Bill Chadwell, who was standing in the middle of the street firing like a maniac into the buildings on the opposite side, went down a moment later.

Cole Younger threw open the door of the bank and made a leap for the horses which were tied to a rail only a few feet away. One of the animals had already been killed by the gunfire, but he managed to make it astride another one that seemed uninjured. Frank and Jesse James were out of the bank building and mounted only seconds after Cole.

Far down the street Cole spotted his two brothers and Charlie Pitts riding in to help. They were firing their guns wildly into the buildings on either side of them as they approached, and the confusion they provided gave Cole, Frank and Jesse the opportunity to escape the hornet's nest of gunfire which was buzzing all around them. In a ragged, howling mob, all six outlaws put the spurs to their horses and thundered away toward the edge of town.

Cole Younger made it about thirty yards before his horse was shot out from under him. He was thrown clear as the animal went down, and then he scurried back on his belly toward the carcass so he could have at least a small amount of shelter from the steady gunfire across the street. Both of his revolvers were empty now, and he had already suffered two minor bullet wounds, one on the forearm and another across the top of his left shoulder.

Over the din of the gunfire a wild rebel yell sounded down the street to the west, and Cole glanced up to see a horse and rider thundering at full speed toward him. It was Frank James. Cole waited until the last possible second, then leaped to his feet and reached out to grab a handful of the horse's mane. He was immediately knocked off his feet as Frank spun his mount around and started back the other way, but he hung on desperately and let himself be dragged away. After they had cleared the worst of the gunfire, Frank stopped long enough for Cole to leap up behind him, then put his spurs to his horse again and raced out of town.

CHAPTER NINETEEN

They were holed up in a small creek cut which twisted through a dense tangle of scrub oak and nearly impenetrable brush. The cut was over six feet deep and ten wide, and along one side there was just enough of a sand bar for them to make a camp on. Charlie Pitts had found the place just before dark, and they hoped that it would be remote and unapproachable enough to give them some respite from the determined posses who had been dogging them ever since the aborted Northfield robbery three days earlier.

Frank and Jesse James had abandoned their companions, so now there were only four men left in the small, desperate band. All four had been wounded during the shootout in Northfield, but Cole's brother Bob was the most seriously injured of the lot. He was suffering terribly from a bullet wound in his abdomen, and now after such a long stretch without medical attention, he was out of his mind most of the time and scarcely able to ride more than a mile or two without stopping to rest.

Although Cole's and his brother Jim's wounds were less severe, both were still in considerable pain. Jim had a nasty hole in his shoulder which would soon become a problem if it wasn't properly cleaned and dressed, and Cole had three minor wounds which were all beginning to swell and fester. Of the four of them, only Charlie Pitts was still in reasonably good shape, and he had assumed most of the scouting and foraging responsibilities since Frank and Jesse's departure.

Cole was crouched over the small twig fire which the cold had finally forced him to build, thinking despondently about the continued danger and suffering which the next day would undoubtedly hold for them. He was nearly naked now. He had sacrificed some of his clothing for bandages, and most of the rest of his ragged garments lay draped over his feverish, unconscious brother Bob. None of them had eaten a bite of food in over forty-eight hours, and now the hunger pangs in Cole's stomach were becoming nearly as vicious as the pain of his throbbing wounds.

It seemed like half the state of Minnesota must be out combing the roads and woods looking for the bank robbers. Not only had the posse from Northfield been relentless in its pursuit, but word must have gone ahead by telegraph because in every direction they turned it seemed like there was another roadblock to avoid or another band of armed and determined farmers to elude. Thus far, Charlie Pitts had done a pretty good job of keeping them out of sight and out of trouble, but Cole knew that it was probably only a matter of time before they were finally discovered and trapped.

They had already decided that they would fight to the last man when the time came. If they were captured, they knew there wasn't much chance of any of them making it back to Northfield alive, not after the bloody mess they had left the town in, and none of them wanted to suffer the humiliation of being lynched by their captors. But despite their vow, Cole realized that even the questionable privilege of dying with guns in their hands might be denied them if the final shootout took very long. Among the four of them, not more than three dozen pistol and rifle cartridges remained.

As a precaution, Cole scattered the embers of his pathetic little fire when he heard the sound of someone approaching the camp up the stony creek bed. He knew it was bound to be Charlie returning after a reconnaissance of the area, but the habits of a lifetime still prevailed. He picked up his revolver from the ground at his feet, then reached out and silently shook Jim awake. They waited with their weapons ready until Charlie Pitts came into sight around a bend in the creek cut. He was on foot because he had decided earlier that it would be too difficult to scout the dense brush which surrounded them on horseback.

"I think we've got problems," Pitts announced, his voice low and urgent. "There's a posse about half a mile east of here and they're headed this way. When I spotted them, some of them were on foot and they were carrying lanterns. It looked to me like they were working out our trail."

"Damn!" Cole muttered. "We must have been spotted as we started into the woods before dark."

"That's my guess," Pitts agreed, "and whoever saw us must have gone for help because there's at least a dozen men in the group."

"So what do we do now, Cole?" Jim asked. "I don't think we'll be able to get Bob back on a horse."

"Maybe we can rig a travois," Cole said. "Some of these pine saplings should work for that, and we can stretch a blanket across them for him to ride on. How long do you think we have, Charlie?"

"Half an hour, maybe," Pitts said. "It's slow going for them trying to work out our sign through this brush."

"All right then. Let's do it," Cole said, rising to his feet. "Charlie, you head on back and keep an eye on them so they won't get right on top of us without our knowing. When we leave here, we'll head due west until we reach the edge of these woods, and then we'll turn back south again. If you aren't back by the time we're ready to go, we'll leave a horse here for you. You shouldn't have any problem catching up with us."

"Don't worry. I'll find you, Cole," Pitts promised. "I'm not about to take off and leave you fellows behind like those yellow-bellied James boys did."

"It never crossed my mind that you would, Charlie," Cole replied. "You're too good a friend for that."

After Pitts was gone again, Cole and Jim busied themselves assembling a travois and strapping it onto the stoutest of their four remaining horses. Bob's only response when they lifted him onto the makeshift stretcher was a low, delirious moan of pain. Jim rolled his blanket up and put it under his brother's head for a pillow, then he and Cole tied Bob securely in place on the travois.

"I think we'd better lead the horses for a while, Jim, at least until the brush starts to thin some," Cole instructed. "You take two of them and go on ahead, and I'll take care of Bob."

After they had gathered up the rest of their meager camp gear, Jim untied two of their mounts and started west along the creek cut. A minute later Cole took the reins of the horse which bore his unconscious brother and started up. They followed the creek for a couple of hundred yards, then Jim found what looked like a trail and headed out into the thick woods. The ground was smoother once they left the creek bed, but the trail itself was narrow, and the thick brush on either side grabbed and clawed at them every step of the way.

Cole had no real idea where they were going, but he could tell by the position of the moon that they were staying on a generally westerly course. That was the most he could hope for at the moment. He began to warm up somewhat now that he had put his clothes back on and they were moving, but the brush and briars were sharp and scratched his arms, adding greatly to the discomfort of the trek.

Within an hour the woods began to thin, and then finally the outlaws emerged into what seemed to be the edge of a large open pasture. The way ahead seemed clear, but in the darkness it was impossible to tell for sure.

"South?" Jim asked.

"I guess so," Cole replied. "Let's follow the tree line for a while so we can get out of sight if we have to. When Charlie catches up to us, we can work out what direction we want to go in after that."

They had gone only another fifty yards or so when the sound of a rifle shot barked out in the woods behind them. To Cole's well-trained ear, it sounded like a shot from the lever-action Winchester that Charlie Pitts carried. A moment later, the lone shot was answered by a barrage of gunfire from several different types of weapons. Other than the fact that Pitts had obviously stopped to confront the posse, the most alarming thing about the gunfire was its surprising nearness. As best Cole could judge, the men who were after them were no more than three or four hundred yards back now.

"Damn, Cole! They're right on top of us!" Jim called out urgently. "What are we going to do?"

"Well, there's not much use in trying to hide from the bastards," Cole said, glancing briefly behind him to their back trail. Even in the moonlight, the two parallel ruts that the travois had dug into the earth were clearly visible. The only way he and Jim could possibly hope to escape at this point would be to leave Bob behind, and that alternative was so unthinkable that neither of them even bothered to mention it. "I guess this is as good a place as any to die, little brother," he added.

"I suppose it is, Cole," Jim said. His voice less steady than his brother's.

They moved into the edge of the woods and gently lifted their unconscious brother onto the ground. Then they turned the horses loose, checked their weapons, and took shelter behind the trunk of a fallen tree near the edge of the open pasture.

The gunfire behind them had stopped by then. Both knew what that meant. Charlie Pitts was dead.

"Save one bullet for Bob," Cole said quietly, "and I'll do the same. Whichever one of us is the last alive will have to finish him."

"I don't know if I can do it, Cole," Jim said obviously horrified at the thought. "I don't know if I have it in me to shoot my own brother."

"If it's you that has to, then you'll do it," Cole said. "Just imagine them tying a rope around Bob's neck and hauling him up off the ground. You'll manage it when the time comes."

After that they waited in silence for the posse to emerge from the woods. The worst part about all of this, Cole decided, was that now he must die knowing that he was responsible for the deaths of his two brothers. Except for him, they would never have taken up the outlaw life and now the blame for their deaths lay squarely on his shoulders.

But there were other regrets as well . . . the many heartaches he had caused his mother and family and the trouble that his wild living had occasionally brought on his friends. Yes, there would be a lot to answer for in the next life, Cole thought grimly, and now that final reckoning seemed only moments away.

And then, of course, there was Mollie. At last it had all seemed right for them. For the first time, Cole had thought that he could settle down and become the kind of man that Mollie deserved to have in her life. But maybe the fact that he had to go out just one more time said more about him than all his good intentions. If he and Mollie had ended up together, there might have always been those "one more times" for him despite all his promises and his desire to change for her sake. He was a gunman and an outlaw, and those were things that a man couldn't always put behind him simply because he wanted to.

At last it became evident that the posse was not going to ride boldly out in the open where they would be an easy target. After their recent exchange of gunfire with Pitts, they were probably convinced that more of their opponents were nearby, and they were being extremely careful about their advance.

Finally a deep voice boomed out in the distance. "This is Marshal Patrick Norwood. You men might as well give it up now. It's over. Your friend back here is dead, and you're next unless you lay down your guns and come out." There was a brief silence, and then the marshal added, "If you surrender, I promise you'll receive fair treatment and that you'll be taken back to Northfield for trial. No posse I've led has ever lynched a single man, and I'm not about to let it start now."

"What do you think, Cole?" Jim asked. "Do you think he might be telling the truth?"

"There's no way to tell," Cole replied. "It could be true, or he might just be saying whatever he thinks it will take to get us out in the open."

"You're right," Jim agreed, "but you know what I've been thinking, Cole? I've been thinking that I just don't feel like killing any of those men out there. They're doing what they're supposed to, and I don't hold anything against any of them because of it."

"I don't really feel like it either," Cole admitted wearily.

"You men!" the marshal called out again. "We know you've got wounded with you, and I promise they'll be taken care of. Anybody that needs medical care will get it. But I just don't want to see anybody else get killed. Not any of us, nor any of you either. At this point, there's just no need of it anymore."

Cole looked over at his two brothers, and he pictured the overwhelming grief that their mother would suffer when she heard that all three of her sons had been killed during one night in a shootout with the law. If there was even a chance that they could spare her that, if there was even a possibility

374

that this marshal was telling the truth, then maybe they should surrender.

"Talking about fighting to the death is one thing," Jim said, a pleading look in his eyes. "But then actually doing it when the time comes is something altogether different. I don't want to die, Cole. I'm not afraid and I'll stick with you no matter what you decide, but I don't really want to die."

"I don't guess I do either, Jim," Cole said. He slowly lowered the hammer of his revolver and laid it on the ground beside him. Then he began to rise, favoring his injured leg and shoulder as much as possible. "I guess it is over now, once and for all."

Morgan Hartman reclined on the bed in his hotel room, smoking a cigar and rereading for the third time the newspaper account of the capture of the Younger brothers. He had been away in Texas checking out a reported sighting of Jesse James when news of the Northfield robbery and shootout first began to circulate. Though he'd started north immediately, he had been too late to participate in the manhunt for the surviving members of the gang.

At this point there was little doubt in anybody's mind that the Northfield raid was the work of the James Gang, and the newspaper story was filled with speculation about which gang members, besides Frank and Jesse, remained at large. As best as the authorities in Northfield could guess only eight men took part in the actual raid, and yet a larger party, composed of perhaps as many as ten to twelve men, had been seen traveling north across Minnesota prior to the incident. That meant either more than eight men were involved in the raid, or that some additional men had gone along but had not participated in the abortive bank robbery and subsequent shootout.

Morgan thought it likely that there were more than eight men, and he had a pretty good idea that two of those additional men were his cousins, John and Daniel Hartman.

His job as a Pinkerton operative required him to seek the capture of all the members of the gang, but even more important than that mandate from his employer was his own personal obsession with pursuing John and Daniel because of his hatred for their father. It would have been easy enough, of course, simply to kill Jason Hartman, but he knew that in the long run he could punish his uncle far more by causing the deaths of his sons and then making sure he knew why they had died.

Now, in the aftermath of this Northfield

business, Morgan Hartman recognized the opportunity he needed to gain the revenge he had yearned for these many years. At this particular time there could be no doubt in anybody's mind about the collective guilt of the members of the James Gang. No one would be likely to protest the killing of two men associated with that gang, no matter how questionable the circumstances of their deaths might be.

It was time to go after John and Daniel Hartman, but unlike their cronies in Minnesota, there would be no trial and imprisonment for the Hartman brothers after they were caught. In the mind of their cousin they were just as good as dead already.

He had come as far as Independence, which was as close to Clay County as any Pinkerton agent dared to venture alone these days, and he was waiting now to receive the reports from the spies he had sent north into the home county of the gang members. The men who were gathering information for him had lived in Clay County for most of their lives and were acquainted with both the Hartman and the James families. Because they were free to travel around the county without arousing any particular suspicion, they could gather information which a stranger might die trying to obtain.

Throughout the long afternoon, Morgan Hartman waited patiently in his hotel room. Since arriving here three days ago and dispatching his spies, he had ventured out only once, at night, to replenish his supply of food and whiskey. Now he was getting ready for something to happen.

Finally, shortly after dark, there was a light knock on the door. Hartman rose and picked up his revolver from the table beside the bed, then went over and unlocked the door to his room. Two men slipped furtively into the room, both acting as if the walls of the hall outside had eyes and ears. They liked Morgan Hartman's gold too much to pass up the assignments he gave to them, but they were also well aware of what would happen to them if word ever got out about their activities. Even here in the next county, it would still be risky to be seen talking to a Pinkerton agent.

Their names were Bill Ford and Henry Maddox. Both were slovenly, characterless rogues, the kind of men who spent their lives searching for any sort of scheme or device which would help them survive without the encumbrance of honest labor. Morgan despised both men and considered them far below him, but professionally, they served their purpose and he was usually careful to disguise the disgust he felt when in their presence.

The three of them gathered at the small table in the room and Hartman poured healthy shots of whiskey into three glasses. Maddox gulped his down quickly in the manner of an alcoholic too long deprived of his vice, but Ford took his in three measured gulps, like an invalid swallowing medicine. Both seemed nervous about being here, so Hartman gave them a minute to compose themselves before he began his interrogation.

"We had us a close call yesterday afternoon," Maddox explained, "and my nerves've been shot ever since."

"What happened?" Hartman asked.

"We got seen in the woods out behind Sarah Parkman's place," Maddox said. "We'd been up close watching the house and we were headed back toward where we'd left our horses when we came across the youngest Hartman boy, Benjamin, out in the woods looking for a lost hog."

"We had a story all made up and we put it on him," Ford said, picking up the thread of the tale. "We told him we'd been hunting rabbits in there the day before and that two of our dogs had run off, so we'd come back the next day looking for them."

"Did he believe you?" Hartman asked.

"He acted like he did," Ford answered, "but there wasn't no real way to tell. Since that Northfield business, folks around there have been pretty jumpy, but we were quite a piece from his aunt's place so he might not have made any connection. But anyway, both me and Henry had rifles and he wasn't armed, so he didn't give us a hard time about it."

"Did he say anything about his brothers?"

"Nope, and we didn't ask neither," Ford replied. "The way things are up there right now, if those two found out that we were asking around about them, there's no telling what they might do. Even if they didn't suspect us, it could be they might decide to shut us up just for safety's sake."

"But anyway, we didn't need to ask Benjamin nothing," Maddox added proudly, "because we already found out what we wanted to know. That's why we were headed back to our horses."

"So what did you find out?" Hartman asked, finally growing impatient.

"Oh, they were there all right," Maddox said. "It took us nearly two days to find out even that much, but when we did finally catch sight of them yesterday afternoon, it was when they came out to leave. They saddled up two horses, packed some gear on a mule, and left about four yesterday afternoon."

"From the sound of that, they must have a long trip in mind," the Pinkerton said. "I don't guess you have any idea where they might be heading, do you?"

"Sure, they're going to Texas," Maddox revealed. "We found that out from Tyler Wilson. He's got a little store about two miles south of Sarah Parkman's place, and they stopped in there for some supplies on their way out. They told Tyler they aimed to be passing through Dallas where his sister lives and promised to stop in and pay her a call. Later in the day when we stopped by the store we mentioned to Tyler, sort of casual like, that we'd seen the Hartman brothers leaving out for someplace, and he told us all about it."

"They must have decided that things would be getting too hot for them around here after that business up in Northfield," Ford speculated. "Now that the Youngers are out of commission and Frank and Jesse James have disappeared to God-knows-where again, I bet they decided that Clay County won't be quite so safe as it used to be for them."

381

"Well I've got news for them," Hartman replied. "Texas won't be safe either, that is if they even manage to live long enough to get to Texas. Now what else do you have to report?"

"Well, they spent the night at Deacon Spear's place outside Liberty, and this morning they started south again," Maddox said. "We would have followed them, but it just seemed too risky, and besides, we had to come here and tell you what we found out."

Morgan Hartman was very pleased with the intelligence his two informants had provided. The mere fact that John and Daniel Hartman seemed to be on the run lent strength to his supposition that they had probably been involved in the Northfield raid, and the fact that they had left Clay County gave him a great advantage because that placed them farther away from family and friends who might help them if trouble started. They should be easy enough to trail as long as they didn't know anyone was after them, and by the time they discovered that they were being pursued, it would probably be too late for them to do anything about it. He had them at last!

After paying off Ford and Maddox, Morgan Hartman sent his two informants on their way. Their type would be little use to him during the next step of his plan. They were valuable enough for weaseling around and sticking their noses into others people's affairs, but for the actual kill he needed another breed entirely. He needed men who were good with guns, men of little conscience who had few qualms about shedding blood when the need arose . . . and he knew just where to find them, too. All that would be required would be a telegram or two to the right men in Lawrence, Kansas.

Chapter Twenty

Daniel Hartman tried to divide his time equally between the card game and the woman on his lap. She was a cute little redhead with dancing green eyes and a saucy smile. As long as he kept slipping an occasional tip down the front of her low-cut costume, she kept the attention coming. She told him her name was Iris.

He was doing fairly well in the low-stakes poker game, too, and though he knew he wasn't likely to leave the Lucky Dollar Saloon a wealthy man, at least he was winning enough to pay for his drinks and for female companionship. That was all he had come for anyway.

John had left the saloon a short time before, explaining that he was going to return to his hotel room, write a letter to their parents, and go to bed. Under other circumstances, Daniel might have gone with him, but the idea of spending some time alone with Iris later in the evening had begun to intrigue him, and he had decided to stay on and explore the possibilities.

The two brothers were a three-day journey from home now, and tonight was the first they had chosen to sleep in a hotel rather than on the trail. They were in a town called Joplin, which was about a hundred miles due south of Kansas City. Nobody knew them there, and this deep into the state the furor over the Northfield robbery seemed less intense, so John and Daniel felt reasonably safe in checking into a hotel under the assumed names of John Hill and Robert Daniels. They posed as horse traders, which was always a safe ruse in this part of the country.

It had not been an easy decision for them to pick up stakes and start for Texas. Everyone they cared about lived in Missouri, and they knew when they headed out that it might be years before they returned home again. But in the end, it seemed the only sensible alternative.

Although they had not participated in the Northfield raid, it had been a sobering experience for them nonetheless. Four of their friends were dead and three others, including Cole Younger, faced decades of imprisonment as a result of the abortive robbery. Both John and Daniel felt that the problems the gang ran into were probably the fault of Frank and Jesse James, and they realized when they read the newspaper accounts of the shootout in the streets of Northfield that, had the two of them been there, they too would probably be either dead or in jail right now.

But even though they had not taken part in the raid, John and Daniel were beginning to believe that Clay County was no longer safe for them. If they continued to live there as they had in the past, they would not only be endangering their own lives, but also the lives of all the people they were closest to.

The old days were over, and if the Hartman brothers expected to survive, they knew they needed to face up to all the new realities in their lives.

But Texas wouldn't be so bad. John and Daniel were taking along several thousand dollars in cash, their split from past robberies, and they knew they would find good opportunities to invest in the business they enjoyed the most: horse breeding and trading. Their new life would not be without its rewards.

When Iris finally began to fidget after more than an hour on Daniel's lap, he decided to cash out of the poker game and devote his full attention to more amorous indulgences. Carrying his half-full whiskey bottle and the stack of money from the game, he led the way to the rear of the Lucky Dollar where he and Iris could talk. After sitting down at the table, he peeled off ten dollars and gave it to the girl — for bringing him luck, he explained — then stashed the rest of the money in his coat pocket. The girl watched the cash with hungry, calculating eyes as it disappeared from view.

"I suppose they'll be closing this place down pretty soon," Daniel said.

"They have to close at twelve," Iris explained. "It's a town ordinance."

"Well, I hate to think we'll have to part company when that happens," Daniel told her. "You're a mighty pretty girl, and it's been a pleasure spending the evening with you. I don't want it to end, not just yet."

"Maybe it will and maybe it won't," Iris said smiling seductively. "After midnight I'm on my own time. I can do what I please with whomever I please."

"I have an idea, then," Daniel suggested. "I'll get another bottle of something, maybe some brandy, and we can have a nightcap in my room. The hotel is just next door and. . . ." His voice trailed away as his eyes settled on a man who was just passing through the Lucky Dollar's batwing doors.

There was something about the man that made Daniel uneasy. It was something in the eyes, and in the way he wore his gun. A minute later another, similar stranger came into the place, and then a third. After looking carefully around the room, they all strode over to the wooden bar and ordered drinks.

"Do you know those men, Robert?" Iris asked Daniel. She had obviously worked in places like this long enough to recognize trouble on the hoof.

"No. Do you?" Daniel replied.

"I've never seen them before. I don't think they're from around these parts. Their kind would be in the Lucky Dollar all the time if they lived nearby."

Daniel quickly took stock of the situation. He hadn't had so much to drink that he couldn't shoot straight and fast if the need arose, but he would still be outnumbered three to one if trouble started. He worked through a couple of scenarios one at a time in his mind, considering the practicality of each. *Draw as you shove the girl out of the way, dive for the floor and take them out one at a time, right to left . . . draw as you stand up and then start shooting as you leap for the*

388

back door . . . draw and charge.

They were curious about him, too. That became obvious after only a minute or two by the way they kept glancing over their shoulders in his direction. As yet they had given no indication that they intended to start trouble; still, Daniel could smell it in the air.

"Has this place got a back door?" Daniel asked Iris.

"Yes, over there," the girl answered, nodding to the left. "It goes through the storage room, and there's another door that leads to an alley out back." By now she had picked up on the fact that the romance was over. She had not quite figured out what was going on yet, but she did understand that something serious was unfolding.

"I want you to do something for me, Iris," Daniel told her, "and I'm going to make it very much worth your while to do it. In another minute or two, I want you to get up and stomp away from me like I said something to make you mad. Then, the first chance you get, I want you to slip out the back door and go wake the man in room 213 in the hotel next door. Just tell him there's trouble and that I need him."

"What do you mean by 'very much worth

my while?' " the saloon girl asked suspiciously.

"When you get back, I'll give you all the money I put in my pocket awhile ago. It's about forty or fifty dollars," Daniel promised.

"Better give it to me now," she said. "From the looks of those three, you might not be around when I get back, or you might have 'forgotten' what you promised me by then. You understand, don't you? A girl like me just has to get her money up front."

Reluctantly Daniel pulled out the folded wad of bills and passed it to her under the table. She was right, of course, but now that she had the money, there was no guarantee that she would carry out her mission. Once she was out the back door, all she had to do was go home instead of going for John. Iris somehow managed to make the money disappear into her undergarments. Then she slid her chair back from the table, leaped to her feet and slapped Daniel hard across the left cheek.

"Nobody calls me a name like that and gets away with it!" she said shrilly. "You men are all alike!"

"I . . . I'm sorry . . ." Daniel stammered.

Iris flounced away indignantly, flipping her

skirts as she walked as if to give him a glimpse of what he was missing. She headed straight for the back door, opened it, and stormed out.

The scene did not escape the attention of the three men at the bar, but none of them seemed to suspect anything. They continued to sip their drinks and to keep an eye on Daniel. It was as if they were waiting for something to happen, he thought. It occurred to him that maybe they wanted him to go outside so they could take care of their business with him in the street rather than her in the saloon where others might interfere or be injured by stray gunshots.

But if that was the case, they were going to have to wait a while longer. If he could manage it, Daniel didn't want to make anything happen until his brother was there to back his play. And so he remained at the table, raising his glass to his lips occasionally but no longer drinking, staring off forlornly into space like any jilted, half-drunk fellow might.

The fourth stranger to enter the saloon brought a whole new wave of tension with him. As soon as Daniel laid eyes on him, he realized that here was the real force to be reckoned with. The other three were just hired guns, but this was the man who told them when to shoot and who to shoot at. The newcomer conferred with the others for a moment, then turned to stare at Daniel with fierce, open glee.

"I've been looking forward to this moment for years now," the stranger said loudly, looking Daniel straight in the eye across the thirty feet which separated them. "But you don't even know who I am, do you?"

"Don't know, and don't much care to," Daniel answered nonchalantly.

All around the place, men were beginning to realize what was happening and to move away from what would soon be the line of fire. A number of them simply left the saloon, but quite a few others remained, willing to risk the danger in order to witness the gunplay and bloodshed. Even the bartender seemed more interested than concerned by the confrontation that was shaping up.

"Any man should be interested in knowing the name of the man that kills him," the stranger said coldly.

"Well, you seem to know who I am, so I guess that takes care of that," Daniel replied. Generally he hated a lot of talk before a fight. It didn't serve any purpose and it just delayed the inevitable. But in this case he was glad to swap tough-talk with this stranger because every second that passed only brought his brother that much closer to being on hand when the bullets started flying.

"Well, maybe it might interest you if I told you that I was there the day that godless old reprobate of a grandfather of yours was killed. In fact, I was the one who killed the old bastard. I gut shot him on purpose because I didn't want him to die right away. I figured a man like him deserved to go slow."

Daniel had all he could do to keep from reaching for his gun, but he realized that at this critical moment, he couldn't afford to let the rush of anger and hatred he was feeling affect his judgment in any way. Years ago, even before the war was over, he and his brother had sworn a solemn vow to kill this man, their cousin Morgan Hartman, on sight. Now here was the man and the opportunity, but Daniel knew he must keep his head if he expected to survive the evening.

"You're right, that does interest me," Daniel admitted. "I always wanted to see how a skunk who was so low that he would kill his own grandfather managed to walk upright on his hind legs and pass himself off as a man. Hell, when I kill you, Cousin Morgan,

393

you ought to die thanking me for finally putting you out of your misery."

Morgan simply sneered.

Daniel set his jaw and tried not to let his relief show when he saw his brother ease in the front door and blend into the crowd. Although he had missed everything that had been said up to this point, it took John only a moment to size up the situation. He began working his way gradually to the left, placing himself as close as possible to the three men who were with Morgan Hartman.

The time was close now. They could all feel it. The talk was over, and all that remained was for hands to reach for guns and triggers to be squeezed. It might take two seconds, or maybe even three, for this handful of men to sort themselves out into two categories . . . the living and the dead.

John started it. When he was close enough, he simply drew his gun and started blasting away at the backs of the three hired gunmen. It wasn't fair and it wasn't honorable, but it worked. John killed two of the men outright, then felled the third as he spun and drew in a desperate attempt to defend himself.

At the same instant, Daniel reached for the revolver at his side and made a dive for the floor. Some instinct had told him that

Morgan was fast with a gun, far too fast for a seated man to outdraw, so his only alternative was to provide a moving target. The two of them flung a couple of wild shots at each other, but no one was hit, and there were people between John and Morgan so he had no way of helping Daniel during those first few critical seconds.

Morgan Hartman was no fool, though. With his own men down, he realized immediately that he was dangerously outgunned, so after snapping off his first two shots he made a dash for the front door. He had plenty of company near the exit, and again John and Daniel were prevented from shooting at him by the presense of so many uninvolved bystanders.

But even as he was retreating, Morgan again showed his cunning. "They're outlaws! They're part of the James Gang!" he shouted out to the men around him. "A thousand dollars will go to the man who kills either one of them!"

There was, of course, no way to respond to such an announcement except to flee. John and Daniel both dove for the back door as the startled townsmen grasped the weight of Morgan's words and began to draw their weapons. Bullets peppered the door and walls of the storage room as they leaped across it and dashed out the back.

"This way!" Daniel said, bounding across the alley and then turning between two buildings. They could hear the sound of many men coming around the sides of the saloon behind them but neither paused to look back. They reloaded their weapons as they ran, knowing that in another few seconds they would probably have to shoot again.

When they reached the next street, they spotted a lone horse tied to a rail about twenty yards to the left. Without even discussing it, they both leaped onto the animal's back, John in front and Daniel behind, and galloped away down the street. Again shots whizzed past them before they had rounded the first corner, but the street was dark and the townsmen pursuing them were too excited to do any accurate shooting.

"Who were those bastards?" John asked his brother once they were momentarily out of the line of fire. Having come in on the tail end of things, he still had no clear idea why it had been necessary for him to walk into the saloon and gun down three men.

"The tall one, the one we didn't get, was Morgan Hartman," Daniel told his brother. "He told me right there in front of everybody that he was the man who shot our grandfather. It was one of the craziest things I ever saw, John. He seemed proud of it!"

"Well I wonder how he managed to find us here?"

"I don't know, but I do know one thing, and that is that we aren't through with him yet. Now that he's put a price on our heads, we're going to have a hundred men on our trail before another hour has passed." They rode along in silence for another moment or two, then Daniel thought to ask his brother, "What about the money, John?"

"I crammed some of it in my shirt before I left the room. I don't know how much. I told the girl that if we didn't come back, she could have our gear and whatever cash we left behind."

"I'm glad," Daniel said. "If it wasn't for her, I guess I'd be laid out on a slab right now."

As they neared the eastern edge of Joplin, the opportunity for them to get another mount presented itself. When John saw the lone horseman ahead of them, he slowed to an easy trot. The man they were coming up behind seemed to be heading home after a hard night of drinking because he weaved slightly in the saddle, and he seemed unaware that anyone else was nearby until the brothers had almost caught up with him. Then he looked around, bleary-eyed but seemingly unalarmed. "What's all that shootin' about back there?" he asked.

"Fight over a whore, I think," John replied.

"Well, I'm glad I got out of town when I did," the man commented. "I don't need no trouble tonight, not as drunk as I am. Sometimes when I get a snootful I get a notion that I can whip the world, and then the next morning. . . ."

As soon as they were close enough, Daniel drew his revolver and caught the man in the side of the head with a smooth backhanded blow. He toppled sideways out of the saddle like a felled tree, and John hardly needed to slow the pace of the horse he was riding as his brother leaped astride his new mount.

"What now?" Daniel asked.

"Well, if that bastard was able to find out we were here," John reasoned, "then he probably knows where we were heading, too, so I'd say Texas is out for the time being. We're headed east now, and it seems as good a direction as any other."

"All right, then," Daniel said, digging his heels into his horse's sides, "We've got the wind at our back and a decent lead. Let's just follow our noses for a while."

Sometimes Morgan Hartman found himself getting so angry at the men he was leading that it was all he could do to resist taking hold of one or another of them and beating the hell out of him. During the trek eastward from Joplin his posse had swelled to a virtual army of men, but still there did not seem to be a solid thimble full of competence in the whole lot of them. The scouts he sent out frequently managed to trample their horses over the very tracks they were trying to follow, and he couldn't impress on anybody that in order to track down and catch their quarry, they had to ride longer and harder than the men they were pursuing. Even the lawmen among them, mostly country constables and hick-town sheriffs, seemed more obsessed with who had authority over whom in the posse than in the actual pursuit of the outlaws themselves.

The only thing that kept them from losing track of the two outlaws was the burst of telegrams which Morgan sent out in all directions each time he arrived at any settlement large enough to support a telegraph office. It would be virtually impossible for the Hartmans to board a train anywhere nearby without being spotted and questioned. Even when they stopped to buy supplies or trade horses, somebody usually reported their passing to the local authorities.

Using the reports which filtered back to him, Morgan was able to track the course of the fugitives with a reasonable degree of accuracy, and somehow, incredible as it seemed, after three days of riding the net seemed to be tightening. Even as he led his makeshift posse eastward, other groups of men were beginning to fan out south and west from Springfield to prevent any possible escape in that direction.

What made Morgan Hartman the angriest, however, was the fiasco that had taken place in the Lucky Dollar Saloon in Joplin. He could hardly believe that he had been so close to victory and then had seen the whole thing fall apart. But it was his own fault, he had to admit. His own eagerness had caused him to close in with too few men and too little preparation. He should have waited until the rest of the men he had summoned from Lawrence and Kansas City caught up with him, and then he should have sprung the trap with no warning or senseless chatter.

At the very least, he knew now that he

should have drawn his gun and shot Daniel Hartman the instant he walked in the saloon. But somehow when the moment of confrontation had arrived, he had not been able to resist the urge to tell Daniel who he was and to let his cousin know why he was about to die. He had ignored all the lessons he had learned while dealing with the bushwhackers during the war, and the deaths of his three best men had been the result. But it wouldn't happen again, he vowed. Every man who now rode with him had standing orders to shoot first . . . and shoot to kill.

They had camped the previous night near the small town of Billings and now, by mid-morning, they had pushed about five miles to the east. They were passing through an area of rugged hills covered with some of the most inhospitable scrub brush and forests he had ever seen. The roads through this area were few and treacherous. Had the circumstances been different, Morgan would have been constantly worried about the possibility of ambush. But he knew how unlikely it was that the Hartman brothers would slow down to harass their pursuers. There were too many men after them. The only way they'd stop now would be if they were cornered with no chance of escape and no alternative but to stand and fight.

Shortly before noon, a small band of half a dozen men approached Morgan's group from the east. It was then that he received the first good news he'd had since learning that the Hartman brothers had stopped for the night in Joplin.

"By damn, we got 'em!" one of the new arrivals announced excitedly as soon as he rode up to Morgan.

"Are they dead?" Morgan asked immediately. He was hardly able to disguise the disappointment he felt at not being in on the kill, but he told himself that at this point, anything was preferable to the complete escape of their prey.

"No, I don't mean that we've got 'em dead or caught already," the man said, "but it's almost as good. We've got them trapped like possums in a pit."

"Are you sure it's them?" Morgan demanded. For the first time in days, a note of excitement crept into his voice.

"Well, it's either them or two fellows who don't care for the likes of us any more than they do," the man said. "They've already killed two men, including Lem Stokes, the sheriff of Christian County, and they've wounded four others. Either we've got the right ones or some others that need killin' just as bad."

"Where are they?"

"They're holed up in a cave about five miles east of here, a place called Wiley's Revenge. Folks in these parts tell a story about how back in the twenties a man named Stub Wiley took his brother-in-law in there and killed him. Not many people are interested in going in, but I've heard tell that there's a pit back in there that's maybe four or five hundred feet straight down. They say that's where Stub did the deed."

"They're definitely trapped in the cave?" Morgan asked sharply to end the man's discourse on local folklore. "And you're sure there's no other way out?"

"None that anybody's ever found," the man assured him. "And we've got about twenty-five men covering the entrance. I'd say we've got them for sure, unless they figure out some way to dig through maybe three miles of solid bedrock and come out on the other side of Eagle Mountain!"

John Hartman drew a careful bead and plucked a straw hat off the top of a careless farmer's head. It was a good shot, and he smiled to himself as he dropped back behind the sheltering rock and waited out the ensuing barrage of return fire.

403

Despite the casualties their pursuers had already suffered, the swarm of yokels outside seemed to consider this whole affair to be quite a lark, and they were making the most of it while they could. Each shot he fired was answered by dozens from the other side, and across the hundred yards of open space outside the cave entrance he could hear his opponents whooping and cheering after each pointless fusillade.

The exchanges of shots had not been quite so harmless at the start of the siege, however. Realizing that they were nearly surrounded early that morning, John and Daniel had chosen to make their stand in the cave because of its easy defensibility. A tangle of fallen rock near the mouth of the cave provided enough good cover for a score of men, and the field of fire overlooked all possible avenues of approach. The land in front of the cave sloped downhill at about a thirty degree angle, and a recent rock slide had swept the area clear of every tree and bush that could possibly be used for cover.

Moments after John and Daniel reached their refuge, the posse decided to charge. The brothers had turned them back with a scathing volley from their repeating rifles and revolvers. The carnage was distasteful to both outlaws, but they had tried to make up for it as best they could by allowing their opponents to come out and drag off their casualties as soon as the fight was ended. That had all taken place several hours before, and from then on there had been no more suicidal heroics. It was a stand-off now, and would be at least until dark when John thought there would probably be another attempt to overrun their position by force.

Daniel was somewhere back in the cave now, trying to find a way out. Just inside the entrance they had been fortunate enough to find some torch materials — sticks, burlap and coal oil left by some previous visitor — so he had no shortage of light for his explorations, but John cherished no real hopes that he would have any success. He was familiar enough with these Ozark mountain caves to realize that the spreading tentacles of some of them went miles down into the earth, so even if there did happen to be another way out, it could take weeks or months of exploration to find.

But they didn't have weeks or months. At most, John thought, the duration of the siege would probably be measured in days, but hours was more like it.

For the time being, though, supplies would be no problem. Anticipating a long stay in the wilderness, John and Daniel had stocked up on food and ammunition the day before, and they had enough of both to last for several days. But considering the man who was after them, John thought the chances were slim that this business would drag on that long. Morgan would find some way to bring an end to it, even if it cost the lives of still more of his men.

Nestling his rifle in a three-inch crack between two fractured hunks of rock, John drew a bead on an elbow which was carelessly protruding from behind a tree down the hill. He was considering whether or not to squeeze off a shot when he heard the sound of his brother returning from his explorations. When he neared the entrance. Daniel extinguished his torch with a handful of dirt, then moved forward cautiously on his bands and knees until he was at John's side.

"Any luck?" John asked.

"Not a damn bit. I explored two of the most likely looking passageways, but both turned out to be dead ends. There's a couple more areas that I still haven't checked, but it doesn't look good. It looks like we're stuck here."

"Well, at least we've got plenty of food and ammunition, and that little pool back where the horses are should provide us with plenty of water."

"Listen, John," Daniel said. "I was thinking about the horses while I was stumbling around back in there. There's not a damn thing in here for them to eat, and it doesn't look very likely that we'll ever need them again. . . ."

"I know," John replied. "I was thinking the same thing. We might as well run them out of here. If this thing lasts for very long, there's no need for them to suffer in here with us."

"All right then. I'll take care of it after a while," Daniel said. He sat there for a moment, chewing on a piece of jerky he'd taken out of his shirt pocket. Then he said, "You know, there's a big deep hole back about a quarter-mile in there, near the rear of this long main passageway. It looks like a sink hole of some kind, but it's deep as hell. I pitched one of the torches down into it, and it seemed like it fell for three or four seconds before it finally went out. It sounded like it might have hit water way down at the bottom, and it seemed like I could almost smell water on the updraft."

"These hills are bound to be laced with underground rivers," John noted. "That's probably what carved most of these caves in the first place. But this one doesn't sound like it would be much use to us. Did you see any way down into it?"

"Not really," Daniel said, "at least no way any sane man would want to try. I just thought it was interesting. Later on if you feel like stretching your legs, you might want to go back and take a look at it."

"Maybe later," John agreed, although he really wasn't too interested. He had given up on the idea that there might be a back way out of these caves.

When he was finished eating, Daniel went back into the cave, and a few minutes later he returned leading their two mounts. Moving cautiously so he would not enter the line of sight of the men below, he got the two horses lined up on the narrow pathway through the rocks. Then he shouted out and slapped the rear end of one of the animals. Immediately the horses sprang forward, bursting out into the open and starting down the hillside. Several rifle muzzles rose into view among the rocks and trees below, but no shots were fired. Slowing finally, the animals disappeared into the woods.

It made John feel good to think that at least their horses would survive all this. He had lost a lot of good mounts during his lifetime, especially during his years with the bushwhackers, but he had never killed or caused the death of one needlessly.

Early in the afternoon John saw some increase in the activity below and began to brace himself for another charge. Daniel had returned to his explorations so John figured he would have to withstand the onslaught alone, but he was not too worried about it. He had both rifles with him, and he was confident that he could shoot enough men by himself to blunt the charge long before they reached the rocks where he was hidden.

But no charge took place, and finally John decided that the movement was made by some new arrivals working their way up the hillside to get a look at the cave. He squeezed off a few rounds just to keep them cautious, then reloaded the rifle and laid it aside again.

Full darkness had almost arrived by the time Daniel returned again to share the nighttime guard duties with his brother. His second exploration was no more productive than the first, but he said that there were still more areas to be checked out the next day . . . if there was to be a next day for either of them.

Morgan Hartman refused to let his hillbilly

army charge the cavern entrance during the night, as many of them were so eager to do. With as many men as he now had assembled outside the cave, he knew that such a tactic stood a good chance of succeeding, but it staggered him to consider how many casualties they might accumulate during the process.

It wasn't that he was particularly concerned about whether the men with him lived or died. Most of them were dolts and morons anyway, living out their pointless lives here in these hills. What did bother him was how bad it would make him look if the band he led suffered inordinately high casualties during the killing of the Hartman brothers. Whether it was his fault or not, he would be blamed, both by the press and by his superiors with the Pinkerton Detective Agency. Five men had already died and several others had been wounded. Now it was time to proceed cautiously so that, if possible, the embarrassing statistics would not climb any higher.

During the afternoon, Morgan Hartman had made a thorough survey of the vicinity, and a plan had started taking shape in his mind. Shortly after dark he had sent some men to a nearby town for the necessary supplies, and now, in the early hours of the

410

morning, everything was in readiness. All that was needed at this point was for daylight to arrive so he could set the whole thing in motion.

When the first hints of morning light appeared in the eastern sky, Morgan issued his final instructions to the men on guard below the entrance to the cave. Then he mounted his horse and started on a roundabout route toward the steep cliffs above the cave opening, where five men were waiting to carry out their part of the plan.

Hartman made a quick inspection of the preparations the men had made. Near the edge of the cliff, directly above the cave lay ten bundles of dynamite, each lashed to a stone about the size of a man's head. Fifty feet of rope had been tied to each bundle, and the free ends of the ropes were secured to a tree nearby. A few feet back from the brink sat the remainder of the two cases of dynamite which the men had brought from town during the night.

The idea was for the men to light the bundles one by one and fling them over the edge. If the ropes were cut correctly, the bundles of dynamite should end up swinging in the air directly over the heads of John and Daniel Hartman when they went off. With any luck, the fugitives would be killed by the concussion or the flying shards of rocks sent out by the explosion. Even if that didn't happen, Morgan thought, they would be driven so deeply into the cave that they would no longer be able to guard its entrance.

"Once I get back down below and give you the signal, I want you to light one bundle and throw it over every two minutes until I signal you to stop. I'll watch each one when it goes off, and if it's too high or too close to the ground, I'll signal you 'up' or 'down.' Then you can adjust the length of the rope a foot or two before you throw the next one. I want them going off about ten feet above the ground."

"How're you going to know whether or not you killed them?" one of the men asked.

"We'll find that out soon enough. The dynamite should get them, but even if it doesn't, they won't be able to cover that slope with their rifles anymore. And once we cross that open area and get inside the cave, I think we can deal with them easily enough. That's their last advantage, and after we take that away from them, they're ours!"

Most of the men were awake and ready by the time Morgan got back down. Although the posse now numbered over two hundred men, he had decided to take only a dozen hand-picked men in with him. That size party would be large enough to get the job done, yet small enough for him to control and direct personally. Each would be armed with a rifle and two pistols, and each would carry some rope and two torches which could be lit once they were inside.

Moving carefully through the trees in the growing morning light, Morgan advanced as far up the wooded hillside as he dared go. He could clearly see the five men on the cliff above. His attack party was gathered behind him, and everything was ready.

Morgan took a handkerchief from his pocket and waved it in the air. An instant later a bullet sang past his hand, proving that his prey was still awake and alert, but he withdrew his hand before a second shot could be fired.

Atop the cliff he saw one of the men pick up a bundle of dynamite and hold it out so a companion could light the fuse. Then the man advanced to the brink of the cliff and pitched the bundle over the side and scrambled back several feet to be clear of the blast. The rope on the first charge was too long, and the dynamite and stone fell clear to the ground.

Smoke and rock dust rose around the

413

entrance to the cave like billowing storm clouds and the roar of the explosion echoed across the broad valley. From Morgan's vantage point, it seemed impossible that any living thing could have survived such a blast, but he knew better than to take such a thing for granted. He raised up slightly and pointed upward with his hand, signaling the men on top of the cliff to shorten the rope before throwing down the next charge.

During the next few minutes, the stillness of the peaceful mountain valley was shattered again and again by the thunder of the exploding dynamite charges. After the first couple of blasts, the men got the rope length right and the next three charges exploded above the ground as they were supposed to. Soon the men in Morgan's attack party began to urge him to let them move forward, certain that by now their quarry must be dead or have moved deep into the cave. But he refused. He was determined to detonate the full ten charges before advancing.

No further signals were needed by the time the men on top of the cliff were ready to toss the sixth explosive bundle over the edge. They simply waited two minutes as instructed, then a man picked up a bundle and held it out for his companion to light.

No one was ever certain what happened up there, and there were no survivors among the five men atop the cliff to tell the tale. The most common speculation was that the man with the bundle of dynamite in his hand slipped on the gravel near the edge and that the lit charge he was carrying was accidentally pitched back near the cases of extra dynamite.

All that anyone knew for certain was that in the next moment the whole side of the mountain seemed to shatter as a deafening, bone-jarring roar blasted out from above the cave opening. Morgan Hartman watched in utter disbelief as the entire face of the cliff seemed to shear away from its anchorage and start downward. In one incredible moment, thousands of tons of fragmented limestone tumbled down, obliterating the entrance of the cavern as thoroughly as if it had never existed. Boulders the size of houses rolled sluggishly down the hillside, cutting swaths of death and destruction through the scattered trees and men in their paths, and for a few seconds the sky rained deadly showers of stone.

Before the echo of the explosion and the resulting avalanche faded in the distance, the screams and moans of the injured and the dying began to rise up from the chaos

415

like the lament of lost souls on their way to
hell.

Chapter Twenty-One

"It amazes me to see how much this part of the state has changed since we came here twenty-two years ago," Mollie told her cousin Ridge. "Back in 1854 when we first arrived from Virginia, nobody had ever heard of a place called Kansas City. And now look what a city it's become. There weren't any railroads, either, and no decent roads to speak of except a post road here and there running from one little jerkwater burg to another."

It was a chilly October afternoon and the two of them were riding northward in an open buggy, heading toward a tragic reunion at Jason Hartman's farm.

"You know, things were wild and dangerous for all of us back then," Mollie went on. "Nobody with any sense went anywhere without being armed, and it was a lot more common for two men to settle their disputes with fists, knives and guns than it was to let

417

the law take care of it. Most little boys, and a lot of girls as well, learned to draw a bead and pull a trigger before they learned the alphabet, and it wasn't all that uncommon back then for a boy to have killed his first man before he'd kissed his first girl."

The rolling hills around them were brown and bare, and the leafless trees stood starkly like skeletons against the backdrop of the gray sky. Mollie had a blanket wrapped around her legs and shoulders, but even that failed to prevent the damp October chill from reaching her flesh. The road they were traveling was practically deserted. No doubt the unpredictability of the weather served to keep all but the most determined travelers off the roads.

"When I talk about what those days were like, they sound really awful, and they weren't times that I'd ever want my children to have to survive," she continued. "But you know what's so odd about the whole thing, Ridge? Sometimes I really miss that part of my life."

"It was your youth, Mollie," Ridge said. "We always miss our youth." Those were the first words he had spoken in a long time.

"Maybe that's what it is," Mollie agreed. "I was young and free back then, and I didn't have any responsibilities to tie me

down . . . no house, no business, no children, and no husband. . . . I could go
wherever I wanted to go and do whatever I
wanted to do, and frequently Cole and I
used to do just that. The two of us were
really a scandal in those days."

"You were well on your way to outraging
the entire family long before you came to
Missouri. Don't forget, we grew up together
and I was there to witness firsthand some of
your early adventures," Ridge chuckled.
"But the thing I've never understood is why
you and Cole Younger never married."

"I can't tell you how many times I've
wondered that very same thing," Mollie
said. "Early on the notion never really occurred to us, I guess. Neither of us wanted
to settle down so soon. Then the war came,
and there were too many other things to
think about. And, of course, along the way
there were other men for me and other
women for Cole. I almost married a Union
Captain named Kurt Rakestraw, but he was
killed in the last year of the war in a skirmish
against George Todd's bushwhackers, and a
couple of years later I made the mistake of
marrying Bedford Lee. As for Cole, I guess
the other great romance of his life was with
his cousin, Belle. He never told me much
about it, but I got an earful from other

sources. I know they were together off and on for years, even after she and Sam Starr married and settled in Texas. I'm sure there were many others as well. But they were all in the past, as were mine, and just before he left for Northfield, we had talked about trying again. . . ."

Mollie fell suddenly silent. Glancing over at her briefly, Ridge could tell by her furrowed brow and by the tears which glistened in her eyes that her thoughts had taken an unexpectedly disturbing turn. He held his tongue, letting her deal with the moment in her own way.

"My hindsight has always been marvelous," Mollie said at last, smiling past the gathering tears. "I can see now that I should have begged him not to go, that I should have promised anything to keep him with me. Today I would gladly give everything I own to have him back at my side. . . . But my God! Who could have predicted that it would go so badly? It's still hard for me to believe that Cole is in jail right now, and that he and his brothers Jim and Bob will probably spend the rest of their lives in prison. I guess if there's anything good to be found in this whole mess, it's the fact that Minnesota doesn't have a death penalty. Otherwise, I guess Cole and his brothers would be facing a gallows instead of long prison terms."

"The time came for them to pay up," Ridge said matter-of-factly. "It happens when you lead the kind of lives that Cole and the rest of that bunch chose to lead. And the same is true for John and Daniel. I regret their deaths for Jason's and Arethia's sake, but at the same time there's no denying that there's a certain justice to it. Their debt came due, and their bill was a heavy one."

"I suppose," Mollie said sadly. "But it doesn't make it any easier for those of us who loved them."

Two days ago, Ridge had been in Wichita, Kansas when he heard the news about the massive manhunt which was underway in southern Missouri to apprehend his cousins. He started almost immediately for Clay County, not knowing whether there was anything he could do but feeling the instinct to be with his family while this drama unfolded for them. The announcement of John and Daniel's deaths, spread in huge letters across the front pages of every local newspaper, greeted him when he arrived in Kansas City, and when he located Mollie, he found her preparing to leave for Clay County the following morning.

They knew that there was not much that either of them could do at this point. If the newspaper stories could be believed, there was little chance that John and Daniel's bodies would ever be recovered. The entrance to Wiley's Revenge had been obliterated, and there was little interest in trying to reopen it simply to recover the mangled corpses of two outlaws. In fact, the only thing that made the story so sensational was the fact that so many lives had been lost in the explosion at Wiley's Revenge. At last count, the death toll had mounted to sixteen, and some others injured during the incident were not expected to live. It was a dark day for the Pinkerton Detective Agency, whose agents were being blamed, at least in print, for the entire tragedy.

Mollie and Ridge were simply concerned with the suffering of Jason and Arethia Hartman. They had set out on their trip to Clay County early in the morning, and now ten hours later they were less than an hour's ride from Jason's farm. They wouldn't quite make it by dark, Mollie thought, but they should be there soon after.

Mollie was not particularly looking forward to the sad, emotional scene which would undoubtedly take place when she and Ridge arrived at the farm, but she knew that it was her responsibility to be there for her brother and sister-in-law, just as they had been there for her during the most trying times in her life. The Hartmans were a family that stood together as one when trouble struck.

Jason Hartman had been sitting in the same chair for more than an hour now, smoking his pipe and staring reflectively into the fire. Across the room Arethia was busy with her knitting, her hands working the needles mechanically as her thoughts, like those of her husband, roamed far afield.

Although all their children had been gone from home for years, the house had never seemed more empty than it did at this moment, Jason thought. Memories assaulted him . . . the glow of excited faces on Christmas morning . . . the sound of muffled giggling in the back bedroom long after bedtime was past . . . the sudden uproar of an argument over the ownership of a slab of pie . . . the soft kiss of young lips expressing unconditional love. . . .

News of John and Daniel's death reached them late the previous evening, delivered by a friend from Liberty, but as yet, the realization had not fully sunk in. Both Jason and his wife were still somewhat in a state of shock, still wanting to believe in the back of their minds that some mistake had been made and that the men who were killed in the cavern outside Springfield were not their sons. But in their hearts, they were beginning slowly to accept that it was true, and that their two eldest sons were gone forever.

It seemed inconceivable, though, that only two of their five children remained alive, and Jason found himself wondering what terrible thing he might have done to make God punish him in such a way. His life had been filled with strife, he had to admit. In the past there had been periods when he had been a violent man, and many times he had stained his hands with the blood of other men. But he had never fought simply for the sake of fighting or killed for the sheer exhiliration of it as some men did. When he fought, it was to defend himself and his family, or for a cause that he believed to be worthwhile and just.

The day had been a busy one for Jason and his wife. His sister Sarah had been over for much of the day, as had their son Benjamin and his young wife. A number of people from their community and their church had also stopped in to express their condolences and to leave various gifts of food. It was almost a relief when everyone finally left, but then the stillness set in, bringing with it dark thoughts and depression. From this time forward, Jason thought, their lives would never be the same again.

When Jason heard the knock on the door, he thought it was probably another neighbor stopping by with some food and a kind word of sympathy. He would have preferred to be finished with company for the day, but he knew that whoever it was probably meant well. . . .

"Hartman! Jason Hartman! Open the door!" The demand from outside was accompanied by an even louder and more insistent knocking on the front door. Jason and Arethia exchanged worried, confused looks, unable to guess who might be making such a rude, alarming demand.

"Wait here." Jason instructed his wife as he rose and crossed the room to open the door.

Only one man, a stranger, stood on the porch, but beyond him Jason saw half a dozen other men standing in the moonlit yard. Their horses were tied to the fence out by the road, which accounted for their silent approach to the house.

"We're in mourning in this house," Jason told the men at the door. "What do you want with us?"

"Who's in there with you?" the man demanded.

"Just my wife and I are here," Jason answered. "Now tell me what you want or go away. I'm in no mood to be bothered with anything this evening."

"Come out of the house, Hartman," the man ordered him. "There's someone out here who wants to talk to you." The man wore a revolver in a holster at his side, and though he had yet to draw the weapon, his right hand was resting on the hilt of the gun, as if to lend authority to his order.

With each passing second, Jason liked the whole situation less and less. He still had no inkling of who these men were or what they wanted, but their attitude and their manner of approach reminded him of a period, years ago, when violent nighttime visits back and forth across the Kansas-Missouri border were commonplace and frequently deadly.

Jason stepped out onto the porch and pulled the door closed behind him, then walked to where the other men waited. He knew there was no use refusing the demands of these men. There were enough of them to do anything they wanted to him.

One man stepped out from the others to meet him as be approached. He was a couple of inches taller than Jason, with broad shoulders and a strong, muscular build. His hat was pulled down over his eyes, partially concealing the features of his face, but despite that there was something unsettlingly familiar about him. He wore a deputy sheriff's badge on his chest, and some of the other men in the group had badges on as well, but Jason didn't recognize any of them as Clay County deputies.

"Do I know you?" Jason asked.

"We only met once briefly, and that was years ago," the man told him. "But I'm not surprised if I look familiar to you because you looked me over pretty good that one time. And besides, they tell me I look quite a bit like my father did when he was about my age. My name is Morgan Hartman."

Jason felt an almost painful tightening in the pit of his stomach at the mere mention of that name. He should know him well enough, he thought. Hadn't he been there the day Morgan Hartman drew his gun and put a bullet in the stomach of his father, Will Hartman?

"I don't know what you want or why you picked this particular night to come here," Jason told him, "but if you have any decency at all, you'll go away and leave us alone. My wife and I just received word that two of our sons are dead. Please, let us mourn our loss in private."

"I know all about your dead sons," Morgan Hartman told him. "I should know about them, because I'm the one who killed them."

Jason glanced in confusion at the badge on his nephew's chest, then up at his face, then back at the badge.

"Don't mind that thing," Morgan said. "It's just a convenience. I got myself and my men here sworn in by your county sheriff this afternoon so we would have some authority when we came out here. But my real job is with the Pinkerton Detective Agency, and I'm proud to say I'm the man who tracked down and killed your two outlaw sons, John and Daniel Hartman."

But why?" Jason asked, thunderstruck by the announcement and his arrogant tone. "The last I heard of you, you were a lawman over in Kansas somewhere. Why would you come back here for something like this . . . to kill your own cousins?"

"Because of you, you bastard!"

"But why?" Jason demanded again. "Damn you, why?"

"It seemed like the best kind of revenge . . . it seemed even better than killing you outright to kill your sons first and then let you know that you're the cause of their deaths as well as your own."

"I don't understand," Jason said. "Revenge for what?" But even as the words were coming out of his mouth, he began to understand. He could imagine only one thing that could inspire the kind of hatred that now inhabited Morgan Hartman's heart.

"I know you thought you got away with it, and that nobody else ever knew what you did," Morgan began to explain. "But I was there that night twenty years ago and I saw it all."

As Morgan spoke, the scene began to recreate itself in Jason's mind. It was back before the war in the late 1850's, at the height of the border trouble between the residents of Missouri and Kansas Territory. In a desperate attempt to seek some sort of truce, Jason had crossed over into Kansas on his own and had headed to John Brown's fortified stronghold near Osawattamie, where his brother Charles and his family were staying. He wanted to reason with Brown and Charles and the other abolitionists, to persuade them to stop all the fighting, and all the attacks and counterattacks across the border. But close on his heels had come an army of angry Missourians determined to take the stronghold by force and kill all the abolitionist fanatics in it.

They had attacked while Jason was still inside.

". . . I had already been hit, and I was lying by a wall, shot in the leg and the side, waiting for somebody to come along and take care of me," Morgan was saying. He too was being swept away by the intensity of the recollections. "I saw my father go into the building where you were. . . ."

They took Jason prisoner when the fighting started, he remembered. He was locked in a small log building, but somehow Mollie and Cole managed to sneak into the compound and overpower his guard. But as they were attempting to escape, Charles saw them and came after them. He was insane with rage, and he was determined to kill his brother Jason and his sister Mollie.

". . . Then a minute later when he came back out, his whole body was on fire." So vivid was Morgan's recollections that his eyes seemed to glow from those twenty-year-old flames, and his voice, smooth and even, filled with bitterness, had a hypnotic quality to it. "And then I saw you shoot him in the back and kill him. I know you thought you got away with it, that only your whore of a sister and her murdering friend, Cole Younger, knew about it . . . but I knew too, and I swore revenge that night. All the years

430

that I was out West, I never forgot and I never forgave. . . ."

"It was a terrible thing, Morgan," Jason agreed, his voice filled with honest regret. "Of all the thing I've done in my life, that is probably the one I am most ashamed of. But since that night, I've never doubted even once that it was necessary. My God, Morgan! Charles was crazy by then! Didn't you know that? Couldn't you see it in his eyes when he looked at you or hear it in his voice when he spoke? All we wanted to do was get out of that place alive, but he was determined to kill us, his own brother and sister."

"I'm not concerned with whatever lies you've told yourself so that you can bear to live with your treachery all these years," Morgan sneered. "All that interests me is seeing you get the punishment you deserve. And tonight you're going to face the final reckoning for what you did to my father twenty years ago."

"Even with that badge pinned to your chest, if you kill me it will still be murder," Jason said.

"That's all taken care of. I have a warrant for your arrest. Harboring known fugitives and accessory to bank robbery. But unfortunately you're never going to make it to jail.

You're going to be killed trying to escape . . . and then, finally, Uncle Jason, this business between us will be finished once and for all."

"But what about all these witnesses?" Jason asked. Realizing how close he was to being killed, a note of desperation was beginning to creep into his voice, but he suppressed it as best he could. "You won't be able to count on this many men to back up your lies when you tell your story to the sheriff."

"Every man here has my gold in his pockets," Morgan replied. "They do what I tell them to do, and see what I tell them to see. Any one of them would not hesitate to draw his gun and shoot you right now if that's what I told him to do, but that's a pleasure that I've reserved for myself."

Even as he spoke, his hand dropped down and closed around the hilt of his revolver. There was no hurry about his movements, though. Jason was unarmed and had no way to defend himself. . . .

The rifle shot split the night like a clap of thunder, and Morgan Hartman spun suddenly to the right and fell as if some unseen adversary had felled him with a powerful blow. His men began to scatter immediately, drawing their guns as they dove for cover, knowing only that the unexpected shot had come from somewhere in the vicinity of the house. A second shot nailed one of them as he ran, and a third bullet nipped at the heels of a man who was diving for cover behind the great elm in Jason's front yard.

Those first three shots, fired by Arethia, bought Jason enough time to fall to the ground and scramble back under the front porch of the house. Once there he began to make his way back under the house itself, moving carefully through the pitch darkness, trying to locate a particular spot under the floor of his home. The gunmen Morgan had brought along were beginning to pepper the front of the house with pistol bullets, but he heard no more from Arethia's rifle. That fact didn't bother him, though, because he had a pretty good idea what it meant.

His suspicions were confirmed when he heard a scraping sound on the floor almost directly above where he was. That, he knew, would be Arethia moving the chest in the bedroom which they kept sitting on top of the trap door. Then he heard the faint squeak of old hinges, and a dim wedge of light appeared above him.

"Did you bring any guns?" Jason whispered up urgently.

"Two rifles and your pistol," his wife answered.

"Good. Pass them to me, and then climb down. It won't be long before they realize you're not firing back, and then they'll probably storm the place. We need to be in the brush by then."

Arethia had already passed Jason's revolver down to him when, quite unexpectedly, a man's voice called out from somewhere nearby, "Hey! They're under the house! They're trying to slip out through a trap door!" He accompanied his announcement with a random shot which ricocheted off a couple of the structure's stone piers before singing off into the night. Jason responded with a quick shot fired at the man's muzzle flash. He was rewarded with a yelp of pain and an oath.

"Help me up," Jason told his wife. "They've spotted me down here, so I guess we're going to have to make our stand inside after all."

As soon as he was up in the bedroom, Jason slammed the trap door closed and slid the dead bolt so that no one could follow him inside.

"All right, you watch the back door and I'll take the front," he hurriedly told his wife. "I didn't see a man in the whole bunch that looked much like a hero, so with Morgan down, maybe they'll decide to cut their losses and leave. We might not have to turn back an all out attack."

The last thing in the world Mollie and Ridge expected to hear this close to Jason's house was the rattle of gunfire. It erupted so abruptly that the first instinctive thought which entered Mollie's mind was that it must be Jayhawkers. But of course it couldn't be Jayhawkers. The last time such a deadly raiding party had crossed over from Kansas was more than ten years before, and it was inconceivable that it could be starting up again in this day and time.

But Ridge Parkman, a man accustomed to such sudden eruptions of violence, wasted little time in wondering who was causing the trouble. Instead, he began immediately preparing himself to deal with it. He stopped the buggy in the middle of the road and turned to reach for his rifle, which was on the floor behind the seat. He was already wearing his gunbelt.

"How far are we from the house right now?" he asked Mollie.

"See that break in the brush up ahead?" she said. "About fifty yards up on the right? That's the turnoff to the house."

"All right, there's a shotgun in with my bedroll and other gear on the back of the buggy," Ridge told her. "Load it up and then move off into the brush at the side of the road. You should be alright there until I come back for you."

"I'll take the shotgun," Mollie said, stepping to the ground. "But I'll be damned if I'll stay here hiding in the bushes while you go up there by yourself. You don't know whether you'll be going up against two men or twenty up there, and one extra gun might make all the difference. I'm going." She quickly found the pump shotgun that Ridge had mentioned, checked the load, and jacked a shell into the chamber.

Ridge knew there was no use arguing with Mollie so he didn't even try. He led the way at a trot down the road toward Jason's house, slowing only when he neared the turnoff that Mollie had pointed out to him. By the time they reached that point, the gunfire had dwindled to an occasional random shot.

They spotted the intruders' horses tied to a fence as they entered the yard, and by their count discovered that they were up against eight men. A moment later Ridge saw two dark, motionless forms lying on the ground down near the house, so he figured the odds had already been improved some before be and Mollie got there.

"Look! Look over there, Ridge!" Mollie said urgently, pointing to the big elm tree which stood off to the right between them and the house. "There's one of them, and I think that's another hunched down by that clump of bushes off to the right."

As they watched, the man behind the tree raised his weapon to fire at the house, but Ridge Parkman was faster. Slapping the butt of his rifle to his shoulder, he squeezed off a quick shot which slammed the man against the tree and then flung him to the ground like a rag doll. The man on the left saw happened and turned to try to defend himself from the assault from this new direction, but his fate had already been sealed. The bullet which killed him was in flight even as be brought his pistol up to fire at Ridge and Mollie. When, as a dying act, he pulled the trigger of his gun reflexively, the bullet furrowed harmlessly into the ground at his feet.

"You men out there," Ridge called out finally. "This is United States Marshal Ridge Parkman and the people who live here are under my personal protection. Half your number are down already, and the rest of you are going to be in the same sad shape if you don't give up on this and get the hell out of here."

"If we agree to go, are you going to let us have our horses?" somebody called out from the darkness.

"I guess not," Ridge responded. "Me and my men figured on keeping them for our trouble. But think about this. You can buy another horse, but where are you going to buy yourself another life?"

"All right, Marshal, we're leaving," came the answer back at last. "Hell, the man who hired us is dead anyway. There's no profit in staying around here any longer."

Ridge and Mollie waited where they were for the next few minutes, marking the progress of their opponents' retreat by the sounds they made passing through the thick brush on the east side of Jason's house. Then at last they stepped out into the open and started moving cautiously toward the house. As they drew near, Jason eased the front door open, and met them on the front porch, pistol in hand.

"Man, are you two ever a welcome sight!" Jason said. "I thought for awhile there we were going to get burnt out again, just like we were back in 'sixty-two."

"Who were those men?" Ridge asked. "From the way they talked, it sounded like they were being paid to attack your home,

438

but who would go to all that trouble?"

"He would," Jason said, pointing across the yard at one of the dead men lying face down on the grass. "It's Morgan Hartman."

"Our cousin from Kansas?" Ridge exclaimed. "That Morgan Hartman?"

"None other," Jason answered. "He claimed he was the one that tracked John and Daniel down and killed them, and he came here tonight to kill me. But I guess that wife of mine figures she's not through with me yet because she shot him before he could get the job done."

With Mollie at his side, Ridge walked over and turned the body of the dead man over to look at him.

"Funny," Mollie commented, gazing down at the corpse impassively. "I never saw him myself, but I'd always heard that he looked at lot more like Charles than this."

"It seems to me he looks just like him . . ." Jason began as he strolled over to examine the corpse of his dead nephew. "My God! That's not him!" he exclaimed as he reached his sister's side and looked down at the body at their feet. "That's not Morgan Hartman's body!"

"I guess this woman's not as good a shot as you thought," a deep voice announced from behind them. "The fact is, that couldn't be me because I'm still far from dead!"

They could scarcely believe what they saw when they turned toward the house. Morgan Hartman stood there with his right arm wrapped around Arethia's waist and a pistol pointed at her neck. His face, coated with blood, sweat and dirt, was a devil's mask of pain and hatred, and the entire right side of his body was soaked with blood from the wound on his right shoulder.

"I'm sorry," Arethia muttered to her husband. "He came up behind me from the kitchen. I didn't hear him or see him in time. . . ."

"It's all right . . ." Jason responded quietly.

"You might think it's all right," Morgan stormed, "but I still aim to do what I came here to do. Now lay that gun down, Jason, and step over closer to me."

"Don't do it, Jason!" Arethia pleaded. "Kill him! Shoot him while you have the chance!"

"I can't. I just can't risk it," Jason answered. "I'm sorry honey. . . ." He took his revolver out of his holster and leaned forward to lay it on the ground, ignoring the pleas of his wife to go ahead and risk her life to save his own. He knew that in another moment he would probably be dead, but oddly enough the prospect was not that frightening. It just didn't seem to matter much anymore.

It was probably one of the finest draws Ridge Parkman would ever make in his life, and certainly it was one of the most important. Had Morgan Hartman been looking straight at Ridge with his gun drawn and his attention focused, there was a good possibility that he still could not have reacted in time to save his own life.

But as it was, Morgan was looking at Jason. He was injured and exhausted, and his mind was muddled with rage and pain. He never really had a chance. His head snapped sharply to the side as the bullet entered his temple, and he immediately fell backward away from Arethia. His arm fell away from her as he went down, and the pistol slipped harmlessly from his grasp. He never uttered another sound before he died.

The letter arrived a few days later like a message from beyond the grave. It was dated October 3, 1877, and in his opening paragraph, John revealed that he was writing from a hotel room in Joplin, Missouri. He explained that, although he and Daniel had been gone from home only three days, he felt as if there were words that needed to be put down which neither he nor his brother had been able to say during their final farewell with their mother and father.

The four-page missive was filled with a variety of regrets, both for the pain he and his brother had caused the people they loved, and for the multitude of unjustifiable wrongs they had committed against so many people that they neither knew nor bore any ill will toward.

The Northfield business had been the turning point for them, John explained. On their way home from Minnesota, even before the news arrived about the death and capture of so many of their friends, they had decided that their outlaw days were over once and for all. Although there was no way they could undo the many sins of their past, they wanted to find out how it felt to live open, honest lives and to look every man in the eye without guilt or fear of discovery.

But they couldn't do that in Missouri. Too many people knew them, and there would always be too much danger for them there.

The letter was not awash with remorse and apology, but John did ask his parents to forgive him and his brother if a long time passed without any communication from them. They wanted to prove to themselves that they could do what they set out to do, and that they could make something of their lives through honest labor rather than always simply taking what they wanted at the point of a gun. And they wanted to be free of all their past associations with men like Frank and Jesse James.

A few tears came to Arethia Hartman's eyes as she read the letter aloud to her husband, but considering the situation and the unexpectedness of the letter's arrival, she was surprisingly composed. For a while after she was finished, the two of them just sat side by side on the worn sofa in the front room of their home, holding hands and sharing their grief in silence.

Later she shared the letter with the other members of the family. By now, Ridge was spending most of his time with his mother, but the two of them drove over almost every day to visit, and Benjamin and his wife came almost as often. Mollie had decided to spend at least a month with her brother and sister-in-law to help them through their period of mourning, and she had sent word to Walter Perry to bring her children to be with her in Clay County.

On the third day after the letter's arrival, Arethia decided that it was too much of a treasure to be left lying around the house. With a heavy feeling of finality in her heart, she carefully returned it to the envelope it had arrived in and carried it into her bedroom to be put away in her big cedar chest with her collection of other priceless treasures from her life and the lives of her children and grandchildren.

She spent a long time in there by herself, sitting on the floor in front of the chest, going through the collection of baby clothes, school grades, letters, photographs and other memorabilia. Each item held a special place in her heart, each was the repository of some splendid or poignant memory from the past, some moment in time which was more valuable to her than any rare jewel could ever be.

At last, when all the items in the chest had been returned to their places, she gently laid the letter from John on top. She reached for the lid of the chest to close it, but she could not bring herself to do it . . . not just yet. Her eyes lingered over the bold, unpretentious letters on the envelope, made such a short time ago by the hand of her loving son. She pictured him holding the pen as he carefully wrote the address on the envelope. She imagined him touching the stamp to his tongue and placing it in the corner . . . and then, for the first time, she saw it.

"Jason! Mollie! Come here!" she cried out.

Her husband was just in the next room reading his Bible and Mollie was only a few steps farther away in the kitchen, but they might have been miles away for the frantic volume in her voice. Tears rushed to her eyes, and a joy as sudden and unexpected as any she had ever felt flooded her heart. "The letter, Jason! The postmark . . . !"

The letter had been mailed in Springfield on October 8th, two days after the entrance to Wiley's Revenge, and the lives of her sons John and Daniel along with it, had been sealed forever from the scrutiny of the outside world.

ABOUT THE AUTHOR

Over the past thirty-five years **Greg Hunt** has published over twenty Western, frontier, and historical novels. A lifelong writer, he has also worked over the decades as a newspaper reporter, photographer and editor, a technical and freelance writer, a tech project manager, and a marketing analyst. Greg served in Vietnam as an intelligence agent and Vietnamese linguist with the 101st Airborne Division and 23rd Infantry Division.

"Writing fiction has always been my true obsession," said Greg. "I tried to give it up a couple of times when things got rough, but it always kept its grip on me until I finally realized that I could never not be a writer."

Greg currently lives in the Memphis area with his wife of twenty-six years, Vernice.

The employees of Thorndike Press hope you have enjoyed this Large Print book. All our Thorndike, Wheeler, and Kennebec Large Print titles are designed for easy reading, and all our books are made to last. Other Thorndike Press Large Print books are available at your library, through selected bookstores, or directly from us.

For information about titles, please call:
(800) 223-1244

or visit our website at:
gale.com/thorndike

To share your comments, please write:
Publisher
Thorndike Press
10 Water St., Suite 310
Waterville, ME 04901